The Union

Gina Robinson

Gina Robinson
SEATTLE, WASHINGTON

CHAPTER ONE

Thompson's Falls, Montana
May 1892

McCullough was dead.

Dietz watched as a fresh bead of blood dripped from McCullough's neck, trickling down to redden the collar of his white cotton shirt. McCullough's blue eyes reflected the clear skies above and nothing else. No life, no emotion. His raven hair was powdered with dust from the street, his head pillowed by soft dry dirt as he lay sprawled. His last living expression, confounded shock, had frozen on his face, giving him the ghoulish look of a caricature.

Damn! When did my aim go bad?

The detective agency had taught Dietz to shoot for the largest target, the body. How had he hit the bastard in the neck? Dietz must have squeezed the trigger too tightly, jerking up as he swung around to fire. Back to target practice or next time he'd be the one dying in the dirt.

Dietz's hands shook. That coward McCullough had surprised him from behind. To hell with him—with any luck, literally. If McCullough hadn't been cocky and yelled a warning, Dietz would be in his place.

What were McCullough's last words?

Dietz's safety, possibly his life, hung on two simple words he couldn't recall. Had McCullough yelled *die* and called out Dietz's alias, or his real name? And had anybody heard?

Sympathy for the miners' union ran high in Thompson's Falls. The air hummed with it, the saloon overflowed with talk of backing the men in Idaho, a mere thirty miles away, in their battle against tyrannical owners. They'd string Dietz up if they even *suspected* he was a private detective hired by the mine owners to break the union stronghold.

The Colt's 45 suddenly felt heavy in his hand. Who had leaked his identity to McCullough? Or had McCullough had another reason for wanting Dietz dead?

Dietz tried to appear dispassionate as he studied the dead man, masking his expression while coursing with anger. A crowd gathered in front of the saloon, circling Dietz. He looked up from where he squatted beside McCullough's body to the circle of blue sky above him rimmed with faces. Not a familiar one among them. The question remained—who was the betrayer?

Dietz pushed up from his squat and stood slowly. A meaty hand clamped his shoulder. He turned to stare into the eyes of the town sheriff.

"He fired first, but killing a man still feels like shit." Dietz stayed in character, acting as if he regretted killing the union terrorist, when nothing could be farther from the truth. Dietz had been undercover so many years, sometimes it seemed like his real identity was only another alias, anyway.

The sheriff released his shoulder. "I saw. You two were traveling together?"

Dietz nodded.

"Looks like you made him mad."

"Looks like it."

"You brothers?"

The lawman's question caught Dietz by surprise. He tried to feign indifference. "No. Just friends, so I thought. Why do you ask?"

"Two Scotsmen. Same hair, same eyes, same height." The sheriff nodded toward the body. "He got any kin?"

"We were headed to his fiancée in Oregon." McCullough's fiancée was in Gem, Idaho.

"Then you won't mind taking the young lady his things. Seems the least you can do."

"Seems like it, but I can't take two horses. What do you say I sell his, and take the money to his lady? That is, what's left after we take some out for a proper burial."

"Very decent of you." The sheriff's solemn edge cracked as he gave what Dietz assumed was supposed to be a sympathetic smile. In reality, Dietz guessed the man felt relieved that the incident cleaned up quickly.

"Excepting his temper when he drank, McCullough was an okay sort." He was an asshole.

The sheriff motioned to someone in the crowd. "Dailey, go run for the undertaker."

An old man scampered off.

"Better get this settled so you can be on your way," the sheriff said.

"Sure." Dietz was in full agreement. "Anyone want to buy a horse?"

Gem, Idaho

Lunn Gaffney sat in Keely Byrne's kitchen watching her as she started supper for the men. She felt his gaze on her as she moved about, dragging pots and pans to the stove. Why did he feel it necessary to check up on her?

"You think the men will rebel at having stew and biscuits again?" She hoisted a large metal pot filled with water onto the stove.

"Seems to me they'll eat whatever you serve them and be happy for it, or answer to me. Not a woman in town cooks better than you, Keely."

"Mrs. Shipley across the street does a fair job of it."

Lunn laughed. "Heard some of her fellows complaining yesterday. Maybe Allison will have to fire her."

"Mr. Allison will not fire her. You shouldn't go making fun of her. She's a fine woman, Lunn." Keely didn't understand what Lunn had against Mr. Allison and his storekeeper.

"Not as fine as you, Keely."

She let the remark slide by and peered out the window to check the weather. Gray clouds scudded by, but they looked less than threatening.

Lunn shifted in his seat. "It's odd Mrs. Shipley is out here without her man. Why would he let her come West alone to cook and clean for other men, boarders?"

"To survive, like I do. Mrs. Shipley running Mr. Allison's boarding house is no odder than me running this one. At least she *has* a man." Keely used to have a man around to protect her, and if she still did, she wouldn't be running a boarding house.

Michael! Her heart ached every time she thought of her older brother, dead these last months. Anger, vicious in its vigor, boiled up with the hurt. She bit back a curse at the owners who ran the mine that had taken Michael's life. They held safety in no regard. If they had, Michael would still be alive.

Dietz pulled to a stop on the hill above the creek-hugging mining camp town of Gem, Idaho, with McCullough's saddlebags slung over his own, or rather, that of his alias, McCabe. Ironically, both were branded with a stylized Mc.

Damn McCullough! Dietz had counted on McCullough being his ticket into the union bosses' confidence. Eight months spent befriending the asshole back in Pennsylvania and another month traveling across the country with the union terrorist, wasted.

Charlie Patterson, aka Leo Allison, the detective agency's operative in the Silver Valley, needed backup.

The union suspected a spy in their midst. But the union labor strike made infiltrating by posing as a miner looking for work impossible. If Dietz strolled into town and applied for a job, the union boys would take him for a scab, non-union labor. He might just as well announce he was a detective. Either way, the mining boys would string him high. Now what was Dietz supposed to do?

Dietz pushed his annoyance away and surveyed the town below him. It didn't differ much from his expectations. Railroad, saloons, boarding houses, a store, a small cluster of houses. Didn't look like much of a place to raise a family. Not that he, being a bachelor, knew anything about raising a family.

Wild, mountainous terrain, covered with white pine and underbrush the likes of huckleberry bushes and wild syringa, surrounded the camp. Dietz clucked to his horse. Time to be riding in. First things first—find Keely Byrne, McCullough's fiancée, and give her the bad news.

Rifling through McCullough's things, hoping to find some useful information, he'd found a neatly tied bundle of love letters from Keely to McCullough. Maybe a scrupulous man wouldn't have, but Dietz had read every word. Miss Byrne's letters indicated she mistook McCullough for a compassionate, witty man. How a man as violent and vile as McCullough had pulled off such deception, Dietz didn't know. But for some reason the woman wanted to marry that bastard McCullough. What kind of a woman could she be?

As unappealing as the task was, he'd better get over and tell her first thing, omitting, of course, his part in the affair. Wasn't that what life was, one distasteful job after another?

"When is McCullough coming?"

With Lunn it always came around to McCullough. "He wired he'd be in any day. He had business in Thompson's Falls."

Lunn looked hurt, almost vulnerable, as he watched Keely.

Why can't I find him attractive? She honestly didn't know. Even now as she studied him, she couldn't say. Many women thought him handsome. Average height but stocky and powerfully built, he kept fit and muscular by laboring in the silver mines. He had dark hair and eyes and pleasant features. But in Keely's opinion, something about him kept him from being truly handsome, something off-center. She could never pin it down. Was his nose slightly too large, or were his eyes too small? Or was it his personality? She wished she knew, but something restrained her from feeling any physical pull toward him.

Michael had always discouraged any relationship between them. It seemed odd, considering he and Lunn had been good friends. Maybe it was nothing more than Michael's sense that she wasn't attracted to Lunn. Her brother had always been protective.

"You are too trusting, Keely. Always have been. Aren't you nervous about a man you've never met, nev-

er seen even a photograph of, coming to claim you?"
Bitterness edged Lunn's tone.

She smiled sympathetically at him. "No. I can always
reject him. McCullough always made it clear I could.
My nerves, if any, come from the thought that I gave
him the same option."

"Even so, Keely. It doesn't seem right." He cleared
his throat.

She knew what he meant. It didn't seem right to
Lunn, with him right there waiting for her. But she
was not anxious over McCullough's arrival. She was
eager and excited. Though they'd never met, she and
McCullough had corresponded for nearly two years
now. He wrote letters sparkling with wit and intelli-
gence. Maybe that was the problem with Lunn—he was
all brawn and no thought.

For nearly a year before he died, Michael had
begged McCullough to come out and help with the union difficulties. Then, in the last month or so before the
accident, he'd stopped pleading. Keely assumed Michael had reconciled himself to McCullough's disinter-
est in their situation.

McCullough came from the Pennsylvania coal re-
gion and had held many prestigious offices in the mining union there. During the years Michael had worked
back East, McCullough had taught Michael everything
he knew. If Michael had trusted it him, so would she.
Michael had never placed his faith foolishly. When
McCullough came, he'd straighten out the owners,
smooth over the troubles. Keely had no doubt that he'd

shoulder her problems, take on her battle. The mines would be safe once McCullough was through.

McCullough. His name quickened her pulse. He had proposed through the mail before Michael's death. But uncertain whether the admiration she felt for him could blossom into love, Keely had turned him down and they had remained friends. Once he had found out about Michael, McCullough immediately proposed again and made plans to come take care of her. She smiled. The second time she had accepted. A man who would drop everything, all his important work, and come to look out for her, what could be better? Lunn looked edgy.

A horse whinnied outside near the road.

"That someone you're expecting, Keely? Looks like a stranger hitching his horse outside." Lunn stared out the window.

"Most likely someone looking for a room." Though her heart skipped a beat, she forced herself to stave off anticipation. With so many strange men streaming into town lately she couldn't go getting her hopes up for McCullough every time another stranger hitched his horse to a post. She had dinner to get on.

"Looks like he's sure he's getting one. He's coming up the walk, carrying his saddlebags."

"We don't have any vacancies." She went to the window to get a look at the fellow. His height, the mustache—everything about him fit the description. "McCullough," she whispered softly. Suddenly, she peeled off her apron and ran for the door. "McCullough!"

Dietz wasn't halfway up the walk when a young, auburn-haired woman came tearing out the door and lunged into him, wrapping her arms around him and whispering McCullough's name rapturously into his chest.

McCullough? Dietz stood frozen in the walk, stunned into silence. He patted the woman awkwardly on the back, like the stranger she was. "Keely?" How he formed the word he couldn't say.

The woman pulled herself away from his chest and dabbed at her eyes before looking up to meet his gaze. She was a petite thing. The top of her head didn't even reach his chin. Her eyes were pale green, the emotion shining in them as fragile as frost. He lost his tongue again, but she didn't seem to mind, almost expected it.

"Oh, McCullough." She laughed, maybe in embarrassment, maybe in joy. On any account it was a pretty sound. She hugged him again.

A man stepped out onto the porch and scowled at them. His glare brought Dietz back to reality. He'd just been handed a silver-plated opportunity. If McCullough's own fiancée mistook him for the man, he should be able to fool anyone. From Keely's letters he knew that no one in town had ever met McCullough in person, so who would dispute his identity? True, McCullough was dead, buried in Thompson's Falls. What if someone who'd been there came to town and squealed? The odds were small. McCullough had gotten himself shot within hours of arriving in town. Few knew him as anything other than an unidentified gunslinger, buried with a plain wooden cross marking his departure.

As McCullough, Dietz had an immediate in with the union. Who would suspect McCullough, union boss from back East, of spying? Time was short. Patterson had reported that things could blow anytime. Trying to infiltrate on his own might take more time than Dietz had. What hardship would it be, escorting a beautiful woman around for a few weeks? His McCabe cover was already tenuous. If this cover were blown, he'd land on his feet as he always did, or die trying.

He decided in an instant, assuming McCullough's identity and personality immediately. "Seeing you took away my tongue. Keely, my lass, you can't know how long I've waited for this moment to lay eyes on you myself. Mick warned me you were a beauty, but I didn't imagine your looks would match the passionate spirit of your letters."

She blushed and took his arm. "You have a silver tongue, McCullough. Michael warned me about that, too." She guided him up the boardwalk toward the house. "Come meet another of Michael's friends—Lunn Gaffney."

Even after McCullough was seated at her table drinking a cup of coffee, Keely couldn't force her gaze away from him. Nor could Lunn, who wore jealousy as conspicuously as a Sunday suit.

She liked everything about McCullough, from the timbre of his voice to the set of his shoulders and his dimpled smile. She could admit, now that she'd seen

him, that she had worried that he might turn out to be
mighty of intellect and spirit and weak in physical
beauty. And she had tried to convince herself that that
would be fine by her. But seeing him now, she realized
she'd been fooling herself.

The man was modest. And Michael, too, deceptive
and humble in his description of him. But McCullough
was everything they described and more. She wanted to
laugh, to burble over with joy.

His eyes were startlingly pale, almost the blue-violet
of sunrise as color begins to seep into the sky. His hair
nearly black. His height slightly taller than average.
His build exceedingly fit and trim. And he looked
younger than his thirty-eight years.

"When you're finished with your coffee, you'll be
wanting to settle into your room. I'll be happy to show
it to you."

"Room? You said there weren't any vacancies."
Lunn looked unhappy. She wished he'd leave.

"Not for a stranger, Lunn. But of course I held a
room for McCullough." She addressed McCullough.
"Lunn saw you tying up your horse and thought you
were a stranger coming for a room." The notion
seemed preposterous now. This man, McCullough, a
stranger! She wanted to laugh.

Lunn glared at her. She was aware her tone had accused him of being a simpleton, but she didn't feel like
apologizing. He could take his bruised feelings and
leave. There was no reason for him to stay around and
torment himself.

"There will be a vacancy soon enough, Gaffney. Soon as me and the lass are married." McCullough's eyes shone with merriment.

Did he know he baited Lunn? Did he enjoy it? She didn't care. His words thrilled.

Lunn pushed his chair back from the table and rose to leave. "I've got to be getting to the union hall. Rumor is the mine owners are going to try and run another load of scabs past us." He glared at McCullough. "Too bad we aren't working. I might have been able to get you on my gang." Lunn's tone was condescending and not in the least sincere.

McCullough smiled easily. "Thank you for the thought, Gaffney, but I haven't worked a hole for years."

Lunn must have felt the insult. He wouldn't let things drop. "And what would you be planning on living off, Keely's wages?"

McCullough laughed full out. "I'm always paid for my services, Gaffney. Exceptionally well paid."

McCullough looked directly at her then and smiled intimately. How could he know how much she wanted Lunn to leave her alone, how uneasy he made her feel? It were as if McCullough had read her mind.

CHAPTER TWO

Dietz dropped his bags on the bed and surveyed the room around him as Keely set a fresh pitcher of water on the washbasin. The bed was neatly made and covered with a plain spread. Unbleached curtains hung open at the window, stirred by a breeze. The room smelled of soap, fresh cleaning, and careful tending. Years back it would have seemed like heaven. Maybe it should have now, given some of the places he'd stayed. But he had seen better, certainly fancier.

"It's a fine room, Keely lass." He ran a finger over the whitewashed wall. "No coal dust. You can't beat that."

She laughed. "This isn't Pennsylvania. We have no coal here, just acres and acres of galena buried in the mountains."

For the first time, he noticed a miniature vase of wildflowers on the nightstand. Tiny, delicate-looking things colored in gentle pastel pinks and lavender.

"Ladyslippers," she said as if she'd read his mind.

"I've never seen anything like them before," he said.

"Oh, they're very rare. Only bloom in May. And they're shy things, hiding and growing in the shade and underbrush where bears like to live."

"Now that you mention it, they do look like slippers." He smiled at her. "You braved bears to get me flowers?"

She didn't look particularly embarrassed, but she didn't reply.

"You shouldn't have, Keely. I don't want any harm coming to my girl."

"I go in the day, when the bear aren't out." She beamed at him again.

She'd been watching him since he'd arrived, admiring him as if he were her hero. No woman had ever looked at him like that before, not even his mother. Damn, but the way she looked at him suddenly made him feel guilty for his spur of the moment deception.

"I'll get you fresh tomorrow," she said. "The blooms last only a day."

He stared at her, trying to assess the kind of woman she was. She picked new flowers every day, anticipating his arrival? No one had ever done that before, either. Come to think of it, no one had still, not for John Dietz.

"You made Lunn mad," she said.

He couldn't help laughing. "I don't take to men who are after my girl."

She shot him a flirtatious look. "Five minutes in the room with him and you determined that?"

"I don't hear you denying it."

"Treat Lunn right and he could be your ally. He knows everyone. With his help, you'd be able to settle in with the union bosses quickly."

He looked her over, liking what he saw, especially the eagerness and sympathy she wore like finery. "I know you're wanting to avenge Michael's death—"

"Not avenge, make sure it doesn't happen to someone else. Make sure some other family doesn't suffer like I have." Tears brimmed in her eyes. She wiped them away with an impatient gesture.

He was McCullough now. He stepped close and pulled her into his embrace. She smelled like flowers, and soap, and supper, everything fine and womanly. She clung to him, her head pressed against his chest. She felt nice, soft and round. Too nice.

He stood nearly a foot taller than her, his chin resting squarely on top of waves of auburn hair. Damn if she didn't fit all too well in his arms. Her manner, the feel of her, the way she looked at him all played against his conscience. Guilt again.

Damn, weak fool. Shake it off, Dietz.

"It's all right, Keely. We'll be taking care of things, but in our own time. You know what they say about fools rushing in?"

She pulled away, wiping at her tears with her apron. He pulled a handkerchief from his pocket and handed it to her.

"Were you warning me about Gaffney?" he asked.

"No, I—"

He winked at her. "Never mind, lass. Believe me, I've dealt with worse. I can handle Mr. Gaffney, at least as far as the union's concerned."

Outside the clouds parted to let a shaft of sunlight out. It cut in through the window, bathing the room with brilliance.

He turned his gaze to Keely. "I've never needed the likes of men like him. I can settle in on my own. Besides, Michael prepared the way for me sure enough."

At his mention of her brother, Keely's eyes misted over.

Dietz allowed his own eyes to cloud. "Ah, Michael." He spoke solemnly. He'd learned long ago to laugh on cue, cry on cue, whatever the hell it took. Once in character, he felt that character's pain and emotion without thinking.

He continued the act, shifting uncomfortably from one foot to the other before removing his gaze from her and returning it to the stream of light coming in. Since childhood when he'd been forced to live in cellars or barns, any dark, out of the way place, he'd loved light like freedom. He might like this room after all.

"Let me give you a lesson. An ally must be someone you trust with your life. A man with eyes for your woman doesn't qualify."

Keely smiled and shook her head. "McCullough, you are your own man."

He didn't refute it. He was whoever he needed to be. "Isn't that best, lass?" He turned from the window and smiled full at her. "Look at the light pouring in. I've always preferred to room on the south side."

"You won't when the days heat up." She paused. "My room is on the north side, cool, and much larger. When we're married, you'll move in with me." Her smile was not timid.

Who is this woman?

"And give up the light? Not on your life. You'll move in with me." Of course that would never happen. He'd delay the ceremony until he'd finished his job, and then move on like he always did. But as he stood there watching her, regret shaded the bright room, sprung from the knowledge that when this thing ended Miss Keely Byrne would most likely be as jaded about life and love as he was.

"We'll see." She spoke confidently.

So it was going to be a battle of wills. Did that fool McCullough know what he'd been in for? For himself, Dietz liked her all the more for her spunk.

"I've got to get back to making supper. I'll leave you to get settled in. We'll talk about the wedding later."

Her skirts rustled as she left, leaving him alone with his smile. He walked to the washbasin, rolled up his sleeves, poured some water, and splashed his face. He watched his reflection as he toweled off. Would Dietz the chameleon be able to pull this new cover off? The

storm of conscience and attraction Keely Byrne stirred
up in him made him wonder.

He dropped the towel onto the edge of the basin.
Better to concentrate on business, anything less dangerous than McCullough's fiancée. He needed to contact Patterson and inform him of his new cover, and
wire the Denver office, and Kinney, of the change as
well. He went to the bed and rummaged through his
duffel.

Where were McCullough's letters from Keely? Better read them over again. This time with a different
eye, one that gleaned information of the personal relationship that existed between them. His heart pounded
with anticipation, as it always did when he started an
operation. Becoming McCullough was a dangerous cover, and a most dangerous game, made even more so by
Miss Keely Byrne. Wasn't that the best kind?

"Drat!" Keely peered into the empty sugar basin as
if staring hard enough would make sugar appear. She'd
have to go across the street to Mr. Allison's store. She
could go to Mr. Samuels' next door. Both stores were
run by good union men. But Mr. Samuels charged
more, and was less companionable than Mr. Allison's
manager, Kate Shipley. Keely had been shopping at
Mr. Allison's since he bought it months ago. Lately
though, Lunn had been encouraging her to switch back
to Samuels'. She didn't understand his interest in
where she shopped. And at the moment, she was in no
mood to consider Lunn's wishes. She didn't want to
think of anything other than McCullough. Just his

name tripping across her thoughts sent her pulse racing.

She hadn't expected something as straightforward and simple as love-at-first-sight to happen to her. But it had, beginning the moment she realized the man coming up the boardwalk was McCullough, her McCullough. It built and grew as she watched him handle Lunn, dismissing him as nothing more than an unworthy competitor. Any man unafraid of Lunn showed bravery worth admiring. Thinking back on the scant hour McCullough had been here, she could only recall how pleasing he was, sensitive, honorable, smart—handsome.

Her newly realized feelings put her at a terrible disadvantage. Before, they had stood on equal, even ground, each with their own reasons for marrying based more on friendship and common goals than love. Now she wanted to bake him sweets, impress him with her talents, chase away insecure thoughts that he might not want her after all, not the way she suddenly wanted him.

Quick to passion, slow to think, that's what Michael always said about her. Maybe he'd been right.

She put on her bonnet and was reaching for the jar where she hid her spare change when a voice from the stairs stopped her.

"You're off somewhere?" McCullough stood on the steps, all freshly scrubbed and wearing a clean white shirt.

His sudden presence made her feel fluttery and off balance. "I'm out of sugar. I was just going across the street to Mr. Allison's store to get more."

"Allison? Isn't he Recording Secretary for the union?"

"He is. How did you know?"

McCullough grinned and shrugged. "The union's my business. Maybe I should join you and make his acquaintance."

"Isn't likely he'll be in. He's usually out on business this time of day, but I'd enjoy the company. And I'm sure Mrs. Shipley would like to meet the town's newest arrival."

"Let me escort you then." He offered his arm and led her out of the boarding house.

Keely spotted Mr. Allison stepping out of his establishment as they crossed the road that separated his place and her boarding house. "Wouldn't you know it? There's Mr. Allison, just to make a liar out of me." She waved and called out to him.

Though the street bustled with men and activity, McCullough's gaze had fixed on Allison immediately with uncanny perception. Mr. Allison came toward them.

"Mr. Allison, I'd like you to meet Mr. McCullough."

"McCullough, is it?" Mr. Allison scrutinized McCullough, looking almost bemused. An awkward moment followed while the two men sized each other up. At last Mr. Allison stuck his hand out and McCullough shook it. "So the much-talked-about McCullough has finally arrived."

"Much talked about?" McCullough turned to her.

"And why shouldn't a woman boast about her fiancé?"

McCullough smiled, obviously pleased. "Why not, indeed."

"McCullough is eager to get involved with the union. Judge Brown is expecting his arrival," Keely said. "It would be nice if someone on the inside introduced him. Will you be conducting any business with the judge soon, Mr. Allison?"

Mr. Allison didn't jump in with an immediate answer. He seemed to be taking a moment to consider. Keely wasn't offended. Mr. Allison was never quick with an answer, but once he made a promise, he always stuck to it.

"Well, truth be told, I was just on my way to Burke. Representatives from the Gem Union have been invited to the Burke Union's general meeting. I'm meeting our boys for a little conference beforehand." Mr. Allison cleared his throat. "I'm not sure as the fellows will let McCullough stay for the meeting, but if he wants to come along, I'll introduce him to everybody."

"Thank you, Mr. Allison."

"Don't be thanking me, Miss Byrne. If the boys let him stay, likely he won't be back before midnight. There's always socializing at the bars afterward. A new fellow won't want to miss it." Mr. Allison turned to McCullough. "When did you get in?"

Keely answered for him. "A little over an hour ago."

"Then I do apologize, ma'am."

"No apologies necessary, Mr. Allison. Anything for the union." She smiled at McCullough. "I guess Mrs. Shipley will have to meet you another day. You go on, and stay as long as you need."

"You'll want your horse," Mr. Allison said.

"It's across the street."

"Good then. Let's be going," Mr. Allison said.

Keely beamed at McCullough, so proud, so pleased with the way he'd turned out. Things were off to a fine start.

Patterson looked well recovered and more robust than Dietz had expected as they rode through town. Patterson, older than Dietz by a good five years, had always cut a dashing figure. Slender, with dark hair and lively, intelligent eyes, Patterson wore a fine specimen of a mustache that he never shaved off, even to change his appearance for a new mission. The only real difference in him was the smallpox scars that dotted his skin. Patterson was a tough bastard, even cheating smallpox of victory. That's what Dietz admired about him.

Patterson chatted about nothing, like a stranger, until they pulled outside the mining camp town of Gem. "What happened to the real McCullough?"

"Dead."

"Dead?" Patterson cocked a brow. "How?"

"I killed him. Bastard tried to shoot me in the back."

"Where?"

"Thompson's Falls."

Patterson sighed. "This is a dangerous game you're playing, my friend."

"Isn't it always?" Dietz slowed his horse to match Patterson's pace. "We'd just arrived in Thompson's Falls. Only a few folks heard the names we gave them. He and I looked similar, I guess. Sheriff there thought we were brothers. Someone tipped McCullough off to who I was. The McCabe cover was good as blown."

"Someone in Thompson's Falls?"

"I don't think so. There wasn't enough time."

"Who then?"

"I wish I knew. Might have been someone in Butte City." Dietz shrugged. "It's only a guess."

"You're betting whoever it was doesn't know McCullough is dead?"

"Yup."

Patterson sat silent a moment. "Takes nerve to just assume his identity."

"I was desperate for a way into the union. With McCullough dead how was I supposed to infiltrate? Likely as not they'd brand a new arrival as a scab or a spy."

Patterson snorted. "They're suspicious of everybody." Patterson's gaze pierced him. "Still, McCullough?"

"When I showed up, Keely Byrne mistook me for him. I figured if she didn't know the difference, who would?"

"What about the girl?" Patterson looked straight ahead.

"What about her? I'll play nice. Don't I always?" Dietz couldn't hold back a grin.

"All right, ladies boy. Just because you've been able to charm and outwit a few dozen whores and loose women, doesn't mean you'll pull this off with a woman who keeps her legs clamped shut and her head on her shoulders."

"I don't need to charm her. McCullough's already done that for me." Dietz laughed. "Maybe you should tell me about her."

"She's a friend of my manager, Mrs. Shipley. Miss Byrne's an ardent union supporter. You know about her brother?"

"I know he was killed in a mining accident."

Patterson nodded. "Then you know her motives?"

Dietz nodded. "Make the mines safe. Fair wages for miners."

"You've done your homework."

"I've read her letters to McCullough."

Patterson laughed, but it sounded hollow. "Then you know she expects McCullough to marry her."

"I do."

"And?"

"It won't come to that."

"Won't it? What are you going to do, stall?"

"Exactly. Bill McParland from the Denver office keeps yammering at me that things here will explode any day. Shouldn't be too hard to come up with excuses for the delay. I've always been a good liar."

"Aren't we all?" Patterson said. "What happens when the operation is over?"

No good trying to pin me down, Patterson, Dietz thought. "The usual. McCullough goes out of town on business, only to meet his date with death. I'll send his things back along with a sympathetic note from some fictitious lawman. Sound good?"

Patterson frowned. "Miss Byrne is a good woman. Her motives seem pure, and given a legitimate union, righteous. I'd hate to see her hurt."

Dietz didn't like the senior agent's accusation. "You going to wire McParland and send me back?"

"No." Patterson shook his head. "Just cautioning. Marriage is nothing to trifle with."

His words and sorrowful tone set Dietz back. Patterson had only recently lost his young wife. Coming from him, empathy and sympathy for a grieving spouse weren't surprising.

"Won't come to that. Did you know her brother Michael?" Dietz asked, changing the subject.

"Slightly."

"What was he like?"

"You knew McCullough," Patterson said. "I don't expect Michael Byrne was much different, just another violent anarchist."

Considering his first impression of Keely, it took Dietz a moment to digest what Patterson said.

"Miss Byrne thinks he was murdered." Patterson adjusted himself in the saddle.

"Was he?"

"It was an accident as far as I could tell. Tunnel caved in on him. Took hours to dig him out. For obvious reasons Michael Byrne was not well liked by the owners. Though, shortly before his death he seemed to have a slight change of heart, or maybe the depth of the violence finally got to him. Anyway, he started preaching about negotiation. Some of his fellow miners thought he'd gone soft.

"Once they realized that the tunnel had collapsed maybe they could have sent for reinforcements sooner to dig it out. But that should have been the foreman's responsibility, and he was a union man and good friend of Byrne's. On any account, Byrne was dead when they got to him." Patterson looked at him. "How do you feel about unions?"

Dietz shrugged. He held no particular opinion.

"Used to sympathize with them myself," Patterson said. "Almost turned down this job. Didn't want to side against the working man. But these men aren't out for the common good. They're anarchists, plain and simple. Most of the leaders are straight off the boat from Ireland. They've taken their orange and green mentality right to the mining conflict. Their credo seems to be *kill them, maim them, terrorize them until you get what you want.* And when you get that, terrorize until you get more.'" Patterson shook his head. "These men are more than a threat to the Valley. They're a threat to the entire nation. If their mentality takes hold nationwide, we will be in anarchy. No citizen will be safe."

Patterson's words chilled Dietz.

"Make no mistake, Dietz. The mine union leaders are a vicious bunch of murderers. They're at war, and they'll eliminate anyone they perceive to be the enemy. Watch your backside."

Dietz snorted. "Haven't I already?"

Patterson laughed with him.

"So what about you and me?" Dietz asked. "A little bird told me you're under suspicion for being a spy."

Patterson's eyes lit up. "Is that what McParland said?" He laughed. "I'm holding my own so far. No one's been able to gather any irrefutable evidence against me yet."

"Still, it sounds like McCullough and Allison shouldn't become good friends."

Patterson nodded. "Isn't that the point of redundancy? Two operatives, one goes down, the other covers. No, I'd say for safety's sake you have to separate yourself from me. And you'd better mail your own reports. The union men are getting suspicious of my evening walks to the post office in Wallace. And they aren't aware of over half the trips I've made."

"You walk to Wallace? No wonder you're so damned thin. That's got to be close to four miles." Dietz shifted in the saddle. "What about the post office in Gem?"

"No good. Samuels, the fellow with the store next door to you, runs the Gem post office from his store. He's a rabid union man."

"But he won't be suspecting McCullough of treason against the union."

"He reads all the outgoing mail. And his deputy postmaster, Big Frank, is also a member of the Gem Union." Patterson spoke matter-of-factly.

"So what do I do?"

"You'll figure something out."

"What about maintaining contact with you?"

"Nothing on a regular basis. We don't want to arouse any suspicion. We'll have to trust fate to give us opportunities as we need them. If you must leave me a message, you can trust Mrs. Shipley with a note. She and that five-year-old boy of hers are salt-of-the-earth people."

"She knows about you?"

"Hasn't a clue."

Dietz nodded. They rounded a bend and the narrow town of Burke came into view. "What the hell? Will you look at that one street town."

Burke was built not so much in a valley as in a crevice between the mountains that allowed for only one street's width. Because the mining town relied heavily on the railroad to ship its lifeblood, galena, silver ore, the tracks and the street shared the same space.

Dietz stared at it in amazement. "What do they do when the train comes through?"

"Businesses fold up their awnings so they don't catch fire or get scraped off." Patterson laughed, then slowed his horse to a near stop. "I ought to warn you. This isn't any common business meeting we're going to. They're going to use this meeting to plan their next act of violence. What that will be, only the bosses know right now. I haven't even been privy to it. Most likely they'll vote on which scab to beat up next, or who to run off. And they'll take care of it tonight. It won't be pretty."

"You don't need to warn me. Coming over the Bitterroot Range I ran into a scab family the union ran off. The fellow was in bad shape, beat up bad, and the wife and this little kid were starving. I gave them food and money, and help back to within miles of Thompson's Falls."

Patterson gave him a serious look. "I hope no one finds out about it. Wouldn't look good for McCullough."

"Wasn't McCullough who helped them. It was Peter Sullivan." Dietz expected Patterson to chuckle, but he didn't.

"Don't get any noble notions here, Dietz. Last fall, shortly after I came, I saw as fine a specimen of Irish manhood as God makes. Looked a lot like you—jet black hair, intelligent eyes, a mustache—real easy for the ladies to look at. He spoke up at a meeting, and condemned the violent approach, advocating negotiation. After the meeting, the leaders sat down on him so hard he couldn't get his jaws working all winter. There was even talk of branding him a 'scab.' He hasn't said a word since.

"These men aren't interested in solving the differences between them and the owners. They just like to fight. Of course, they'll tell you different. They'll talk the talk. Fair wages for all. But does it make any sense for muckers and common roustabouts to receive three-fifty a day in wages, the same as skilled miners?"

Dietz didn't get a chance to answer. Maybe the question was rhetorical anyway. Patterson was already looking ahead toward town.

"Looks like the bosses are starting to gather." Patterson pointed toward something in the distance. "I recognize Brown from here." He clucked to his horse.

"Let's be going. We don't want to be late." He laughed. "Oh, and Dietz, if they deem you worthy of member-ship, cross your fingers when they give you the Molly Maguire oath and make you swear loyalty to the union on penalty of death."

Patterson moved out, with Dietz right behind him. "Won't have to, Charlie. McCullough took the Molly Maguire oath years ago. He was practically baptized with it."

CHAPTER THREE

D ietz and Patterson met up with Judge Brown in the street outside the meeting hall.

"Judge Brown." Patterson sounded friendly, though Dietz knew he despised the judge.

"Allison, who've you brought?" The judge's gruff manner matched his overall appearance.

What a pompous, egotistical bastard. Dietz disliked him immediately but smiled at him just the same.

As the judge stared at Dietz, not a hint of a smile broke his lips. His eyes reflected nothing but darkness.

"Let me introduce you to Ian McCullough," Patterson continued. "From Pennsylvania. Of union activist fame. Keely Byrne asked me to make introductions."

Judge Brown grunted. "Friend of her dead brother. Byrne always spoke highly of him." The judge squinted at Dietz, studying him at length. "Younger looking than Byrne described you but similar enough." He grunted again. "Can't be too careful. Waters hired you to do some work for us?"

Dietz nodded.

Brown waved a dismissive hand at Dietz. "Come on in. You can stay."

The meeting room filled quickly. Patterson made all the necessary introductions. Dietz had read Patterson's reports. From them he knew how the union operated and recognized many names. Each town, or mining camp, had its own union. All the local unions elected delegates to represent them in the Central Union. Tim O'Brien was president, and Joe Poynton, secretary, of the Central Union. Both were present, as well as Sam Waters, president of the Gem Union, and of course, Judge Brown and Patterson.

Patterson, as Allison, pulled out a pad of paper and a pen and prepared to take minutes. The Burke Union president called the meeting to order, but the judge quickly took over.

"Gentlemen, we're here to discuss our next course of action against the owners. Our men have been out of work far too long, and the owners refuse to capitulate or negotiate. We must act, in the interest of our men, before they lose heart, before they face any more deprivation. We have men leaving the Valley, going off to seek temporary work elsewhere so that they can feed their families.

"Gentlemen, can we afford to let our men go another month without wages?"

A hearty round of no's sounded around the room. Brown's eyes sparkled with passion, or love of evil, Dietz couldn't decide which, and his voice shook with emotion. All apparently genuine. And terribly dangerous. Dietz stared at him with the same rapt attention the others gave, not daring to look any less interested.

"What do you suggest, George?" O'Brien asked.

The judge seemed to tremble with excitement. "We all know the owners won't act without a little prodding, some small incident to show we mean business." Giddy, that was how the judge looked.

"The boys still want blood for that first load of scabs that sneaked past us to the Gem mine. I say it's time we let them have it. Those scabs are trapped up at the mine without supplies—"

"Are you saying we hold up the supply train, George?" Poynton asked.

"I don't see how we can get around the law to do that just now, Joe. It's one thing to have a phony warrant written out to arrest the train engineer for transporting illegal workers, but what reason can we give to hold up cargo? We aren't that desperate—yet. What I had in mind is a little more personal."

Brown outlined his plan to beat up a scab laborer from the Gem Mine. Petty stuff. Nothing worth reporting or risking his life for, Dietz thought. Boring. Dietz yawned. McCullough would have been asleep at such small stuff ten minutes ago. Maybe an eruption wasn't as close as Patterson thought.

The private meeting adjourned. President O'Brien sent the bell ringers out ahead to Gem to signal a meeting of the general assembly so that they could present their plan to beat up a man.

Back in Gem, anger, palpable and impatient, pulsed through the general assembly. Bleak, weary frustration painted the faces of a hundred idle miners with too much time to think and too little sense to do so critically. That was Dietz's impression as he strode out of the assembly hall into the street joining the crowd that wove toward O'Malley's Tavern.

Scruffy beards, faded denim pants, weathered skin, work shirts. The description fit almost every man within sight. When had things become desperate? What had driven these men to mob mentality, to trust violence to solve their problems?

Judge Brown had outlined his plan to the general membership. Dietz prayed that the targeted scab, Jake Waller, had the good sense to stay up at the mine. But he doubted Brown would allow a quirk of fate, or human fickleness, to rob him of his glory. Nothing was said, but Dietz got the impression that Jake would be where he was expected tonight.

Before dismissing the crowd, Brown had introduced Dietz.

"McCullough is an expert in union management negotiations. He'll be advising your leadership on strategies that have proven useful back East."

Yeah, strategies. Terrorism more like. Dietz had bowed to the crowd and taken his seat again.

Then Brown had looked pointedly at his watch. "Men, the hour is upon us." He nodded and spread his arms and the crowd had parted, forming an aisle. The judge walked through with Dietz and the others trailing him. As soon as they broke through the door and out into the dusk, the aisle collapsed as the masses pressed in behind them. Now they weaved to the back of O'Malley's three abreast, circling to the back and arcing around the door.

"How's it feel to have a front row seat, McCullough? Bet you haven't had this much fun in quite a while." Before Dietz could answer, Brown yelled out a command. "O'Malley, send him out."

How long had Waller been held prisoner? This was no last minute, spur of the moment act.

The back door to the bar opened. The stout bartender thrust a terrified man out into the mud, into the center of the arc of men surrounding him.

Premeditated, the whole damn thing planned well in advance.

"Look, boys." Jake's voice trembled. "I just came down for a drink. I didn't mean any harm."

"Thief!" someone yelled.

"Damned scab!" A torrent of insults and obscenities followed as the crowd collapsed onto the man. Lunn Gaffney threw the first punch. With it came the sickening crack of knuckles hitting flesh. Jake Waller staggered. The crowd laughed.

As Dietz watched, sickened, Gaffney grabbed the man and pinned his arms back. "When's the next load of cussed scabs due in?"

Waller trembled and shook his head. "Don't know."

Gaffney wrenched Waller's arm. Waller groaned. "I don't know. I don't."

"Who's next?" Gaffney yelled.

The men didn't bother forming a line. What did Dietz expect, gentlemen? They punched and kicked and spit on Jake as many at a time as they could get to him, repeating their question and retaliating when they got no response.

"Care for a turn, McCullough?" Brown spoke to him.

"Not my style," Dietz said, trying to sound insulted. Didn't Brown realize that participating in a small time beating was well beneath McCullough? "Let the men have their fun."

In mere minutes, Jake no longer looked human. His features became unrecognizable beneath the swelling and blood. He passed out. Gaffney, heavily muscled and strong, staggered under his dead weight, and at last dropped him face down into a puddle. The battle seemed lost. Waller wouldn't be talking now. Dietz watched Waller's blood color the water, mingling with it like red rain. In a minute, he'd drown.

"Get a rope!" someone shouted. "If he won't talk, we'll string him up as an example!"

Cheers echoed off the building. Patterson made no move to help. Dietz couldn't stand it any longer. He wasn't paid to watch innocent men die. He stepped to the center of the half circle and opened his mouth to shout.

"Enough!"

But it wasn't Dietz's voice that silenced the crowd. Keely Byrne came flying around the corner of the building, her hair loose and blowing wildly about her face, her green eyes flashing. In that instant, their gazes locked. Something ephemeral but powerful passed between them. An intimacy so deep and unexpected it caught Dietz off guard and shattered his senses. For a brief moment it was just the two of them—Keely and him. Both on the same side, and wildly opposed to each other.

Fear for her safety, mingled with admiration for her courage, pumped through him, hammering at his heart, surprising him. *Damn that woman for coming out into this crowd!*

The men around Keely looked startled by her appearance. Dietz saw them only peripherally. Without unlocking his gaze from hers, Dietz used his foot to push Waller over onto his back.

"Go on home, Keely." His voice came out deeper, more drawling than he wanted. "This isn't something a lady should see."

Keely's stomach felt tight and sick at the sight before her. How could McCullough just stand there and watch it happen? And yet as her gaze beheld his, she saw the spark of compassion in his eyes, his own horror at the spectacle before them. Maybe she could trust him.

"No, indeed! This isn't something a *human being* should see!" Keely's heart pounded in her ears. Her hands trembled as she glanced around the crowd.

"Shame on you! Shame on you all. Violence against the innocent and the weak never overcomes tyranny. Save your anger for the real culprits—the owners. Go after them where it hurts, in their pocketbooks."

Keely nodded to McCullough, turned on her heel, and retreated. But only around the corner, to the shadow of the building just out of McCullough's sight. She'd not go one step closer to home until she made certain they didn't kill the scab, until McCullough saved him as she'd challenged him to do. She pressed herself tightly against the building and dared to peek around the corner at the action still unfolding.

Damn, a woman who obeys, Dietz thought. *What an enigma that woman is turning out to be.*

Relieved she'd left, he looked down to the man at his feet. In a glance, he took in the delicate rise of Waller's chest. Maybe it wasn't too late to save him.

Waller coughed, spitting up blood and water. "Thursday," he said only loud enough for Dietz to hear before his head rolled to the side and he passed out again.

Dietz held his arms up with his palms out toward the crowd. His heart thudded in his ears. One wrong move and he joined Waller. "Thursday," Dietz shouted.

The crowd roared.

Dietz couldn't get the picture of Keely from his mind.

"What time? Get the time!" Someone screamed from the audience. Another man moved in with a rope. Dietz pushed him away.

"What's the point? He can't tell us more." Dietz cleared his throat. "Take this man." Dietz nudged Waller with the toe of his boot. "And dump him at the entrance of the Gem Mine."

Several men stepped forward and hoisted Waller up.

Brown clapped Dietz on the back. "Good thinking, McCullough." The judge nodded, smiling. "Let the boys take him." He chuckled. "Can you imagine those scabs up there at the Gem quaking in their boots? Wonder how long it'll take them to get up the nerve to open up and bring Waller in."

Dietz forced a smile. "Thank you, Judge."

The judge nodded toward the bar. "Let's get us something to drink while we plan what to do about that train load of scabs we're expecting. First drink's on me."

The judge prattled on, gloating about their triumph, but Dietz wasn't listening. In his mind, he kept seeing Keely coming around the corner, kept feeling the stun of it. He had trouble on his hands with that woman. Big trouble, and most of it deep down in his own core where she stirred something in him that he didn't like feeling—not one bit.

As the crowd dispersed, Keely darted back around the corner and turned to tip her head back against the wall and release a pent up sigh. "Yes," she whispered and pounded the air in victory. The scab had a chance now, all thanks to McCullough's quick thinking.

McCullough! He was everything she'd imagined— courageous, honorable, compassionate. She smiled

broadly, so proud of him, so happy to be proved right in
her regard for him. Why had she doubted him?

Men began coming around the building in her direction. Time to get home. Remembering the looks of hatred, the bloodlust in the eyes of the mob, she shook off
a shudder and quickened her step. Her hands trembled
like white pines in the wind as she picked up her skirts
to avoid dragging them in the dusty street. The enor-
mity of her hasty actions overcame her. What had she
been thinking by jumping unarmed and with no plan
into the midst of such evil? She couldn't have stopped
the men on her own. When would she learn to think
before acting? When men stopped hurting each other?
She shook her head. Probably never. On all counts.

She hurried across the street. Because she was a
woman, the men probably would not have harmed her.
They hadn't beaten up a woman yet. Tossed her out of
the way—certainly. Pawed her up, yes. Burning the
boardinghouse, running her out of town, terrorizing
her—in that frenzied mood, now spent, she believed
them capable of all of that. Thank God for
McCullough! What would she have done without him?
In the future she must check her indignation. After all,
she sympathized with the union, if not always with
their methods.

Dietz staggered up the boardwalk to the boarding
house. It was late. The sky had clouded up again. Nary
a star lit his way in. Too much whiskey swirled his
thoughts in an ugly direction. Blood. The sight of Waller beaten, maybe dying. He tried to push the images

away, but they remained, distorted and inflated by drink. Usually alcohol numbed his senses, but not tonight.

He wasn't squeamish. In his days as a cowpuncher he'd seen good men gored by bulls, trampled by runaway cattle. Working as a private detective he'd seen his share of killing. Thoughts of McCullough's vacant stare came to him. Killing in self-defense was one thing, but this blatant bloodlust...

He shivered. Patterson was right. These union men were rabid anarchists. And Keely Byrne lived right in the midst of it all.

Keely. Now that's what made him squeamish. His reaction to her. She lived in a world on the opposite side of his. He shouldn't be feeling a thing for her, not one. So why couldn't he shake the impact she'd made on him that afternoon?

He stumbled up the front step and collided with the front doorframe, cursing. He paused at the door. Well, one thing was certain. Miss Keely Byrne wasn't going to be happy with McCullough's behavior tonight. He'd be lucky if she didn't throw McCullough out. But Dietz wasn't so pleased with her antics earlier, either.

He pushed the front door open, anticipating slipping quietly upstairs, but his boots clunked noisily on the wooden floor. As he slipped them off, he paused, trying to remember what room was his. That was the problem with being so many people. You were always trying to recall where home was.

"McCullough?" A gentle, feminine voice sliced through the silence.

Dietz started and turned toward the sound. Keely sat in the dark at the kitchen table. Why hadn't he noticed her? Damned whiskey.

In the dark, he couldn't make out her features, only her silhouette. Her hair fell loose over her shoulders. He heard the clinking of glass, like the lid of a kerosene lamp being removed, then the strike of a match. Suddenly, she was illuminated at the table. She wore nightclothes, a white wrapper with gown peeking through. To his surprise, she didn't look angry. Her green eyes sparkled in the light, like she was happy to see him. After he'd ordered her home and caroused all night, how could that be?

"Keely. You shouldn't have waited up." Did his voice sound slurred?

"Have a seat, McCullough." She kicked a chair out for him opposite her.

He should have apologized. At least, he felt that's what McCullough should have done. John Dietz had never operated by the clock and had never been keen on commitment or asking forgiveness. Probably had to do with being on his own so young. But Keely didn't seem to be expecting an apology, so he didn't offer one.

"How was the meeting?"

"The meeting?"

"After I left."

She *was* cool.

"Productive." Dietz dropped into the chair. It felt good to sit, but disconcerting to be stared at so obviously. What was the woman looking for? Worse still, he had a hard time focusing on her face. His gaze kept drifting to the well-formed nipples poking through the thin cotton of her wrapper. Damn whiskey. It always made him amorous.

Maybe it *had* been too long since he'd been with a woman. It sure had been too long since he'd been with a good woman, if, indeed, he ever had. But he couldn't fool himself. Keely Byrne was attractive. He'd always been partial to dark, auburn hair and green eyes—and curves.

"Productive," Keely repeated. "You'll have to be more specific. Does the scab live?"

Dietz nodded, too tired and too drunk to keep up pretenses with Keely. If anyone would find him out, she would. "But we sent a message to the owners. One they can't well ignore."

Keely nodded, looking hesitant. "I'm sorry. I owe you an apology. I should have trusted you—"

"Damn right, lass."

"But I didn't know if you were still back in Burke or not." She hardly looked contrite.

"You could have gotten yourself run out of town." Maybe it was only the drink, but the conversation made little sense to Dietz. She apologized when he should have?

She smiled and shrugged. "Wouldn't have happened. You would have protected me."

"You have great faith in my abilities, especially considering you didn't think I'd be there."

"Lunn wouldn't let them harm me either."

Damn that Lunn. Dietz needed to shift topics.

"Why aren't you mad at me?" Damn, that was Dietz talking, not McCullough. What did it matter anyway, other than it was blasted odd? Even the whores he kept company with on other missions got possessive. And this woman had every right to be, but wasn't. He was supposed to be her fiancé, and he sure hadn't acted like it. He'd have to remedy that before she got suspicious. He hadn't brought her a present or anything. He tried to think, but the whiskey fog blocked him. Did McCullough have a present for her among his things? Women liked gifts.

"Mad at you for what? For being late? For being drunk? Why should I be? You saved the scab and still managed to make a point to the owners. What is a little drunkenness compared to that? You like your drink, like Michael did. I wouldn't have expected different. Besides, once we met Mr. Allison, I knew you wouldn't be coming back for supper. And after the incident by the tavern, I realized you might not come back till dawn. I never made that special pie. I'll make it tomorrow."

What kind of a life had Keely led? How had Michael schooled her to be so blasted tolerant? He resisted the urge to shake his head. Keely stared at him intently. "I'm glad you're not mad, but what in the devil are you staring at?"

"You." She smiled, looking almost shy for the first time.

"Me?"

"You don't look exactly like you described yourself."

Dietz's heart thudded, pounding so loud it hurt his head. If she decided he wasn't McCullough after all...

He forced a lopsided grin. "How so?"

"Your eyes." Her voice grew soft. "They're not plain old blue, like you said. They're, well, they're nearly violet." Her voice became breathy, too alluring. "Ian McCullough, you're so beautiful, you're nearly perfection." Her gaze fell from his face.

What the hell? No woman had ever spoken of him so tenderly before. He was oddly moved, and damned uncomfortable. Coming on top of all that had happened today, he didn't like it one bit.

She stood. "Let me make you some coffee. Michael always liked to chat over a cup of coffee when he got back from a meeting." Her words were simple enough, but she sounded almost forlorn, a shade uneasy. What had he done now?

Dietz shoved his chair back and came around the table to stand in front of her. "Don't bother about the coffee, Keely. I don't need any." He caught her chin and pulled her face up, forcing her to look at him. Her fair skin felt soft against his rough hand, as soft as he imagined. "Something wrong, Keely?"

Her eyes misted, making him uncomfortable. He'd always been a sucker for a vulnerable woman. "I'm just a camp cook and a boarding house worker. Why would a man as powerful, smart, and handsome as you want me?"

Dumbfounded, he dropped his hand from her chin.

"What will I do, McCullough, if you don't want me?"

Dietz couldn't believe her words. Either the woman was amazingly coy, or she really believed what she said. On any account, her words sliced through him like a stiletto. Damned guilt again. "You'd be the same strong, independent woman you've shown me through your letters these last years. You'd get by. But that isn't going to happen, darling." What was he saying?

She looked up at him. Almost without thinking, he bent to kiss her. Her lips were moist when they met his, and there was nothing shy about the way she pressed herself against him. He felt himself go long and hard. All the ugly thoughts and incidents of the night faded away. The soft, round feel of Keely against him, and the innocent probing of her tongue consumed him. He crushed her to him in a long embrace, tracing her shapely backside with his hands. The heavy thudding of boots on the boardwalk outside brought him to his senses. Damn, he had to pull away before he went too far. Another bolt of conscience come from nowhere.

As the footsteps receded into the night, he separated from Keely. The light made her eyes emerald, and she looked wild and flushed, and eager. He liked the sight of her far too much.

She cleared her throat and straightened the folds of her wrapper. He couldn't help himself from speaking. "You have nothing to worry about, Keely."

She laughed self-consciously, sounding genuinely happy. "Seems like we'd better discuss the wedding tomorrow." She looked up at him from under her thick lashes. "Time for bed." She pointed to the stairs. "Third door on the left."

He picked up his boots and walked to the stairs while she picked up the kerosene lamp and went to the hall on the main floor. He turned back to watch her just as she disappeared into the black hall toward her ground floor room.

He hoped it was only the whiskey obscuring his good sense and stirring his desires, but Keely was having far too great an effect on him. *Watch it, Dietz, that woman could bring nothing but trouble and heartache.* Let her under his skin and he'd lose all perspective about the operation and his cover, maybe even his jaded heart, along with it.

Back in her room, Keely latched the door shut and plopped onto her back on her deep featherbed, sighing happily as the bed squeaked beneath her weight. McCullough's kiss still sang on her lips. The feel of his hands caressing her body was a memory so pleasant it felt real. What a day this had been! A day unequaled in all her life.

McCullough had come and was more than mere man. Handsome, devastatingly so, smart, strong, brave, honest, compassionate. A knight, her knight. A dream realized so completely she barely dared to believe it true. Yet it was!

Like Lunn had done this afternoon, people always accused her of being too trusting. But in this instance, her faith had not been misplaced. It might be true that a man could impersonate traits in a letter, pretend to be something different than his true self. But a man's actions showed his real character, and from what she'd seen, McCullough had plenty. Deep down she knew that if she couldn't trust McCullough with her heart, there wasn't a man alive she could.

CHAPTER FOUR

What had come over Keely? Why had she admitted her fears and insecurities to McCullough when she needed to show him strength? But she *had* always wondered why McCullough had chosen her from all the women of his acquaintance, women he had seen and known. Why go with a blind choice?

McCullough stood above local men in power and reputation. He could have any woman he chose. Why her, a poor girl without position or connections?

Before he came, she half-feared he must be hideously deformed, or uncommonly hard to get along with in person. Of course, Michael had always claimed the contrary. But when McCullough arrived and she saw how handsome he was, her insecurities resurfaced.

At first he hadn't acted like the McCullough of her letters, not until the kiss. Then she knew that he felt all he had expressed with his pen. Keely sighed. "McCullough," she whispered into the darkness. She couldn't wait to become his wife.

Dietz woke. The unfamiliar surroundings didn't disorient him. He never stayed in one place long enough for things to become homey. But the thick pounding in his temples felt all too familiar. He rolled onto his side and reached for the water pitcher on the bedside table. Drinking plenty of water helped fight off the effect of too much whiskey. Man, had he had too much.

The night had tormented him with sensual, drugged dreams of Keely. He rubbed his temple. If one lousy kiss could cause all this discomfort—he was indeed a desperate man.

He fell back onto the pillow, trying to remember the events that had occurred before he'd come home the previous night—without the gory details. Hazy memories flooded back.

Waters had put him in charge of planning the holdup of the scab train on Thursday. But they'd all been too drunk to think clearly. Still, he'd better wire the owners right away. Damn, a clandestine four-mile walk to Wallace didn't sound the least enticing. He'd save himself a second trip if he came up with his plan for the holdup and wired that along with his first report. The owners better be smart enough to foil the union's plan without casting suspicion on him.

Keely drifted back into his thoughts. Stick to business. Search McCullough's saddlebags for a present and a ring. He seemed to recall a wrapped package. He hadn't paid much attention when he'd perused McCullough's things before. What kind of a suitor had McCullough been? Keely wrote uninhibited, intimate letters to McCullough, letting her ideas and thoughts flow freely, but speaking little of love. How had McCullough responded? Did he keep his feelings to himself or embarrass her with fond sentiments?

McCullough hadn't spoken much about Keely. Not much more than to admit she existed, which had surprised the hell out of Dietz the first time McCullough had mentioned that he had a fiancée. Why did he need a wife? He had a mistress of long standing whom he abused on a regular basis and any number of one night encounters and relationships of short duration.

His mistress had provided the reason for McCullough to flee Pennsylvania. One night, thoroughly pickled after a night of heavy drinking, McCullough had beaten her up, not for the first time by any accounting method. New and surprising, however, was her sudden desire to see him prosecuted for his crimes. That in itself would not have worried McCullough enough to send him scurrying to Idaho. But all the terrorist secrets he'd shared with her over the years had him worried a good piece. Angry and scorned, she might be tempted to use his confidences against him. So McCullough had fled, Dietz at his side, intent on heading to Idaho to stir up more trouble and marry a girl there. Maybe McCullough thought a wife would add an element of respectability to him? That's all Dietz could figure.

McCullough ranked as a first class bastard, which made Dietz feel only slightly less guilty about deceiving Keely than he otherwise might. No matter how low Dietz's deception ranked, it paled when compared to how McCullough would have treated Keely.

Still, odd as it was, McCullough wrote to Keely every night, mailing the letters when he could. Dietz sat up and swung out of bed. He washed up at the basin, toweled off, pulled on his clothes, and combed his hair before digging into McCullough's bags.

There, wrapped in brown paper and tied with twine with her name scrawled across it in a bold, sloppy hand sat the parcel. McCullough's? Dietz studied it, trying to memorize the way it looked before he passed the package on to Keely. His own writing looked nothing the same. Could he avoid writing anything she'd see until his mission ended? He hoped so.

Dietz hefted the package—a book. He hoped something touching like poetry or sonnets. He had no choice but to trust McCullough's taste in gifts. He rifled through the rest of the bags looking for a wedding ring. Nothing. Dietz frowned, McCullough hadn't had a ring on him either. Quite the romantic—a book, no ring. He stuffed McCullough's things back in his bags and glanced at his pocket watch. Time to head downstairs for breakfast.

He found Keely frying ham and potatoes and serving two old men. She looked up at him and called a greeting as he clumped down the last steps. She looked fresh and pretty, all flushed from the heat of the stove.

"Come meet two of my other boarders, Sly and Pickins. McCullough."

The men grunted and nodded as Keely bent to set their breakfast before them. Before she straightened, Dietz got a quick view of the ample curve of her breast—whoa! She wore a white apron covering a worn, faded work dress, shapeless and old, but still unable to hide her voluptuous figure. If she had just one outfit like those of the fancy ladies Dietz usually associated with on missions, she'd put them to shame.

"Since the mines shut down Sly and Pickins have been my only early risers," Keely said.

"We work our own claim," Sly cut in.

"You don't say." Dietz took a seat at the table. "Hope you use union labor."

The two weathered men laughed in unison. They looked like brothers. "We don't work for silver," Sly said.

"Nah," Pickins said. "We got us a gold stake."

"Gold?" The old men amused Dietz. "Aren't you boys about twenty years too late for that? Last gold I heard about in Idaho was up in Murray, about that long ago."

"What would you know about that, young man? You had to be nothing but a boy twenty years ago." Sly sounded insulted. "We'll find us our gold, mark my words."

You had to admire their optimism. Dietz smiled and nodded.

"All the gold taken was by placer mining and pan-
ning. I ask you where all that gold came from," Pickins
said.

Dietz shrugged. Keely winked at him behind the
men's backs.

Sly nodded. "There's got to be a vein."

"Might be," Dietz said. "Where's your claim?"

Keely came around to set a plate of food in front of
him and smiled boldly. He liked a brash woman. Unfortunately, he liked this particular one too much for any
good to come of it. How was he supposed to postpone
the wedding and keep to himself when his body reacted
to her the way it did? He wanted more than a look—he
wanted a feel, a good one. He hadn't imagined he'd be
fighting himself, too.

"The boys never reveal the location of their latest
stake," she said.

Dietz laughed. "Didn't mean any offense. I hope you
fellows are looking on the south side of the Valley. Isn't
that where legend says it should be?" One thing about
private detectives—they knew their subject. Dietz had
always been a quick study. He had picked up the history of the Valley without much trouble.

"We'll never say, young man," Pickins said.

"What's that tucked under your arm, McCullough?"
Keely asked.

Dietz handed her the package. "For you. I meant to
give it to you yesterday, but I got distracted. My apologies."

Keely wiped her hands on her apron and took it. She
pulled up a chair next to his and stared at the package

a moment before carefully removing the twine and paper. Dietz read the title as she pulled the book from its wrapping, *A Connecticut Yankee in King Arthur's Court.* What kind of a gift was that to give a woman you intend to marry? But Keely's eyes misted. She opened the cover and traced the written inscription lovingly, reverently. Though he strained, the angle she held it at prevented him from reading it.

"Michael's copy. How kind of you to remember and return it."

Dietz fought to hide his natural astonishment. The bastard McCullough hadn't bought her a present after all. While he understood her happiness at getting her brother's book back, it didn't lessen his anger at McCullough. McCullough should have brought her a real gift, something from himself. It had been Dietz's experience that women loved, and expected, gifts, nice ones. Any one of the women he seduced on the job, or even the few he'd courted as himself, would have flung such a "gift" back in his face. But Keely seemed satisfied—why?

He didn't like the empathy for her that crept over him unbidden. Had she been a child like him—discarded, abandoned, unwanted? What scars, like his own, did she live with?

Fortunately, Sly and Pickins rose to leave, muttering gruff grunts he took for goodbyes. Their departure broke his contemplative mood. No good ever came of becoming attached to a woman during a mission.

Keely rose and cleared away their plates before re-joining Dietz at the table. Her mood seemed less reflective, which suited him.

"How's Thursday?" she asked.

He frowned, confused. "Thursday? For what?" He filled his fork with potatoes.

"The wedding."

He set down the fork, still heaped with food. This was a fine fix. Her stare disconcerted him. She looked too—what? Honest, hopeful?

"Ah," he cleared his throat, "this Thursday?"

She laughed. "You're hedging, McCullough. You suddenly getting cold feet?"

"No, darling. I have an important union meeting Thursday."

"Will it take the whole day?"

"Probably."

She looked skeptical. "Then when? Thursday is the only day the circuit minister comes to the Valley."

"Just this Thursday? One Thursday a month?" Did he sound too hopeful?

"No." When she laughed her eyes danced. "Every Thursday. But I don't want to wait."

Her innocence and straightforward manner rattled him. He cleared his throat. For some unaccountable reason this discussion frightened him more than any situation he'd encountered in his eight years as a private detective. "Well, then, how about a wedding with the justice of the peace? Then we can pick our day." *Months from now*, he added silently. Even before the words slipped out of his mouth he frantically tried to think of a way to postpone it indefinitely.

Keely's face fell. He couldn't understand the hurt.

"No. McCullough, you agreed to be married by a man of God."

When had he agreed? Dietz couldn't remember Keely asking such a thing in any of her letters. He had to get ahold of the letters McCullough wrote before he blew his cover. And he'd better give her letters a closer study. "Uh, well." For once John Dietz was speechless, unable to come up with a lie as he looked into her guileless eyes.

"I won't be living in sin before Him."

"No, of course not." He didn't need to try to sound contrite. His voice quaked and stuttered all on its own. "I'm sorry."

She smiled again. "Thursday next—no union business. You'll have a wedding to attend."

He nodded like a fool. "Thursday next." At least he had another week to weasel out of it. Out of her presence he'd be able to think better. With luck, the fireworks would be over by then anyway and he could head back to the spartan hotel room he called home in Denver and wait for a nice, exciting mission somewhere far away from Idaho.

Dietz sat facing the judge in a cramped room in the temporary Gem Union headquarters building located just down the street from the boardinghouse. He, Judge Brown, President O'Brien, Joe Poynton, Gem Union President Sam Waters and several other dignitaries crowded around a circular table going over plans to hold up the next scab train.

"How do we know Waller told us the truth?" O'Brien asked.

"For cripes sakes, he was trying to save his own skin. Why would he lie? He didn't have enough wits left at that point to think to try." The judge was as gruff and impatient as always.

"What if Waller talked to his fellow scabs, and told them what he told us?" Waters looked pointedly at Dietz, like he should be blamed for this new worry.

"What if? What does it matter? We've got scouts everywhere and the canyon blockaded. How are the scabs going to get to town to wire and warn the owners?" The judge glared at Waters, his disgust for the man evident.

"We still don't know the time," Waters argued.

"Doesn't matter," Dietz said. "We'll place lookouts down the canyon to watch for the train. The men need something to keep them occupied and out of trouble, even if it's just twiddling their thumbs on lookout duty."

"McCullough makes a good point," O'Brien said. "It's best to keep the men busy. But whatever the plan, it's got to be legal, or at least look legal, or we risk turning public sentiment against us."

"We arrest and turn back them blasted scabs in Wallace, just like we planned to the first time. It's still just as illegal to import armed thugs today as it was last month," said Poynton without the slightest trace of irony.

"The owners ran their train through Wallace without stopping last time. Why would they change their minds now?" The judge drummed the table.

"Let's blockade the entrance to the Gem and get them there," Waters said.

"Nah. Too risky. The scabs have that place armed and guarded like a fortress."

"Ambush them between Wallace and the Gem," Dietz said.

"How is that legal?" O'Brien asked.

"Have the Sheriff's posse waiting, blocking the tracks ready to arrest them. If they don't submit, we get them for resisting, or firing at an officer of the law." Dietz stared at the intense faces around him.

"Where?"

Dietz pointed to the map spread out in front of them. "You men know the area better than I do. You tell me." The men around him smiled.

"What if they don't stop?" Waters asked. "How do we know they won't just plow over our men?"

"It won't be our men on the tracks. We'll stage a small landslide. They won't risk derailment to go plowing over that, but they won't suspect us either. From what I've heard, you've had a wet spring. Lots of hillsides eroded and gave way earlier this spring, giving the railroad fits. It's rained heavily off and on over the last week. It's not beyond the imagination that an already weakened hillside would collapse now." Dietz stretched back and tapped his pencil on the table. "We'll need to select a spot near a hillside but with plenty of cover. And we need someone with dynamiting experience. We'll have to blow the hill tomorrow night. Either that or we get a crew of men to dig it out. We must move quickly, under cover of darkness."

"I don't know. It sounds risky." Waters hedged again. "Those damned owners are bound to be suspicious of just about everything. Won't the engineer be warned to be cautious?"

"Sure. He'll be nervous about slowing, but we'll be well-concealed. Besides, what option will they have? Our main concern will be the scabs. They'll be heavily armed this time around," Dietz said.

"And so will we," the judge said. His smile reached ear to ear. "So will we."

Waters finally smiled, looking pleased with himself. "See why I hired him, boys? McCullough knows his stuff."

Keely wrapped the leftover biscuits from the night before in a clean cloth and set them in the basket she'd prepared for Lacy Hardrow. She pulled the cookie jar to the front of the counter, lifted the lid, and peered in. Three cookies stared back at her. She scooped them out and wrapped them with the biscuits. Time to bake again. The men got fussy if they didn't get their sweets, but Lacy and the children needed the cookies more.

She frowned at the basket. What she'd packed looked like a pitifully small amount, but she couldn't afford more. Then, as she had agreed to with the owners of the boardinghouse, she dropped a nickel into the cash jar to pay for the food before covering the basket with another cloth and removing her apron.

Poor Lacy—ever since Jim had died in the mines, she'd had a hard time supporting those children. Taking in wash brought in too little money. Keely sighed. Lacy should have had this job, but the owners didn't want a woman with children. Too unreliable. That was silly, of course. Mrs. Shipley ran Mr. Allison's rooms and store smooth as you please and she had that cute little five-year-old boy. Providence smiling on Keely meant greater deprivation for Lacy. Keely felt obligated to help her out. But then, she felt called to help out whomever she could. And without the men working, many families needed help.

Soon Lacy would be forced into marrying again. There were few women and plenty of men, but with the mines shut down not many men felt like marrying. And with no income for two months, most men were liabilities anyway.

Times couldn't be stranger. Usually, men had the great hankering to get married. Marriage improved a man's life, but doomed the woman to a baby every other year and with it more and more work. A man got a housekeeper, cook, and companion, with the immeasurable bonus of easy, frequent access to sex. Around these parts, a wife and a set of children didn't cost much more than a whore. Marrying was a sight more convenient than standing in line down at the Lux Building in Wallace on Saturday night, waiting for a turn with a fancy lady. But a man could rid himself of a whore easier than a wife. Rumor had it that even the

Lux suffered in the face of the strike. Men had no spare change, and what they did have, they spent on whiskey.

Of course, women had their own reasons for marrying—survival being chief among them. At least men had a means of providing for themselves, but women had few options. You took in wash, or cooked, and survived at the poverty level, or you ended up on your back at the Lux. And most presumably died early, either of disease or shame. Keely shuddered. None of them pretty options.

How grateful she felt for McCullough. He stirred in her a deep, earthy longing. As silly as it sounded, when she looked into his eyes or listened to his deep voice, she knew she'd found her mate. With their shared beliefs and goals, and the strong attraction she felt to him, how could their union be anything but perfect?

Her only concern—McCullough's stalling. Earlier in the morning, she hadn't missed his reluctance. She watched him struggle to come up with some plausible excuse to delay the wedding—why? She saw desire when he looked at her. Was it as he'd said, devotion to duty and union business? It had to be, and she had to admit that was what she most admired about him. Well, it used to be. Now she wasn't so sure it wasn't his fine, tall physique and nearly violet eyes.

Forgetting she'd removed her apron, she wiped her damp palms on her skirt. Oh, blast! Thinking about McCullough was making her daft. She picked up the basket and headed for Lacy's.

Lacy's small, unpainted cabin sat at the edge of the camp. Her children played on the solitary step out front. When they saw Keely coming, they ran to meet her. She pulled the cookies from the basket and handed them out. Watching their joy warmed her.

Lacy must have heard their happy squeals. She appeared in the doorway. Plain , round-faced Lacy Hardrow had a florid complexion, red hair to match, and a stout build. Not a beauty by any stretch, she was nonetheless a kind woman and good friend to Keely.

"Hello, Keely. What's this? You haven't even set foot in the yard and you're feeding my children cookies?"

"I had to, Lacy. They expect it."

Lacy waved Keely into the house. "Come on in and tell me all the news. I hear your man McCullough arrived yesterday."

"He did. Who told you?"

"Mrs. Shipley."

"And what did she say about him?"

"You know Mrs. Shipley. She doesn't run on or gush. But she did say he's not bad to look at."

"Not bad! He's the most beautiful man I've ever seen!"

Lacy laughed. "He's gotten to you already, has he?"

"Oh, Lace, I can't tell you. I shouldn't tell you. But you know how I worried before that I wouldn't be attracted to him. Well, it seems it was all for naught."

Lacy laughed again. "Poor Lunn. I imagine his hopes are dashed. I think he wished McCullough would turn out to be ugly."

"Too bad for Lunn. McCullough's looks wouldn't have stopped me from marrying him. I'm a person of deeper honor and convictions than that. Now I don't get a chance to prove it, is all."

"So, handsome face aside, is he like his letters?"

Keely hesitated. Lacy noticed immediately. "What's wrong?"

"I haven't had much chance to talk with him. He had barely put his bags in his room when Mr. Allison dragged him off to some union doings. This morning he left early. So, in a way, I guess you could say he is. He's a true union man." Keely bit her lip. "Something's brewing. Something big."

"These days, isn't it always?" Lacy sounded almost sad.

Worried, Keely frowned. But Lacy cut in before she could speak. "So when's the wedding?"

"A week from Thursday."

"So long? You don't sound happy."

"I wanted to get married sooner, this Thursday. But he claims to have an all-day engagement with the union." She paused. "I can't put my finger on it, Lacy. Maybe it's my imagination, but it seems like he's stalling."

"I'm sure he does have a meeting." Lacy laughed. "Take a good look in the mirror someday, Keely. If you aren't the prettiest woman in the Valley, I don't know who is. Not like others of us." Tears welled in Lacy's eyes.

"Lace?"

Lacy wiped angrily at her eyes. "Didn't mean to sound self-pitying." Keely heard her draw a deep breath. "Got my own news." Her smile seemed half-hearted. "I'm getting married myself on Thursday. I was kind of hoping for a double wedding."

Keely shouldn't have been shocked, but her senses reeled. "To whom?"

"Kyle Vandergaard."

Kyle Vandergaard was dull, dumb, big, and lumbering. The best that could be said of him was that he worked ploddingly and tirelessly, like the endlessly cud chewing cows he cared for. Keely fought to keep her disappointment to herself. "How nice."

"No, it isn't. But my babies got to eat. Working at the dairy like he does, Kyle's got work. The children like him. He'll be a good father. For me he won't be like, well, like Jim." The tears that brimmed earlier spilled onto Lacy's cheeks. "I'll always miss that man." It was the merest whisper, but it choked Keely with an odd combination of sentiment and anger. The mines took so much.

"And he's got himself a nice, safe job," Lacy continued.

"A woman does what she has to do. What else could you do? Jim would understand. You'll be fine." At that moment, Keely was never so thankful to providence for giving her McCullough.

When Dietz returned to the boardinghouse, Keely was out. He strode down the hall and let himself into her room. When you were somewhere you shouldn't be, it always paid to look like you belonged. With one ear cocked to the door, he visually mapped the room, marking an escape route. Rule number two—know your exits, in case she came back unexpectedly. A window at the rear of the room opened to the back of the building and a dense stretch of woods. He tried the window latch. It swung open easily. A leap, a couple of long strides, and he'd be hidden in underbrush and evergreens before she realized anyone had been there.

Plain and sparsely furnished, her room didn't surprise him. Two dresses hung in the cupboard, both of them old and worn. He wondered what she planned on wearing to the wedding that wouldn't be taking place. He didn't see any other options.

A framed photograph of a man sat on her bedside table next to a vase of flowers that matched the one in his room. Michael—it had to be. The resemblance to Keely was striking. His gaze moved on and he went to work. Searching rooms had become routine well back in his early detective days.

The search lasted mere minutes. Nothing under the bed, no trunk of any sort. The bedside table had only the book he'd given her earlier in the morning. The chest of drawers—only two contained anything. One, a second set of undergarments too thin and threadbare to conceal anything. The next, a hanky, an embroidered pillowcase, a small purse holding a handful of change, and a sachet of dried lavender. Keely Byrne owned next to nothing. He didn't know why it should, but her poverty upset him.

He shook his head ironically. Plenty of room for McCullough to move in. Both into this room and her life. He'd buy her a few trinkets. Maybe then she wouldn't be so suspicious about McCullough's sudden cold feet. He moved toward the door.

No letters? Maybe she wasn't as sentimental as he presumed. Maybe she hadn't kept the letters. He had no way of knowing, but they weren't in her room. He slid out, latching the door softly behind him, and went back through the kitchen to his own room.

It was always possible she'd hid them somewhere else. But he couldn't risk searching the public area in the middle of the day.

Dietz dug a notebook and pen out from his bag. Within minutes he'd detailed the union's plan of attack for Thursday. Time to make a trip into the big city of Wallace, Idaho.

CHAPTER FIVE

As far as towns went, Wallace wasn't much. To the extreme north, just across the river, the long flat railroad depot dominated the landscape. Trains pulled in and out on tracks located on the north side of the building. Beyond that the wilderness crept in. Conveniently located just across the river, on the opposite side of the street, the local brothel beckoned to the mostly male clientele who rode the trains down from the mining camps. Farther up the street several woodplank buildings, including the general store and the post office, faced off across a patch of mud.

Dietz went directly to the combination post office and general store that Patterson had told him about. As he walked in, a bell tinkled over his head. An old man behind the counter looked up from a newspaper and adjusted his glasses for a better look at Dietz.

"Help you?"

Dietz smiled. Always appear friendly. "I need to mail a letter."

"And who might you be?" the old man asked.

Suspicion ran deep in these parts. "Ian McCullough."

"McCullough, you say?"

"Arrived yesterday. I'm staying in Gem. Going to marry Miss Keely Byrne. Know her?"

"Miss Byrne? Why didn't you say so? So you're the fellow she's been waiting for." He scrutinized Dietz before nodding to himself in apparent approval. "You treat her nice, young man. That little gal is poor as a church mouse, but the biggest angel of mercy I ever seen. Always working at the union hall, serving food to them that's got none. Bringing baskets of supplies to others. Nursing those that get sick." He winked at Dietz. "And she's mighty pretty to boot."

Dietz's laugh boomed through the building. "That she is."

"Well, you got a letter. Hand it over."

Dietz gave the old man his letter and followed him from the counter to the barred mail window. The old man let himself into the post office through a door on his side of the counter. He glanced at the address. "California, eh?"

"Got friends down there." Before leaving Denver, Dietz had been instructed to mail all reports to an operative in California, who then forwarded them to the owners. Mailing them directly to the owners would have been foolhardy and dangerous.

The old man weighed out the letter. Dietz handed him the postage due. "You got a telegraph office in town?" he asked. The report wouldn't reach the owners in time. In case of an emergency, like now, he could wire the New York office in code. He had to chance it.

The old man pointed to a telegraph machine at the back of the office. "There it be. But it won't do you no good. I don't know how to run the blasted thing. My assistant postmaster is sick, didn't come in today."

"Oh."

"You need to wire someone right away?"

"No, no hurry. Got friends back East. Just want to let them know I got here safely."

The old man nodded.

Dietz took a chance. "I know how to run those things."

"Do you?" the old man said. "Then help yourself." He lifted the hinged counter and let Dietz through. "The rate schedule is on the board. Leave the money in the till beside the machine."

Dietz barely contained his amazement. Keely's reputation spoke for itself. He couldn't have picked a better cover. No one came in while he telegraphed his message and the old man didn't seem to pay any attention to it. Not that the innocuous sounding code words should alarm him. When Dietz finished, he left the money as instructed and went to the counter. He cleared his throat and tried to act self-conscious.

"You know, I came to town for more than to just mail a letter. That's the excuse I gave Keely for leaving."

"Oh?"

"Yes. I actually came to buy her a present. I meant to bring one from back East with me, but I couldn't see hauling one across the country. So I came in to buy her something. You have anything nice and pretty? Something that would make her happy?"

The old man laughed. "Fair wages and decent mining hours would make Miss Keely happy. But I'll see what we have."

Half an hour later Dietz walked out of the store with one of just about every feminine, dainty thing the store carried. The old man was a salesman, that was certain. Dietz laughed to himself. Presents for today, presents for the wedding. And it was all on the mine owners. What the hell? They owed her a little something.

Keely hummed as she came down the hall, her hand full with a fresh bouquet of ladyslippers for McCullough's room. She'd stopped by the flower patch on her way home from Lacy's. Picking flowers always calmed her nerves. Poor Lacy. Keely couldn't get her out of her mind. To have to marry someone she could barely tolerate! Keely came around the corner into the hall. McCullough's door was closed. She didn't think much about it, just turned the handle and stepped inside.

"Oh, I'm sorry." She stammered over herself. "I thought you were out."

McCullough sat on the bed reading some letters. In that brief moment, she recognized her own handwriting and stationery. He shoved the letters aside, looking like a boy who just got caught sneaking his daddy's whiskey.

Seeing the look she gave him, he smiled and cleared his throat. "Just doing a little light reading." He picked the letters up again and showed them to her.

"My letters to you?" she asked.

"Yeah. Come in."

She walked in slowly.

"Just trying to put the beautiful woman you are together with the intelligent woman of the letters." He sounded sincere enough.

"Do compliments always drip off you like warm honey off a spoon?"

His laugh filled the room. Such a pleasant sound. "Just around you."

She smiled back at him. "You kept my letters?"

He looked sheepish. "Every one." He held up a stack large enough to account for two years' worth of correspondence.

He began reading aloud. "April 23, 1891. Dear McCullough, I went out flower picking today to get away. The pressures of running the house and the always present strain swirling through the Valley kept my dreams weighted down.

"I found the first purple birdbills of spring and a few lingering buttercups—"

Keely sat down next to him. She hated to stop his mesmerizing voice, or draw attention back to herself, but embarrassed, she pulled the letter from him. "You shouldn't be reading these again. You'll embarrass me."

"Shy?"

"No. You ought to know that." She squirmed. Did he notice? "They're not worth repeating."

"Aren't they?" McCullough nodded to the bedside table where she'd laid the ladyslippers. "I think you bared your soul more than you know. I see you stopped to pick wildflowers today. Something bothering you?"

She imagined herself staring at him with her mouth popped open. But she managed to keep it shut. It was like the man read her mind. "I told you yesterday I'd get you fresh flowers."

He laughed. "My coming bothered you. Or were you dreaming out there? Maybe about me."

"Maybe." She looked down, afraid of further inspection.

"I did the best I could to represent myself accurately in my letters. At least, the essence of who I am. I hope seeing me didn't disappoint you?"

His words startled her into looking up. How could he imagine any woman would find fault with his looks? She opened her mouth to speak, but he cut her off.

"Don't answer that." He laughed in a self-deprecating way. "I'm always sticking my foot in my mouth. That wasn't any kind of question to ask a woman. What I meant is, are you having second thoughts?"

"Oh, no!" Her words rushed out faster than she intended. She felt a blush flash over her face.

"Good." He was still smiling and those fabulous violet eyes of his were dancing with what? Amusement?

Joy? She didn't care, as long as they were happy. She looked down again.

"So, were you daydreaming out there among the flowers? Or is something else bothering you?" He stood up. She watched him remove the old flowers from the vase and replace them with the new. "No use letting these die." Bless him. He was trying to put her back at ease.

"It's my friend Lacy."

He sat back down beside her. She told him the story.

"Sounds to me like she made the right decision. Isn't that what marriage is about? It isn't always love and romance. Sometimes it's just survival. Isn't that part of our reasoning, too?"

She must have looked shocked.

"Part, I said. It's part of any marriage. In some a larger piece than others. Your friend Lacy might have a bigger slice of it than you'd like, but she'll make out all right, I think."

"You're probably right."

He covered her hand with his, and squeezed. His simple touch, so caring and innocent, sent a current of warmth over her. Before she could fully savor or understand it, he pulled away and reached across the bed. An instant later he held a paper wrapped package out to her. "Brought you something." His eyes twinkled.

"You're full of surprises, McCullough."

"I am. Open it."

She pulled a dainty lace hanky from the paper and a pair of lace gloves to match. "Oh, McCullough! How beautiful. Thank you."

He nodded. "Thought the hanky would look pretty tucked in your apron pocket. Add glamour."

She laughed to hide her self-consciousness. "You got these in Wallace, didn't you?"

He nodded. "Caught."

What a rogue! "Mr. Blakely is quite the salesman. What else did he talk you into buying?"

McCullough laughed. "Give me some credit. I had the idea of buying you something in the first place." He nodded toward the package in her lap. "How'd you recognize them?"

"I've had my eye on them awhile. Just never could afford them myself."

His smile lit his eyes. "Then I did good. You can wear the gloves in the flower patch. To fuel your dreams, Keely." His voice broke with tenderness.

"Is that what Mr. Blakely told you?" Men—they'd never understand feminine things. "I can't wear these picking flowers. I'll ruin them."

"Sure you can." He sounded emphatic.

"No, I can't."

He looked resigned. She didn't understand his exasperation. "Then I'll get you a pair of gardening gloves and you can wear these whenever you want."

Stupid little sentimental tears of happiness piled up in her eyes. Wide-eyed, she tried to blink them away before he noticed.

"You know, all those years of reading your letters, I had an idea of what your voice sounded like. Sweet and feminine. I heard that same voice every time I read them. But it wasn't your voice. Yours is much sweeter."

He handed her a letter. "Read your letters to me, Keely. Let me hear them as you thought them."

She shook her head and laughed at her own emotionalism.

"Come on." His voice was low and coaxing. "No? I would read mine to you, if I could. I'd lay my soul bare to you, Keely. I want you to know me, and I, you."

"You can read them to me, McCullough. I kept them. I'll let you read to me but not now. I've got to pull myself together and get downstairs and start cooking." She forced herself to stand, clutching her gifts to her bosom like children.

"Thank you for the gifts." She hurried from the room, closing the door behind her. She paused in the hall to take a deep breath and still her heart. What a man McCullough was! Reading her letters in secret like a sentimental fool. He couldn't have touched her any deeper if he'd planned to. She sighed and headed downstairs to start cooking.

So she had kept the letters, Dietz thought, as he watched the door swing closed behind Keely. Where? Did it matter? She'd read them to him.

For a moment, when she surprised him by walking in, he thought he'd been found out. But he read people with innate skill and his smooth tongue had prevailed, like always. A man who couldn't think fast, and lie with equal speed, didn't last long in his occupation. How could it have been so easy?

All he'd had to do was turn on the charm. He didn't even need to lie much. He did want know who she was, and he did want to hear those letters. But this time something gnawed at his conscience. He didn't like examining the reasons, but his inner voice shouted at him just the same. He, John Dietz, wanted to know who she was.

Dietz crouched in the underbrush surveying the railroad tracks. The train would be coming from the south. He hadn't seen the site before. The union boys had picked a good one. The train would round a bend and have just enough time to see the slide and halt.

The landslide looked good, natural. Whoever the dynamiter had been, and the union brass were keeping it secret, had talent. Dietz smiled to himself, remembering the previous night. The blast had sounded just after dark as he, Keely, and the other boarders he'd been playing cards with were about to call it a night.

"What's that?" Keely had asked.

"Sounds like a landslide," he'd said.

"A landslide doesn't sound like that. That sounded like an explosion." Her voice had trembled.

"That's the way a landslide sounds tonight, lass. Trust me."

His thoughts returned to the present. When the coming train stopped, his men, who were perched on the hillside above the slide, would drop onto it. He shook his head, amused at himself. His boys. Sometimes it was hard to remember whose side he was on. He prayed the owners had gotten his message and suspended the mission. But he couldn't be sure they had.

The bushes trembled in the woods around him as the men jostled one another, rocked on the balls of their feet, or spent their energy in whatever manner their personality dictated. He heard the murmured voices of small groups of men. They were nervous and jumpy, agitated, frustrated and ready for action. Any kind. Amateurs! Cripes, what kind of man couldn't wait calmly? The woods pulsed with anxious excitement. The boys would be loose with their trigger fingers and hot with their heads. Dietz shook his head, wondering why any man would risk violence at the hands of this mob to scab up at the Gem or Frisco.

He looked at his watch, aching for a stretch. Four p.m. Another five hours and they could call this nonsense off. Sam Waters and the judge had insisted on posting scouts in Wallace only. All the scabs would have to come from Spokane, Washington, east of Coeur d'Alene and through Wallace to reach the mines. Dietz favored posting scouts along the route, but Waters and the others had laughed at his caution, brushing off his ideas as that of a newcomer. The latest round of scouts hadn't reported in, but earlier reports yielded nothing. The Valley sat quiet.

Just then he heard the unmistakable whine of a steam engine making its way up a grade, followed by the shrill call of a whistle. The woods went silent. Dietz cursed under his breath. Both sides seemed to have failed him. His union scouts hadn't reported in and the owners either hadn't received his message, or had ignored his warning. Dietz crawled on his belly to the rise of the hill and peered out, straining for the first glimpse of the train. Everyone waited for his signal. He held the men back with his upturned hand.

The train rounded the bend and came into view. Dietz frowned. An engine and a single top loading car?

The engineer must have seen the slide, but it looked to Dietz liked he'd been forewarned. The train glided to a smooth, unhurried stop with a minimum of brake squeal. The owners had received his message.

Waters, who'd been hidden nearby crawled next to Dietz. "What do we do now?"

"Wait and see what they're up to."

The brakeman and engineer looked around nervously, then descended from the train, carrying shovels, evidently prepared to clear the slide. A loosely tied tarp covered the top loading car. Something didn't feel right to Dietz. He was about to speak when someone behind him whooped the rebel yell.

"What are we waiting for?" Someone else yelled. "They're not armed."

Dietz cursed again. Before he could stop them half a dozen men piled over the edge of the hillside into plain view of the train.

The engineer shouted something Dietz couldn't quite hear. The tarp flipped off the car, exposing at least fifteen heavily armed men. A shot sounded from the hill.

"Get back," Dietz yelled.

The shot ricocheted off the metal car. Dietz heard the tink, saw the owners' men duck. A volley of return fire erupted. One of the miners toppled face first into the soft dirt of the slide, blood oozing from his shoulder. Startled, the other miners retreated back up the hill, dragging the man behind them. Another round from below and they dropped him and ran. Without thinking, Dietz went down after him. It was an idiotic, foolhardy thing to do, but seconds later he had the man under the arms and almost into the relative safety of the woods when Dietz took a bullet.

Dietz's left arm smarted like it had been stung by a bee. The hit startled him and drained the strength from his left arm. Cursing, he gave a final tug and dragged the man to cover. Several other miners stepped up to help, pulling the man deep into the woods.

"Take him back to Gem. Get him a doctor," Dietz shouted after them.

The sheriff's posse, which had been under cover farther north, came thundering around the corner, alerted by the echoes of gunshot. Dietz slapped his right hand over the aching left arm. As he expected, slick red blood covered his fingers. He pressed against the injury, certain it was nothing but a flesh wound. Bled like hell, but they'd only grazed him. Hit by fellow owner employees!

Dietz flattened, melding with the ground as he watched the action. At the sight of the sheriff, both sides ceased firing. The look on the sheriff's face as he encountered the digging party was worth the price of admission.

Dietz signaled for his men to retreat—an empty gesture. Most of the men had scrambled halfway back to Gem. The battle was lost.

Dietz imagined what the engineer told the sheriff. Dietz lay too far away to hear, but the gist of it must have been that the engineer received word of a slide and had been sent out with a crew to clear it when he was suddenly attacked without provocation. The dumbfounded sheriff couldn't do a thing without tipping his corrupt hand, nothing but guarantee them protection as they completed their task.

Dietz chuckled. Smart sons of guns, the owners. No doubt another train, one filled with scabs and supplies, would come rolling up the hill in an hour or two, along with McCullough's surprised scouts.

By the time Dietz got back to Gem he'd stopped bleeding. But Waters insisted on escorting him to the doctor, and came right into the office while the doc cleaned him up.

"That was a damned foolhardy thing you did, McCullough," Waters said, but his tone held praise.

"Tell me about it." Dietz winced as the doctor washed his arm with rubbing alcohol.

"No bullet," the doctor said. "Just grazed."

"See, I told you." Dietz looked to Waters.

Waters shrugged. "It needed to be cleaned."

"Promise me you won't tell Keely about my escapades," Dietz said. Waters looked skeptical.

"How the hell do you plan on keeping it from her?"

"Just let her think I got hit while hiding out in the bushes, otherwise, she'll be angry and frightened."

Waters laughed. "You and Michael. He always kept things from her, too. 'So as not to scare her,' he'd say."

Dietz stared him down.

Waters held his hands up in mock defense. "I promise."

"And you'll keep the boys quiet."

"Shoot, McCullough. You took a bullet for them. You think they aren't going to talk about it?"

Dietz grunted as the doctor began bandaging.

"All right," Waters said. "I'll keep them quiet as best I can. But I don't promise success."

The doctor finished bandaging. "Put your shirt on, Mr. McCullough. I'm finished. Keep a clean dressing on that wound for the next few days. It's not deep. In a week it won't be more than a small scab."

"Sure feels deep now."

Waters clapped Dietz on the back. "What do you say I take you across the street for a drink to numb the pain?"

"Excellent."

On the way out Waters paid the doctor's bill using union funds. Sometimes the irony of the job almost overcame Dietz. If Waters knew his true identity he'd fill Dietz with lead himself.

CHAPTER SIX

A couple of shots of whiskey at O'Malley's took the edge off Dietz's pain, but looking around him, Dietz realized the alcohol only served to fuel the anger of the miners surrounding him. They had been ratted out and knew it. Dietz listened with half an ear to Waters who perched on a bar stool next to him. The rest of his attention Dietz devoted to eavesdropping on nearby conversations. A fellow never knew what he might hear.

"Another drink?" Waters said as they sat at the bar in the comfortably smoky atmosphere. A player piano tinkled away at the far end of the room, obscuring his words. Or maybe it was only the whiskey obscuring Dietz's senses.

"No, thank you." The agency always taught their operatives to take the offensive if they might be under suspicion. It seemed wise to follow that advice now. "You've got a spy in your ranks, Waters."

"Hell, yes." Waters set his glass on the counter and ordered a refill. "The owners aren't smart enough to send a decoy train up without being warned. That blasted train today didn't suddenly pull the brakes and screech to a halt. He slowed like he knew the slide was coming."

"Yeah." Dietz nodded, assessing Waters. As far as Dietz could tell Waters harbored no suspicions about McCullough, made no connection between his arrival and the owners' newfound knowledge. But then, they already had suspected they had a spy among them. Why should they imagine they had two?

Waters continued. "This isn't the first time we've suspected we've got ourselves a traitor. A year ago we caught a private detective. But we shipped him out of town fast enough." Waters chuckled, leaving Dietz to imagine what he found humorous about that previous situation.

Dietz had read the owners' report. The miners beat Billy Oak nearly to death and shipped him out by train stark naked. Nothing funny about that to Dietz's way of thinking.

"Things were quiet for months after he left," Waters continued. "But suddenly these last five, oh, six, months, the owners have gotten a whole lot smarter. I think we got us another detective." A commotion at the door interrupted Waters' speech. Joe Poynton strode in, anger erupting from his expression, and headed right for them.

Poynton threw his felt hat on the table. A steady stream of expletives spewed from his mouth. "The owners were warned," he said. The irony struck Dietz. Poynton came in and took up the conversation like he'd been a part of it all along. All the miners seemed to have one collective thought today. "Yesterday they sent that first train up toward Canyon Creek like she was headed to the camp up there. Hid her out overnight and ran her up to us this afternoon. Word is a second train loaded with supplies and scabs just went by, escorted by the sheriff." Poynton scowled. "Sheriff had no choice. All the big newspapers have been carrying the story of the strike. We've got the sympathy of folks in Spokane and smaller towns. Don't want to turn them against us."

Dietz and Waters nodded in unison. Why disagree with Poynton? Dietz's shoulder ached like hell. He fought not to slump on his stool.

"We got to catch that spy," Poynton said.

"I was just saying the same thing to McCullough before you came in."

"I agree, men," Dietz said. He straightened and winced involuntarily.

"Good," Waters said. "We've all of us got to make a plan to find the man out. First though, I think we ought to take McCullough home. You look pale, old boy."

Keely's heart pounded as she raced into the boardinghouse kitchen. She slammed down the basket she'd been carrying onto the table with more force than she intended. The house sounded quiet, too quiet to silence her fears. The men were all out drinking, worked up over their foiled attempt at stopping the train. She'd been at the union hall distributing food to needy families when she heard the news of the skirmish. McCullough had been shot. The men couldn't stop bragging about his heroics. Fools!

Mr. Waters had taken McCullough to the doctor. By the time she'd gotten there the doctor had stitched him up and sent him on his way. The doctor's reassurances that McCullough suffered only a flesh wound fell on deaf ears. She had to see him for herself. Wretched fear. Ever since Michael...

Wasn't it enough for the mine owners to shut down the mines, forcing good men to go idle and their families to starve? Did they have to rile up the miners and invite trouble by shipping more worthless scabs up to the Gem, right in the faces of the miners? The owners deserved whatever trouble they got. Unfortunately, today they'd gotten their way. She took a deep breath, suppressing an oath. The money the owners spent on shipping scabs to the mines! They could just as easily capitulate to the miners' request for higher wages and be money ahead, never mind trouble.

Stopping to discard the basket barely slowed Keely's momentum. She swished past the long side of the table, bumping, catching, and righting a chair in her path with one distracted motion. She swung past the table corner, realized belatedly she was too close and pushed her hip out to miss it. Banged it anyway. She lifted her skirt and took the stairs two at a time in a manner her mother had taught her not to do at a young age, rubbing her hip with her elbow to ease the smart.

Fear always made her clumsy. When Michael had been hurt— She pushed the unpleasant memories away. No use dwelling on them. McCullough needed her. Dear God, let him be all right. She reached the top of the stairs.

"McCullough! McCullough, are you home?" She pushed into his room without knocking. He lay on the bed looking pale but not deathly. Thank goodness! She owed God one.

McCullough looked at her quizzically. She exhaled loudly. Could he hear it? It felt like the whole world could. "You look right enough to me. How do you feel?"

"What?" He leaned up on an elbow. She saw the wince.

"Don't pretend with me. Down at the union hall I heard all about your escapades."

"News travels fast." He didn't look happy.

"Around here, it has wings." She walked to his bedside and sat down beside him, being careful not to rock his wound. "You shouldn't have gone out after him. You could have been killed." Why did her voice have to go and crack on her? How often she'd wished for a stoic, placid demeanor. But she'd never been able to manage it. Why did she always succeed in giving every piece of herself away?

McCullough must have seen her worry and concern. He reached out to her and rested his hand on her arm. There was something magnetic about his touch, about him. She felt it the first time she saw him, the purely physical pull between them. Never, never had she known anything like it before. She hoped this fascinating attraction between them would last forever. But why did she think such thoughts now? Being near him rattled her, including her thinking. She covered McCullough's hand with her own and pressed it against herself, trying to ignore its warm, strong presence. He was fine. He would recover. Lush, potent relief washed over her, filling her eyes with moisture.

"The fools shouldn't have fired." McCullough paused to look up at her.

Giving herself away again. Why did he have to catch her blinking away tears?

"I'm all right, Keely. It's just a flesh wound. It'll be healed up fine as you please by next week." He grinned. "At least that's what the doc tells me."

She didn't speak for fear of revealing more of the depth of her feelings for McCullough. He must have mistaken her expression for scrutiny. He looked suddenly guilty. Neither spoke, though McCullough looked thoughtful, like he was measuring his words ahead of time.

"I planned this escapade, as you called it, Keely. You know that."

Her heart thudded in her ears. "I knew you were involved."

"I *planned* it, Keely. The injuries, the violence, are on my head."

What could she say? She nodded, mute. She had expected him to take charge.

"I had a standing order—no shooting. But the train surprised them. The men lost their heads—"

"I'm not blaming you."

His grip on her arm tightened. "Maybe you should."

"Yes, maybe I should." She wished she could have photographed the surprised look he gave her. "But not for that. For your own carelessness." She wiped at her eyes with the sides of her fingers, hoping he wouldn't notice. But of course he did. What else could she be doing but wiping away tears? Suddenly, she didn't care if he did see. Maybe it was best if he knew where she stood. "You're all I have, Ian McCullough."

She didn't understand the look he gave her. Was it surprise? Wonder? Fear? Guilt? Whatever it was, it seemed genuine. But not what she wanted to see.

He cleared his throat. She released his hand and he dropped it back by his side.

"I mean that, McCullough. I won't have you up and dying on me. I refuse to be a widow before I'm even married."

This time, as fleeting as his expression was, she saw the emotion. Guilt, clearly guilt. Why? Well, whatever it was for, maybe it was time he felt guilty, time he understood. "I won't be the pity case of the community again. Not like after Michael. I'll die if I have to endure the silent, embarrassed glances of friends. The shuffling of feet, the downward looks. The out and out uncomfortable feeling of being some kind of pariah because tragedy struck." She took a breath. "Because everyone knows that next time it could be them, and no one knows what to do about it or what to say.

"I won't be rescued again by the likes of Lunn Gaffney—" The look on McCullough's face stopped her mid-sentence.

"Gaffney?"

"Never mind." Oh, blast her rash tongue!

"What about Gaffney? Rescued by him how?"

"I don't want to talk about it."

"But we haven't discussed Michael's death yet. Don't you think we should?"

"Not now. We're discussing marriage. You're going to marry me, McCullough. Alive and kicking. When you've healed, maybe sooner. I'm an impatient woman." After today's scare, more impatient than ever. Blast him, she'd just set a time. She nodded to herself. "Next week. If we have to drive to Coeur d'Alene to do it."

"Yes, ma'am."

His contrite tone and bright grin brought back her sense of humor. If she put herself at a distance, scolding a wounded man about dying held a certain humor. It certainly wouldn't help him recover. She laughed. "That's settled then. What do you need? Can I get you anything?"

"You mean to ease the pain?"

"Exactly."

"Nothing. Nothing but time can do that. But you can distract me. Keep me company."

"I thought I was."

He eased back off his elbow onto the pillow, looking suddenly weary and pale. "Is that what you call it? Sounded more like scolding to me."

"You're tired. It looks like what you mostly need is rest."

"No. I'll just lie here hurting. I need your company to distract me, Keely. But I need you like I know you. I need the kind of companionship you've given me these last years." He laughed. "One sided."

"Like you know me?"

"Read me your letters, Keely." His voice sounded weak. "There is a bundle of them in the drawer of the bedside table. Get them and read them." He adjusted his position and closed his eyes. Little beads of sweat dotted his forehead. He'd overexerted himself. "I need to know you."

"How do you mean?" She couldn't figure him out. What did he mean? Know her how?

He smiled weakly. "Inflection is everything, Keely. I read the words you wrote with my own voice. Now read them to me as you meant them."

Her eyes clouded over again. What a sentimental fool she was. She never suspected McCullough as being the same. She unfolded the first letter and began reading. She read the first, and the second, and began the third. "Dear McCullough—"

"Pardon the interruption." He sounded sleepy. "You never called me Ian. Why not?"

It seemed a strange question. "No one ever calls you Ian. At least that's what Michael said. I didn't think you'd like it."

"Maybe I would, from you."

"Maybe I will. When the time is right."

He chuckled. "You're something, Keely."

"That I knew. If you're only discovering that, then you are getting to know me better."

"I am. For one thing you're an awful good reader."

She laughed. "That's not what I meant."

"Me, either." He sighed.

"You're tired now. You need sleep and I've got to get supper on." She set the letter down and stood. "I'll come read to you later when I bring up a tray of supper."

"I look forward to it."

"I hope so. When I come, I'll bring the letters you wrote me." She liked the surprised look he gave her. "You're not the only sentimental one, McCullough. I'll bring them and read them to you, so you can see how I view you. Later, when you've recovered some, you can read them to me."

Dietz woke slowly, gently lifting to consciousness from the foggy haze of sleep, almost fighting it. He glanced at the clock with one eye. Two hours had passed since Keely had sat with him. He sat up slowly, favoring his shoulder. It must be getting near to supper time. He heard shuffling in the rooms around his. The men were home for that brief interval between afternoon card playing and evening carousing. Downstairs he heard pots and pans clanging together and pictured Keely hard at work cooking, lugging the heavy pans, perspiration spotting her forehead, flour covering her apron. A woman that pretty shouldn't have to work so hard—

Shoot, why should he think that? Thoughts of Keely made him soft in the head. Damn, had he promised to marry her? Their conversation came flooding back with harsh clarity. She disturbed him, in more ways than he cared to count. How could he marry her? His boss would have his ass. Never involve more people than necessary and never become entangled in messy affairs.

It was one thing to roll in the hay with various and assorted ladies of the night, even to engage their sympathy and affection. An agent could court any number of desperate, hard women as he had in the past, to gain important information. But marrying an innocent under an alias? He had few scruples, but this? Being around Keely was robbing him of his edge.

He couldn't marry her, but her words haunted him. *You're all I have, Ian McCullough.* But he was *not* Ian McCullough. What was she to him? Yet he couldn't push the thought or her expression from his mind. Added to it, he couldn't afford to lose his cover. How could he explain not marrying her? Now if she didn't want to marry him—

Someone banged and clanked up the stairs. From the sound of the movements, Dietz knew whoever it was, had to be drunk. He shook his head. Trouble hovered over town. With too little to do and too much time on their hands, the men turned to drink and cards, and plotting against the Mine Owners Association. It wouldn't be long in erupting. The question—how long?

He needed a little time. He should be out drinking and carousing with the miners, operating in the usual way. Being their friend, gaining their confidence, and hearing their confidences. Being supposedly committed stifled him and his detective methods. Suddenly, Dietz smiled. What if Keely refused him, turned him out? A little too much drink consumed too often, too many flirtations with too many women. Shouldn't be hard. Shouldn't be too different than the real McCullough. What a perfect plan. No one would think anything about a girl changing her mind once she finally met her mail-order fiancé. Especially if he turned out to be a rascal, a no good. No one at all. She would come out of the whole mess looking downright honorable, and what did he care how he looked? Still, her words and the hope she assigned to McCullough niggled at him. But it didn't change his mind. He had to pick a fight with Keely, and he had to do it soon.

He sat up, and winced. Wounded. Blasted nuisance. Fortunately, the bullet had caught his left shoulder, not his right. He peeled back the dressing the doctor had applied earlier and stared at the oozing injury. Clear. Didn't look infected. Something bothered him, stirring in him a dim memory, almost from his shady dreams. Had he dreamed of the attempted train heist? Memories came from somewhere. The sting, like the bite of an angry wasp. Slapping at the bullet wound with his right hand. Nearly dropping the man he carried.

He replayed the scene in his mind. The smart of the bullet, nearly dropping the man, being afraid the man would bang his head and fall into the rocky basalt below or get shot again. Turning sideways to the fire to make himself a thinner target and protect his chest. Worried about his own gun arm. Turn around Dietz, you fool. Angle the left shoulder downhill, not the right. Left shoulder hit.

Realization swept over him. He shivered in the heat of the evening. He'd been shot from uphill, by a miner, friendly fire. Or had it been intentional?

The sound of bells ringing startled Keely from her thoughts of McCullough as she cleared the supper dishes away. She needed to prepare a tray of food to take up to him, and she would bring the letters to read to him. His grin, his easy consent to marry next week, all danced through her thoughts. The ferocious clanking of bells grew louder, shrinking away the happy swell of her heart over such thoughts, and replacing it with the rapid pulse of fear. She'd heard the bells too many times before to imagine they meant any good. She set down the plate she held and went to the window to watch as the last of her boarders spilled from the kitchen out into the street, joining the vicious swarm of drunk, rowdy men that formed, weaving toward the Gem Union Hall across the street and two buildings over.

She took off her apron, folded it, and set it on the table. The men craved revenge, in any form, for the foiled attempt on the train. During supper, her boarders talked of nothing else around the table. She shuddered.

The bells. Blast the bells. A bell ringer in the street caught her eye and smiled at her, giving an emphatic shake to the bell he carried, tipping his hat with his free hand. She turned away. The bells summoned the people to the union hall, ostensibly for a citizens' meeting. In reality, they summoned the miners to a meeting of the general assembly. Everyone knew the game. Not a single woman marched with the crowd in the street. Only union members would be permitted into the hall, and the whole meeting would be a sham. Nothing more.

The special council must have met already, probably at J.H. Johnson's saloon, like they always did. She bit her lip. She hadn't heard any mention that President O'Brien was in town. He alone could reason with the men when their ire flew up. Oh, she prayed he had arrived in town. The Special Council would have set the agenda in their meeting earlier. Eloquent men who knew how to turn a phrase, the union leaders never encountered trouble convincing the men that some scab or other needed to be run out of town, which was what these meetings always preceded. But who, who was left? Her thoughts raced frantically.

During the winter months, many scab families still resided in the Valley. The meetings had become routine, nearly monotonous. Keely had little sympathy for scabs. They didn't deserve to be working, earning the same wages as union men who fought to get those wages. And any man who would settle his family in the heart of the battle and unrest was a bigger fool than deserved a family. But that didn't give union men the right to use violence to achieve their goals.

When the strike began in April and the mines shut down, the remaining scab miners hurriedly relocated their families elsewhere, generally under the cover of darkness. The union ran the last stubborn family out over a month ago. Keely felt blessed by the ensuing silence. But her heart pounded now. Was greater trouble coming?

She shook her head, thinking. She hoped not. But she couldn't think. Suddenly, she recalled an innocuous snippet of conversation she'd overhead earlier in the day. Something about old Jack Catridge, the crazy independent miner whose cabin sat up next to the creek at the edge of town. Oh heavens! Were they going after him? She couldn't let them hurt the old fellow. He might be touched, but he was harmless. He didn't belong to the union because he had no need.

Goosebumps pilled on her arms. Her heart thudded in her ears. Cold fear gripped her. Suddenly she wished for Michael. He would have known how to stop them. She reached for her shawl and paused. Should she get McCullough? She bit her lip again in indecision. No, he needed his rest. She'd have to do this one on her own. She wrapped the shawl around herself and headed out, slamming the door behind her.

CHAPTER SEVEN

K eely never appeared with that tray. What kept her? Noise from the street, a mixture of ringing bells and bass voices, roused Dietz from his musings. Damn. Something was up. Reluctantly, Dietz pushed himself up out of bed and went to the window, cursing. Men filled the streets, called to a union meeting. Silently, he watched them stream into the union hall across the street. Nearly five hundred miners, angry and on the march.

He started to turn away, intent on going back to bed. Whatever trouble the union bosses had in mind could be accomplished without McCullough. No one would expect him to participate after his heroics earlier in the afternoon. But a quick glimpse of auburn hair, coifed into a neat knot, slender curves, and a walk with a sway arrested him. Keely. What had brought her out into the mob? Suddenly, his heart thudded wildly.

Directly across the street, Mrs. Shipley came out of her store. Dietz watched Keely swim across the stream of men and join her on the boardwalk. The two women chatted, apparently casually.

Half an hour passed with Dietz glued next to the window, pressed back out of sight from the street, watching Keely. Fatigue tore at him, enticing him back to bed. But fear for Keely kept him in place. The union hall rocked with a chorus of shouts akin to a passionate amen. Something had been decided. Moments later, men poured out of the building into the fading dusk, carrying torches and lanterns, wearing bloodthirsty looks. Keely left Mrs. Shipley on the boardwalk and blended into the mob. Dietz swore. He picked up his trusty Colt's 45, hefting the piece in his hand. Then he slid out of the room, out after Keely.

Following the crowd required no detective skill. Dietz kept to the fringes, in shadow, as the last of the light faded away. The crowd ambled to the edge of town, crossed back over Canyon Creek, followed the high grade railway tracks past the mill, and came to a halt in front of a small untidy cabin that listed to the left. Though a few other women had joined the crowd, it wasn't difficult to spot Keely. Dietz moved into the shadow of an overgrown white pine. As long as Keely remained where she stood, firmly positioned midcrowd, he figured she'd be safe.

His shoulder throbbed like hell. He leaned back against the pine to watch the action, fingering the Colt, eyes trained on Keely and those surrounding her.

Waters stepped to the front of the crowd. "Catridge! Get the hell out here, you damned scab!"

The crowd cheered. Flames from lanterns and torches lit faces in grotesque caricature, aided in their distortion by the ugly emotion of hate. Was it his imagination, or was Keely trembling? At least she had enough sense to be frightened. Or was it rage? Unfortunately, neither emotion proved strong enough to send her fleeing home. He had half a mind to grab her and drag her back there. What compelled her to watch the horror certain to unfold? Just how deep did her support for the union run?

Someone fired a shot into the cabin. Dietz instinctively ducked. Heated laughter drifted to him on the breeze waving the pines overhead. Waters held up his hand to silence the crowd. The listing door swung open, revealing a confused old man. From his vantage point, Dietz couldn't hear the old man's pleas. But from Catridge's posture, Dietz knew plead he did.

On command from Waters, two thugs, one of them Lunn Gaffney, stepped forward and grabbed Catridge, shoving him roughly toward the swarm of miners. Gaffney pinned the old miner's arms back so tightly Catridge winced and wore a pinched expression. Another cluster of men stepped forward toward the cabin, torches blazing, their intent clear.

"Stop!" Keely's voice echoed off the pines. Pushed to action, she bore through the crowd toward the cabin.

As if the miners suddenly remembered their manners, they parted to let her through. The men near the cabin froze.

Dietz swore, and moved out after her, keeping to the outside of the crowd, his gun cocked and ready. He circled round to the front of the cabin, angled to where he could see Keely's face and keep an eye on the crowd at the same time.

"Jack Catridge is no scab." Keely turned and faced the men. Her voice shook. Dietz, trained in observation, noticed everything about her. Couldn't help himself, as his heart thudded away wildly, pounding out a beat of fear for her like he'd never felt for himself. Her hands trembled. Her voice pleaded for sympathy. She licked her lips too often. They shone moist and sparkling in the moon and torchlight. Delectable. Keely— curvaceous, beautiful, and afraid. Damn, he didn't want to, but he had to admire her conviction and courage. She'd more guts than any man in the crowd. With that kind of fortitude she made a powerful ally and a strong enemy. He'd never admired a woman's character before. It was another damned dangerous thing about her.

Scanning the crowd, Dietz didn't miss the looks the men gave her. Some glared with anger, others, hatred, and most, a hearty dose of lust. He had to get her out of here. Whatever her position on violence, she had chosen to fight a battle she'd never win.

"He doesn't belong to the union," someone shouted.

"He has no need. He's an independent. You know he doesn't even mine galena. He pans for gold." She stepped up next to Catridge.

"He's crazy," Waters said.

"He's harmless." Keely leveled her gaze at Waters. "You know that, Mr. Waters." She addressed the men gathered. "Men, I know you're frustrated and angry at the owners. We all are. But why punish an innocent man? Why vent your anger like this? It will only hurt our cause. Don't you see?"

"Step out of the way, Miss Byrne, or I'll have to have you restrained." Rancor edged Waters' voice.

Keely didn't appear to listen. She stepped next to Gaffney and touched him lightly on the arm. "Let him go, Lunn. Please."

Her pleading tone ate at Dietz, especially her begging a man like Gaffney and the apparent intimacy between them. Gaffney's expression softened. He looked like he wanted to please her, and Keely seemed to know it, the wily woman. How was Dietz supposed to get her out of this mess?

Waters nodded toward two men. "Relieve Gaffney," he said. "Gaffney." Waters nodded toward Keely.

"You're making a mistake, Mr. Waters. I don't believe President O'Brien would approve of your methods. How convenient you didn't see fit to notify him."

Gaffney stepped up behind Keely, took her by both elbows, and pressed himself indecently close to her. "Miss Byrne didn't mean any harm. You know women and their delicate sensibilities. Their hearts are always bleeding for someone. I'll see Miss Byrne safely home.

She won't be causing any more trouble. I promise." In
that instant, the look on Gaffney's face as he touched
Keely cut through Dietz. Dietz saw something darker
than love written there. He saw obsession. It sent him
reeling with disgust and an emotion he'd never felt before—jealousy.

As to seeing her safely home, did that include ravag-
ing her? Gaffney craved Keely. That much was obvious.

Dietz stepped from the shadows into the long lan-
tern light with his gun at ready. "I'll take Miss Byrne
home."

Waters smiled at him. "How good of you to join us,
McCullough. Couldn't imagine you'd want to miss the
action." Waters nodded at Gaffney again. "Give
McCullough his woman."

Keely clenched her jaw at Waters' comment. She
didn't like being possessed, huh? With obvious reluctance, Gaffney let her go. Dietz stepped up to take her
arm. Right now the woman needed a protective man.
She needed him.

"McCullough." She threw herself into his arms.

Dietz had to clench his jaw to keep from crying out
in pain. His shoulder throbbed like hell at the jolt.

Gaffney glared at him. His lips formed the word
bastard. Dietz took it as a warning.

"McCullough, make them stop." Keely's eyes sparkled with tears as she looked up at him. He hated that
she used the same method of appeal on him that she
had used on Gaffney. And Heaven help him, he wanted
to please her, too. He was really no better than Gaffney,

except that an overwhelming desire for her safety over-
rode any notion of humoring her.

"What do you think of our little excitement,
McCullough?" Waters asked.

Dietz smiled in reply.

"What should we do next, McCullough? Tell us."
Waters' smile resembled more of a leer, an angry scowl.
With his question, he clearly tested McCullough, and
Dietz knew it. Was McCullough loyal to the union or
his woman?

"Torch the place."

The miners cheered at Dietz's confident reply.
Keely gasped. Behind him, Dietz heard the men who
carried the torches stomp up the board stairs into the
decrepit cabin.

"Run the old man out. But let's be gentlemen. Dis-
patch him to Wallace, and put him on a train. Hell, pay
his fare. Miss Byrne is right. There's no need for bloodshed tonight."

"No, indeed." Waters smiled. Dietz saw admiration
and a sinister form of victory shine in Waters' eyes, like
he'd figured out how to solve a dark puzzle to his own
ends. Dietz didn't like it. "Gaffney, get your men and
take Catridge away." Waters spoke with the ease of a
powerful man.

Gaffney slunk off sullenly with Catridge and a
group of thugs in toe. Keely wrenched free of
McCullough's embrace and ran off toward home, obviously angry and upset with Dietz. Waters laughed.
"Good luck with your woman, McCullough. Looks to

me like you better marry her soon. So as to keep her in line."

"Yeah." Like hell. He didn't need the kind of trouble she brought on him. Usually he'd be enjoying himself to no end over the excitement of the mission. Plotting and planning. Hanging out in bars. Drinking with the boys after the excitement finished up, energy coursing through him giving him the high he lived for. Now he'd have to go make up with a woman and damned if he didn't half want to.

On top of it all, Gaffney appeared more dangerous than Dietz originally had thought. A man obsessed with a woman was a loose cannon for sure, too unpredictable for any measure of safety. Well, maybe Dietz would let that be the crowning glory of this mission. He'd see Gaffney locked up and safely away from Keely.

"Well, go after her, man," Waters said. "I'll clean up here."

Yeah, sure. Waters would clean up good. Dietz didn't like taking orders, but protecting Keely seemed more important than making a point with Waters. Dietz took off after her.

He caught up with her near Canyon Creek. Behind him he heard the gasp of a flame taking life, and then its angry birth cry—a roar. Keely strode on. He let her have her lead and her space until they got to the boardinghouse. Then he'd had enough. He caught her in the kitchen.

"Keely."

She stopped and turned to face him. "How dare you!"

"How dare I? How dare you. Do you realize what a foolish thing you did out there?"

"Do you realize what those miners intended out there?"

"I do." He ran his fingers back through his hair. Could she be that naive? Didn't she know who McCullough was, what he'd done?

"No, I don't believe you do. They meant to kill that man in any hideous, ugly way they could. You haven't seen them. You haven't seen their cruelty. They're so frustrated. They don't know what to do other than show their anger, retaliate."

Oh, he knew about cruelty. He'd seen far more than he hoped she'd ever imagined.

"Michael would have stopped them."

"Michael would never have gone on a fool's mission. He knew which battles to fight."

"How dare you presume to know my brother better than I do? If you were half the man he was, you would have stopped them." She turned on her heel. He caught her by the elbow.

"I trained him. I know what he would have done. The same thing I did myself."

"No." She shook her arm. "Let go of me."

"Not until you listen to me."

"No, you listen to me, Ian McCullough. I will not marry a man of violence. A coward. You pack your things and move across the street to Shipley's in the morning."

He should have let it go right there. She'd given him the out he'd wanted. But something greater was at stake—her safety, his.

"I'm not going anywhere. I promised Michael that I'd take care of you. Call off the wedding if you like, but I'm staying to see to your safety until this thing is over." For once in his life, Dietz spoke the truth.

She wouldn't look directly at him. He softened his voice. "What you did tonight, though brave, was also foolhardy in the extreme. Can't you see that you made Waters test me? He wanted to see where my loyalties lay, with the union or you. To choose you would put both of us in danger." He lifted her chin with his fingers. "You know the truth of it, though, don't you, Keely? Where my loyalty is."

"I'm not sorry for what I did."

"No, I knew you wouldn't be, lass. And I don't expect you to be. You're a hardheaded Irishwoman after all."

"And you're not an equally stubborn Irishman?"

"Not as stubborn as you, lass. I'm only half Irish. My pa was a Scot. They're much less temperamental."

She laughed and blinked away her tears.

"Now do you still insist on throwing me out?"

She didn't answer, just started crying. He hated it when a woman cried, even though he suspected her tears were those of relief, maybe even happiness. He pulled her into his embrace. "I'm here now, lass. Let me do the fighting." He kissed the top of her head. "And stay away from Gaffney. He's trouble."

Dietz didn't speak just for McCullough. Somehow John Dietz had become involved with this woman.

The next day Dietz sat in Waters' office, called in to perform another fool's errand, no doubt. The trouble with Waters seemed to be his love of power and bossing other men around. Dietz didn't like it, but it went with the job. Soon enough Dietz would have the upper hand and Waters would be where he belonged—locked up.

Today Waters seemed a bit too jovial and confident for Dietz's tastes. Who'd he put one over on this time?

"How's the shoulder today?" Waters set two shot glasses on his desk and removed the stopper from a decanter of whiskey. Taking on the airs of the rich?

"The pain's down to a dull roar." Dietz shifted in his chair to emphasize the point.

Waters laughed. "That so. Whiskey? It ought to take that roar right away." He poured without waiting for an answer.

Dietz was in no mood for doing any verbal dancing with Waters. "You called me in for a reason?"

Waters looked solemn and almost too pained. "I did, my friend."

My friend, hell, Dietz thought. *Smile pleasantly.* His face ached from the forced effort of the charade.

Waters inhaled like he was about to speak, then paused. For effect? "I wanted to talk to you in private. I heard some disturbing rumors last night."

"That so?" Dietz's heart bounded around in his rib cage like an exuberant puppy, too rash and frolicking to mean any good. Had someone from Butte come to town and warned Waters of Dietz's true identity? Had someone recognized him? If so, would Waters call him in privately? Dietz didn't think so. More likely Waters would opt for a public party. Still, Dietz sat on guard, weighing his options, contemplating lies and escape. "What about?"

"A price on Miss Byrne's head?"

Dietz would have sputtered into his glass if he'd had possession of it yet. "Keely?"

"You're rightfully shocked." Waters shook his head and clucked his tongue. "She's a sweet, well-intentioned lass."

"By whom?"

"Word is that the Clan-na-Gael has a contract on her. Who hired them, we can only surmise."

Arrogant bastard! Clan-na-Gael, the Irish crime gang. Even a rumor that they were involved was worth heeding. McCullough belonged to the Clan-na-Gael and was only considered a lesser evil by those in the know. McCullough would have heard of any rumors, but Dietz was not McCullough. He had to bluff. "I've heard no rumors."

Waters' true nature emerged with the smile that spread across his face, the power hungry, egotistical son of a bitch. "You would if they wanted you to."

"And why wouldn't they?"

"They are now, which, I assume, is why they let the rumor fly. And because you're one of their own, they're giving you an out, McCullough."

Dietz cocked his head. Just what game did Waters play? "How so?"

"I've heard it said that they'd never hit McCullough's wife."

Dietz thumped back in his chair trying hard to keep the astonishment from his face. "You're implying that I marry Miss Byrne. Isn't that what I meant to do by coming here?"

"Very slowly, my friend. Too slowly for their tastes, and those of the men who hired them." Waters cleared his throat. "There's some who are beginning to think that McCullough's got cold feet."

"And if he does?"

Waters shrugged. "Too bad for Miss Byrne, I suppose."

Dietz cursed mentally but tried to mask his outward expression and sound light and easy. "Look, what should she matter to them? What kind of a threat could she be?"

"She's been mucking around in union business."

"You mean like out at the old miner's last night?" Dietz fought hard to effect a scoff and keep the fear and frustration from his voice. "That's innocent, womanish meddling. Petty, insignificant."

"There's some who fear Miss Byrne is turning turncoat like her brother did shortly before his death."

"Mick Byrne?" A new fear burned in Dietz. Had the Clan been responsible for Michael Byrne's death? Was Keely right in thinking that someone was to blame, that Michael had been murdered? And was she merely misguided as to the source?

Waters laughed. "I'd heard the two of you were somewhat estranged shortly before he died. Judging from your shocked expression I guess he didn't tell you how he was suddenly for compromise, what we call giving up the fight and kowtowing to the owners." Waters picked up his whiskey and took a gulp. "Mick had plenty of friends. Guess some feel that his sister could influence them. The last thing the union needs so close to our final victory is to be divided. The owners are powerful, too strong a foe to be easily dismissed or to fight with an army not of one mind. Civil insurrection requires a rather broad base of support." Waters took another drink of whiskey. "Surely you agree?"

"Certainly."

Waters sounded like a military strategist, and what he said made sense from that standpoint. But did he tell the truth about the Clan? If Dietz were really McCullough there might be a way to find out. But Dietz had no direct ties to the Clan. Worse still, the Clan-na-Gael members back East knew McCullough by sight and could recognize Dietz as the fake he was if he started nosing around. Trying to make contact by mail or telegram seemed too damned risky. Waters would intercept anything that went out of Gem and Dietz couldn't risk trying Wallace, not without jeopardizing his ability to mail out reports. Dietz had known that the Clan operated all over the country, but he hadn't heard anything directly about their involvement in Idaho. McCullough had been amazingly tight-lipped about it. Just another reason for Dietz to be looking over his shoulder. What if someone from the local Clan recognized him as an imposter?

Dietz wondered further about Waters. Just how deep was his involvement with the Clan-na-Gael? If he spoke the truth at all, was he a member or merely teaming with them to get something he wanted? Or was he innocently repeating idle gossip? How would he benefit from Dietz marrying Keely?

"Look, McCullough, I've seen your written protestation of love for our fair Miss Byrne. Surely you weren't lying to the lady?"

Dietz tensed. How had Waters seen the letters? Keely wouldn't have shown them to him. Had Waters had Keely's room searched? That gave some validation to his claims. And put Dietz on greater alert. The union knew how McCullough should act. And who was to say that they weren't still keeping Keely under surveillance? "Absolutely not."

"Then marrying her should be no hardship."

"Not at all, not on my own schedule. A man likes to woo a woman in his own time. We've only just met in person. Miss Byrne has her own right to be certain of the match."

Waters laughed. "From what I hear, she doesn't need any convincing. You know, McCullough, it would be convenient for everyone if our schedules for this wedding were compatible."

"What's your stake in this Waters? What do you gain?"

Waters looked surprised. He set his glass down suddenly. "Very perceptive. I have my own reasons. Miss Byrne distracts one of my men."

"You mean Gaffney."

Waters nodded and smiled. "His obsession has become all too obvious lately. I don't need my men distracted. I want peace in the ranks. And," Waters paused, seemingly searching for the right words, "I want Miss Byrne safely away from trouble. All kinds of trouble."

Waters' none too subtle hint about Gaffney and the union slammed Dietz right in the stomach. Waters knew something about Gaffney, something Dietz did not. A warning? Maybe Waters did mean some good, or maybe it all just suited his purposes. The man proved an enigma.

"How soon?" A few more weeks of stalling, that's all Dietz needed.

"This afternoon." Waters sounded uncompromising. The mere conviction of his manner carried an implicit threat.

Dietz hated being backed into a corner. But there seemed no escape now. Guilty as he felt over the whole damned situation, he had to marry Keely. He knew no other way to save her.

"She won't be married by anyone other than a preacher. And we need a license."

"I can arrange that. Bring your bride and meet me back here at four."

"Know where I can pick up a ring quick and cheap?" Sometimes a man had to make a decision in an instant. Dietz hoped he'd made the right one.

"Oh, yeah. We've got us an amateur goldsmith and jewelry maker in town. I'll introduce you." Waters poured himself another glass of whiskey and raised it in toast. "To married bliss."

Dietz matched him. "To a good time tonight."

Dietz left Waters' office, silently cursing and musing. The whole damned thing could blow up in his face. He'd have to be doubly careful about his cover now. Right after the action McCullough would have to disappear from Gem. Later Dietz would have to send his things and a note of condolence, along with a healthy dose of cash, back to Keely. He'd have to create some honorable end to McCullough, which was better than the man deserved. If all went well, Keely would never discover the truth about Dietz and McCullough. But his noble deception proved poor salve on his bleeding conscience.

He turned his thoughts to the immediate present. For now, other more immediate matters pressed him. What could he say to Keely to convince her of their urgent need to marry this afternoon? Did she have any hint of the danger? What would serve him better, honesty or deception?

Patterson, who was sweeping the boardwalk in front of his store, called out a greeting. "Quite a show you put on last night, my friend."

"Think so?" Dietz barely heard him.

"Nice bit of fireworks, and I'm not speaking of the cabin." Patterson chuckled, then grew suddenly serious as he lowered his voice. "I've been waiting for you. This boardwalk's cleaner than it's ever been. I stay out here

much longer and folks are going think I've turned fastidious."

"You are fastidious, Patterson."

"Yeah, but not generally about boardwalks." Patterson looked him straight in the eye and asked bluntly,
"You going to marry Miss Byrne?"

"What have you heard?"

"Quite a lot while I was out drinking last night.
Rumors about the Clan-na-Gael and Miss Byrne's safety. Rumors that the union wants to run her out, or I
should say, a certain faction of the union wants to run
her out, the militant fringe."

"So Waters wasn't lying."

Patterson shrugged. "He's a smart man. He could
just as easily have started the rumors himself."

"You don't think they're true?" Dietz hoped Patterson had some answers.

"Maybe, maybe not. There's no way of knowing."

"How do we find out?"

"How much time did they give you to get hitched?"

"This afternoon."

"Then we don't find out. You haven't answered my
question—you marrying her?"

"I am." Dietz might have amended his statement to
say he had no other choice, but he hated sounding weak
and out of control. He expected Patterson to censure
him, but his fellow agent masked his expression. Patterson was too damned good at hiding his thoughts.

"What is going on between you and Keely?"

Patterson surprised him with the question. "Going
on? What do you mean?"

"Don't play games with me, Dietz. I have two eyes. Either you're one fine actor, or you're falling in love with her."

"You've got yourself two blind eyes, Patterson." Dietz shook his head.

"Need I quote the rules to you? Never jeopardize an operation by falling in love on the job. A woman will make you lose your objectivity, especially a woman in the enemy camp."

"I'm not in love with her, but I am going to marry her. I have to."

Patterson shook his head. His fatherly attitude irritated Dietz. "The boss isn't going to like it." He leaned against his broom. "But it may all work out in the end. Just don't say I didn't warn you about messing around with matrimony."

Dietz chose to ignore Patterson's insinuations. "I don't plan on staying married long. How soon do you expect whole scale war to break out?"

"Not before this afternoon, but soon." Patterson laughed again. "No later than a month from now. Looks like you may be right—married bliss won't have to last you too long."

"What have you heard?"

"Nothing definite."

Dietz nodded. Patterson slapped him on the back. "Treat Miss Byrne well. A month may have to last her a lifetime."

Dietz grunted. "Yeah. Don't worry. McCullough will leave this world like a hero, at least as far as Keely is concerned. Which is more than I can say for the real

McCullough." Dietz looked toward the boardinghouse. "I've got to be going. I'd invite you to the wedding, but you and I aren't supposed to be friends."

Dietz found Keely in the kitchen cleaning up the last of the breakfast dishes, humming a sweet little tune. It surprised him how well he like the sound of her voice. She looked lovely all flushed from the exertion. His mind drifted to another kind of flush he expected to see tonight. She turned and saw him before he could finish his thoughts.

"McCullough." She sounded startled. "I didn't expect you back so soon. I thought you were meeting with union officials, making plans to end this strike."

It wasn't hard to look sheepish. "Lass. I've been making plans all right, plans of another nature. I hope they don't displease you." He tried to sound light and a bit hopeful.

A look of confused consternation flitted across her face. "What have you been up to?"

"Nothing evil, I assure you." Liar. "Don't sound so suspicious." He gave her a lopsided grin. "It's a fine day. You got any plans for this afternoon?"

"What do you have in mind?"

Dietz stared her down directly, trying to look devilish. He smiled and shrugged. "Nothing much. Maybe a wedding. I found a preacher who isn't busy."

Keely's mouth popped open and then she screamed. An instant later she threw herself into his arms and hugged him ferociously. So much for having to convince her. "I'll take that to mean you're available. How's four?"

"I love you, McCullough." She sounded rapturous.

"We'll see if it lasts when I tell you that I've still got a big meeting to attend this evening." He laughed and for some unexplainable reason felt some happiness along with it. "You won't be mad, will you?"

"As long as you come directly home and we get a real wedding night, I won't care."

A real wedding night—yipes! Damn guilt again. "Keely, you're one in a million."

Oh, what the hell. She looked up at him ripe for a kiss and he took it.

Dietz signed McCullough's name with a flourish to a marriage license, thereby ending McCullough's bachelorhood well after his death. Dietz copied the fancy, dandified moniker from memory, and as for the rest of McCullough's handwriting, as best as Dietz could remember—chicken scratch.

As he watched Keely sign the license with her rounded, feminine script, a sense of relief washed over him. Keely would be safe now, as safe as he could make her. Maybe he should have had regrets, doubts. Yet the only real guilt that assailed him involved lying before a preacher and God. An air of condemnation surrounded the act, despite his noble motives. But who knew? Maybe God did understand his actions. Maybe they weren't so damnable. God knew he'd done worse, with less motivation.

Alone in her room, their room, Keely sat on the bed wearing only her chemise, hugging her knees, waiting for McCullough to come home from the union meeting and consummate their marriage. A kind of abject joy filled her. How could happiness be so miserable? She hugged her knees tighter against herself. Details of the wedding and the afternoon rode through her mind.

Despite his stoic manner, and confusing air of reluctance given his earlier insistence that they marry today, McCullough married her for richer, for poorer, for better, for worse, in sickness, and in health with a garnet and gold wedding ring more beautiful than any she could have conjured up in her imagination. It weighted her ring finger, but by no means restrained her. It freed her to love McCullough openly.

Men seemed to think women felt no physical passions. Come to think of it, she'd felt that way herself until McCullough had showed up. But McCullough set her pulse thudding and her heart hammering. Since his arrival, she had wondered at her own virtue. How much longer could she have hung onto it with him around? Now she didn't have to.

Though a virgin, thoughts of the marital bed didn't cause her any alarm, just a fluttery, nervous anticipation. She had only sketchy instructions, awkwardly given to her by Michael after he'd learned McCullough had proposed. But she came from generations of women with passion. They said that's what had killed her mother. That she had insisted on making love with Keely's father even though he was coming down with the fever. Mam might have escaped the fever except for that last, passionate act. Keely didn't know about that. The fever struck with apparent randomness and cruelty. What one did or didn't do, didn't seem to make much difference. Anyway, as for herself, Keely had no doubt that when McCullough caught her between him and the sheets, nature would have its way and she hers.

It wasn't that particular passion that worried her— it was the way she loved McCullough. If he walked through the door right now with a whore on each arm, she'd forgive him. She forgave him, even admired his sense of duty at attending the union meeting that kept him from her now, on their wedding night. He'd probably stay out late, go drinking with the boys after the meeting, the way Michael always had and McCullough had taken to doing. She forgave him that and waited, albeit impatiently, for his return. He let them burn Jack Catridge's cabin, and though she'd been angrier than she'd almost ever been, she couldn't go through with turning him out. She couldn't imagine anything that she couldn't forgive him for, loving him in the strange, wild way she did. That gave him a kind of frightening power over her.

But today her love brought joy, while the knowledge that she loved him more than he loved her, misery. Self-pity did not prompt the thought. Somehow she knew. His reserve, his calm, his holding back. Even his sudden capitulation and impromptu wedding planning seemed motivated by other reasons, though she couldn't imagine what. No, she loved him more than he did her.

He fought his feelings; any astute observer could see it. Yet he did love her; he had to. What else explained his jealousy over Lunn? Or the looks he gave her when he assumed she wasn't looking? Or the years of letters and their tender sentiments? But what explained his restraint? She wished she knew, or maybe she didn't. Did it matter, as long as she had him?

CHAPTER EIGHT

Dietz crossed the street and stumbled toward the boardinghouse, whiskey from Dutch's Saloon hot on his breath. A man probably shouldn't go out drinking on his wedding night, but he wasn't certain he could face the night cold sober, and the opportunity to be one of the boys had been too good to pass up. Seemed like every man in camp wanted to buy him a drink and toast the bride. Everyone except Gaffney who made a point of following Dietz from bar to bar, fingering his gun, giving Dietz death looks. Sure enough, Gaffney would be trouble. But as long as he didn't hurt Keely, Dietz could handle him.

As the alcohol flowed, so did tongues. Dietz had picked up many useful tidbits. Nothing like a celebration to make quick friends of near strangers.

Dietz slowed as he came to the boardinghouse
steps—a contrast to his usual behavior when a woman
waited for him. He knew where his hesitation sprang
from. Keely wasn't a whore, and as fickle as it sounded,
that bothered him. Not that he doubted his ability to
please her with his lovemaking. He was ladies' man
enough for that. But he'd never had a virgin. What
would she be expecting? How much pain would she
feel? He swallowed.

And not being a whore, Keely wouldn't know anything about contraception. He carried a supply of those
fancy French condoms with him, but how could he explain using one on his wedding night?

He wiped his damp palms against his pants. He'd
never been with a woman who didn't practice some
form of birth prevention herself, or not expect him to.
Marrying Keely was one thing, but leaving a little Dietz
behind, to be passed off as a McCullough, left him cold.
A fatherless bastard. How could he do that to a child, to
Keely? Hadn't the source of his problems started when
his father died? Hadn't that been when he'd become a
liar?

He'd have to withdraw early and hope she didn't
question it, didn't know better. Being an operative was
hell.

He sauntered up the steps, through the dark kitch-
en, and back to her room, pausing to listen at the door.
All quiet. He doubted she slept. What nervous bride
would? The thought of her sitting quietly, waiting for
his return while he went carousing, laid him with a
heavier burden of guilt. *Buck up, man,* he chided him-

self. Time to start play-acting. Time to become McCullough and forget Dietz's existence. At least for a few hours.

He swung the bedroom door open without knocking. The sight that met him took his breath away, stunned him.

Keely stood in front of the half-open window wearing a light cotton, formless white chemise tied closed at the neck. Alluringly backlit by moonlight, she might as well have worn nothing. He shut the door, reminding himself to get hold of his nerves. When he turned back to her, she pulled the chemise over her head, revealing lush curves, and full breasts that bounced as she dropped the chemise to the floor.

How did she do that? Look innocent, unjaded, and horribly seductive at the same time. An erection tugged at his pants. He was losing himself to this woman.

"Michael always told me men were visual creatures. Give your husband an eyeful." Keely laughed softly, nervously. "That's the advice he gave me for my wedding night. That's all I know about this business, McCullough."

"That's all you need to know." Did she hear the hoarse desire in his voice and recognize it for what it was? Be smooth, man, Deitz reminded himself, irked by reacting to her like a boy who'd just gotten his first squeeze of breast.

A soft breeze fluttered the open curtains, drawing his attention, making him feel uncomfortably vulnerable. He denied the obvious—that again she'd rendered him assailable, that he could lose his heart to her.

"For heaven's sake, Keely. Close the window."

She laughed again. "Didn't think you were shy, McCullough. There's nothing but woods rising up the hill behind the building. No one can see us."

"No?" He stepped past her and pulled the thing shut, latching it, suddenly craving privacy. Suddenly wanting them to be the only two people in the world. Crazy. "Maybe not, but half the town will be straining to hear our love sounds. I'm in no mood for entertaining anyone but you, lass." He pulled the curtains together.

McCullough traced Keely's shoulders from behind as he turned from the window. Despite the warmth of his touch, goosebumps rose on her arms. Was it possible to be hot and cold at the same moment? Nervous and eager? Oh, she loved this man, wanted him. Too much, too much.

He kissed the hollow of her neck like no man ever had. The wonder of it. The feelings his touch aroused. She was so innocent. She'd never let any man near enough to kiss her at all. Lunn tried once, but she rebuked him easily enough. In this town any willing acceptance of affection caused a line of suitors to form a mile long outside your door. But she had her man, McCullough. Long distance, where she wanted him. Until he came and snatched away her soul with his violet eyes.

His breath warmed more than body, it warmed her soul with its sweet whiskey scent. He reached around from behind and gathered her breasts in his hands. She melted into him. Her nipples tightened and swelled into peaks like they did when very cold. But they weren't cold, far from it. She gasped. She felt him staring at them over her shoulder as he pressed into her, his bulge, restrained by his pants, splitting her buttocks.

"Keely, ah, Keely."

Her name on his lips sounded like a sonnet, melodic, deep. She pulled away and turned to face him and unbuttoned his shirt. His clothes fell away, shed like unnecessary layers of onionskin. Naked, facing each other, he took her into his arms and began to dance. Slowly, face buried in her neck, deep with breathing, manhood pressed between her legs, they moved together.

On tiptoe she danced, as the passion of generations of Irish ancestors built within her. McCullough spun with her gently and pressed her against him in a fine dance whose steps she didn't know. It didn't matter. He led. He could lead her anywhere. Once around the room. Twice, until her breath came in small gasps. Until a frustrated pleasure built between her legs. He danced them to the bed, scooped her up under the knees and laid her gently down.

"Open up to me, Keely."

"Oh, I have, McCullough." If only he knew. But she supposed at this moment he didn't mean her heart. She flattened her legs open against the bed, revealing herself to him. He positioned himself above her.

His eyes, violet in the night, pierced her with their desire. At that moment, his look made her feel irresistible, the most beautiful woman alive, the only one. He bent to kiss her, found her mouth, and washed away every thought she had, except of him. At the same time, his fingers played between her legs. She gasped again as pleasure built.

With one long, sweet drive, he was in her. As if he hadn't been from the moment she first saw him. He rocked her in another kind of dance. One mixed with pain, and pleasure. One unfamiliar and timelessly natural. One she should have known. But somehow, she got the rhythm wrong. Their bodies arched out of step, in mock battle. One she didn't want to fight.

"Lie still, Keely," he coaxed. "Let me lead the rhythm, then follow me." He pulled her legs up around him. She latched on and let him ride. With each thrust a small love song escaped her, building with the motion and the sensations. A gentle, crescendo of chorus in time to his lovemaking. Tender sounds, passionate sounds.

Keely moaned beneath him. Pull out fool, pull out before it's too late. *Now.*

He made the mistake of delaying, of opening his eyes to study her expression. What he saw astounded him with its innocence, its open honesty. He tried to remember a look in any vague way similar to it on the face of any woman he'd ever made love to, but none came to mind. No other woman had ever opened her soul to him, expressing her rapture in so pure and comfortable and genuine a fashion.

She clamped him in with her legs and arched against him, driving him on. Her staccato scream sliced through the room, reverberating off the walls, echoing through him, throwing him over the edge into pleasurable completion.

I'm coming. I coming, Keely.

Thoughts of all else vanished. Only Keely on his mind.

He thrust and grunted and stiffened inside her. Keely's frustration melted away on waves of pleasure, physical and emotional, too fine to describe. She'd always known there were some emotions too complex for words. This was one.

He collapsed on top of her, warm and sweaty from exertion. His perspiration mixed with hers, tingling and stinging her skin, binding them together in an intimacy she'd never thought possible. Every pore of her being had opened for him. She wanted him no other way, just on top of her like that forever. Never mind his weight or the rawness between her legs.

"Beautiful," he whispered in her ear.

"Close, McCullough."

She couldn't help laughing at his consternation. She hadn't meant to insult him. Quite the opposite. "There aren't words enough, McCullough." She traced his chest with her fingers.

"No indeed," he said. He pulled from her and rolled off her, next to her, pulling her into the crook of his arm, embracing her with the other.

She couldn't stop looking at him. Her gaze traveled the length of his body. She liked the way he looked lying beside her, hard, long, sleek, slick with her love-making.

He started to laugh. "You're something, Keely. You sure you were a virgin?"

"Minutes ago, hours ago, an eternity ago, yes. Didn't I feel like one? My dainty parts ache well enough to prove it." She shifted on the bed, feeling beneath her for the sticky evidence of lost maidenhood. "And I'm bleeding. There's blood on the sheets. Check for yourself."

"No." He shook his head, clearly amused. "You felt like a virgin, as far as I know. Just didn't act like one."

"As far as you know?"

He looked sheepish. "What do I know about virgins, Keely?"

He sounded almost guilty.

"I couldn't say, except that I'd wager you weren't one yourself. You seemed to know your way around the bed," she said with a sudden jealousy she hadn't expected.

"You didn't expect me to be, did you?"

"No. I guess I always expected a ladies' man."

"Good. Then both our expectations were met." He looked toward the window and began chuckling. "Silly of me to close the window. Think that thin pain of glass kept our secrets in this room?"

"Hardly." He was a tease. "I think we gave the town what they were waiting for." She kissed his cheek. "And I'm not sorry or embarrassed."

"No, me either."

"I'd be happy to do it again. Whenever you want." He made her say things she'd never dreamed she would. "I love you, McCullough."

His expression startled her. He seemed surprised and suddenly distant, almost hurt. He hesitated before answering, just slightly, but long enough to leave her clinging to a precipice of emotion and fear.

"I love you, too, Keely McCullough."

She smiled, happy again, content. He'd said he loved her. If he lied, she didn't care. She couldn't let herself believe he'd lied. "Keely McCullough. Nice, I like it." She curled up against him, suddenly drowsy. "I'm sleepy."

"Yeah," he said. She knew he might have said, "It's like that after sex." She was happy he was gentlemanly enough not to remind her of other women. But she liked the thought that sex brought sleep on.

"I should draw you a tub of warm water, Keely. You should take a soak."

"No." She was too tired. How could she leave his side and this comfortable tiredness?

He cleared his throat. "I've heard it helps. You know, after the first—"

"Tomorrow."

"All right then. Tomorrow. Go on to sleep, Keely. It's been a long day."

"Yeah," she said and closed her eyes.

He was a damned liar. If ever there had been any doubt as to his salvation, none existed now. He was a damned liar, emphasis on the damned. Keely slept next to him, her breathing soft and warm against him. She had fallen asleep quickly in what seemed like an eternity. His shoulder ached where the bullet had grazed it, and his arm had fallen asleep long ago. He deserved any discomfort he got. He needed to roll over, but he couldn't bear disturbing Keely. Hadn't he hurt her enough already?

Making love to her had washed away the numbing haze of alcohol that had kept his guilt at bay. Sober, it ate him up. He'd never experienced this kind of contrition before. Why the hell now? Though he knew well enough. All he had to do was look at the dark stain underneath where Keely rested to find the explanation. He'd taken something precious from her that he had no right to take. True. She'd given it willingly. But not to him—to McCullough.

And take it he did, riding it right over the edge, not pulling out like he'd planned. Now maybe he'd done more than take, maybe he'd given.

Damn! He preferred jaded women. They were a lot less trouble. They knew how to take care of things. They didn't let themselves become involved. They didn't look at him with trust and love shining in their eyes. They let him leave.

He took a deep breath and exhaled. They let him leave. Because for John Dietz, there always came a time to leave. And no matter what he felt for Keely, or what he denied, he'd leave this time, too. He'd have to.

Gaffney knew the bars would eventually close up for the night, but it still came as a shock when Dutch final-

ly threw him out of the saloon into the street, locking
the doors behind him. Gaffney landed on his butt in the
middle of the road. He sat, too stunned at first to move.
Across the road, three buildings down, McCullough
was deflowering his Keely. His Keely. Rage the shade
of lightning coursed through him at the thought.
Gaffney's glare followed his thoughts to the
boardinghouse.

After a night of tailing McCullough from bar to bar,
seeing him slapped on the back and congratulated like
some kind of hero, fingering his gun, warning
McCullough, McCullough still didn't get it. Gaffney
wasn't letting Keely go, husband or no. He hadn't let
anyone stand in his way, not even Michael. At the
memory of Michael lying broken and dying at the bottom of the mine tunnel, sweat broke out on his forehead and his stomach rolled with nausea. "Shit,
Michael," he said. "I didn't mean to kill you."

Gaffney wiped his brow with an unsteady hand.
Sawing through the last bracing timber and ordering
his crew to brace another tunnel that day instead had
been so easy. And as Michael's foreman, sending him
down to work the shaft got no question. Gaffney
gulped down the fresh summer night air, but nothing
chased the nightmare away. Michael's scream, the
death rattle of his last breaths. Gaffney shuddered.

He'd only meant to make a hero of himself, save
Michael's life. Then Michael would've been so grateful,
he would have given Keely to Gaffney. He'd have had
to. But something had gone wrong. The cave in was
more serious than Gaffney had thought possible. By the

time he got there, his best friend was beyond help. He could only stand there and let him die. Then he backed up and walked casually back to his post. No one noticed the cave in until hours into the next shift. The whole incident played to the union's hand. Union leaders blamed the owners for allowing unsafe conditions to exist below. Even Keely bought the story. Any regret on Gaffney's part stemmed from the incident turning Keely into a kind of crusader for safety and nonviolence. It looked damned bad for her.

As for suspicion of foul play, someone mentioned seeing Gaffney leaving the tunnel that afternoon. But no one seriously thought he'd kill his best friend. No one but Waters, who offered Gaffney the privileged position of hired gun for the union, explaining that union brass weren't altogether sorry for Byrne's death. Michael Byrne had been stirring up trouble with his preaching against violence, on pacifism. Waters seemed to think Gaffney a hero. And hell, Gaffney had thought, why shouldn't he continue being a hero? He'd killed his best friend, killing anyone else had to be easy.

Gaffney pushed up and tried to stand, but fell right back on his hamhocks. When was the last time he'd been this drunk? He couldn't remember, and it didn't matter. Only the cause of his drunken stupor did. Keely's wedding. He pushed up again, this time successful, and staggered across the street to the corner of Keely's boardinghouse. Tonight, though he gave it chance enough, alcohol couldn't push back the dark thoughts sweeping through his mind. Part of him was numb, had to be. Damn Waters for sending him on a fool's errand today. It was almost like he were in cahoots with McCullough. Slimy, secretive, coward of a bastard McCullough. Marrying his Keely while Gaffney worked on union business out of town. He'd show him.

Gaffney leaned on the building corner; his stomach heaved, rebelling at his sudden upright position. He retched into a bush that capped the corner. When his stomach finished its business, he looked up to the windows overhead. Had McCullough taken Keely to his room? No, he wouldn't, not up there with all the other men. They had to be in Keely's room. Gaffney stumbled around to the backside of the building.

By the time he reached the backyard, his breath came in drunken gasps. His mouth felt dry and sour with his own vomit and the taste of Keely in bed with another man. He closed his eyes briefly before summoning the courage to look at her window. What did he intend to do? Watch them. Listen to their lovemaking? His pulse raced. Maybe, sickening as it would be. At least he'd get to see Keely.

He opened his eyes and fixed his gaze on her dark window. Damn him! That bastard had closed the curtains, shuttered her in. Keely never closed the window on nights like these. Rage overtook him. He scrambled up the bank behind the building, hefted the largest rock he could find, and hurled it at the building. Direct hit. It sailed through the window leaving a pleasant tinkling of glass in its wake. Gaffney laughed and staggered up the hill into the woods where he wouldn't be caught.

The crash woke Dietz, or maybe it was Keely's scream that roused him. He couldn't say. The two seemed to happen simultaneously. He sat up automatically, Colt in hand at ready, senses on alert, sleep forgotten and dusted from his mind. Years with the detective agency had taught him how to quickly shrug off any lasting effects sleep caused. The bed creaked as Keely sat up. He felt her trembling behind him. A crowd of bloodthirsty men did not scare her, but something heaved through her window in the middle of the night evidently did. He reached back with one arm and hugged her protectively. "It's all right, lass."

"What is it?" she asked.

Tiny shards of glass littered the floor, glinting in the moonlight shining through the gently blowing curtains. How thoughtful of someone to open the window for them. A large rock rested in the midst of the rubble, in the darkness looking like blackness itself. Without the buffeting effect of the closed curtains, the blasted thing would have sailed right into their bed. "Vandals," he said. "Stay put. I'll check it out."

Otherwise naked, he slipped his boots on and walked to the window where he pulled the curtains back cautiously, peering into the yard. Nothing, no one. As he had suspected the perpetrator had fled.

"What do you see?" Keely whispered.

"Nothing." Damned nothing. Was the rock the Clan-na-Gael's way of offering their blessing? A warning not to get too comfortable? Or merely a prank?

"Come back from the window, McCullough. Maybe our rock throwing friend is still out there, hiding in the woods. We don't need you making a target of yourself. Though a fine looking one you are."

Despite the situation, he laughed. She charmed him too easily. "Such brashness, Keely McCullough. And such insult to my stealth."

She joined him in laughter. "But such compliment to your form."

He turned to face her, expecting to find her with the bedcovers pulled to her chin. Instead the sheet lay crumpled around her legs and waist. From there up she was most beautifully naked. His body reacted immediately. From the height of her gaze, he guessed she saw it. She laughed again.

"Cover yourself woman," he said, a scant hoarsely. "What if we've got us a peeper out there."

She made no move toward the bedsheet, just giggled. "What if? Look at you."

"It isn't me he'd be wanting to look at, lass." She smiled at him defiantly. Quick as he could he crunched across the glass to the bed, wrenched the sheet free from its tuck, and wrapped his startled wife in it. "Gather what you'll need for the morning. We aren't staying here." Using all his restraint, he let her go, shucked off his boots and pulled on his pants.

"Where are we going?"

"I'm taking you to my room upstairs."

She still stared at his pants. He looked down to see his own obvious bulge. "Taking me to, or taking me in?"

"Maybe both." He forced his gaze away from her, making himself look for something to patch the window with.

"Don't worry about that," Keely said as she pulled her wrapper on. "I always sleep with the window open in the summer. No one's ever stolen anything from me yet."

Her words caught him off guard. Somebody had. He had, with the window closed. "An attractive woman, a town full of drunken men, and a ground floor room— that's foolishness, Keely." Gaffney came to mind. Could he be the arm behind the rock? It was either him, a random act of rowdiness, the Clan-na-Gael, or someone who suspected his true identity. The first and last two options sent a chill through him.

She shrugged. "Michael was always there to protect me." For the first time she looked a bit shy. "And now you."

"And I'm taking you upstairs."

"Oh, please do," she said.

He couldn't help laughing at her innuendo, not so innocently done, he suspected. He swept her and her things into his arms and carried them upstairs into his room. The bed creaked when he deposited her on it, but he didn't care. He began to make love to McCullough's wife for the second time that night, slowly, with no intention of pulling out early. Damn, that woman overtook his senses.

CHAPTER NINE

The bed spring creaked. Dietz rolled over, rebelling against opening his eyes. Sunlight cut through the room, penetrating his closed eyelids. Damn, it was morning. His head pounded with a hangover, nothing new, but nothing to anticipate. Where was he? For the moment, he'd forgotten. Wherever he slept, another person occupied the bed with him. One who smelled sweetly of lavender and rose. In the haze before wakefulness, he hoped he'd bedded a decent looking whore, and gotten the information he'd been after, whatever that could have been. He carelessly reached for her.

"No, you don't, lover. It's morning, and one of us has got to go to work. Since you don't have a regular job, I guess that had better be me." Keely's voice sounded lilting and happy.

Dietz's eyes flew open and his hard-on came back, if indeed it had ever left. Keely sat on the bed next to him pulling on her work shift. His situation came back to him clearly. With the sun highlighting her hair and the deep green of her eyes, she made a beautiful sight. He reached out and rubbed her back. He could have sworn she purred. "Stay in bed."

"I can't. The men will be wanting their breakfast."

"Let them want."

She shook her head.

He dropped his hands and propped up on one elbow. She pulled the bodice up over her shoulders and began deftly buttoning it up.

"You're a hard-hearted woman."

"Aye," she laughed, "and a sore one."

He couldn't answer that; for some reason it embarrassed him. He tugged at the worn sleeve of her dress, so thin a man could nearly see through it. "Looks like one of my first orders of business as your husband should be buying you a few new dresses."

The look she gave him startled him. She was clearly shocked and embarrassed now herself. She looked down self-consciously, fingering the fine garnet ring on her finger. "Whatever you please, when the mines open up and you've got yourself regular work again."

For some irrational reason her assumption irritated him. She thought he couldn't provide for her? "What are you saying, Keely?" Unable to help himself, he pressed her cruelly.

She kept her gaze fixed on her ring. "You've done enough already, McCullough." Keely sighed. "This ring is wonderful, prettier than any I could imagine, and it makes me happy and proud. But I'm no fool. This ring cost you a pretty piece." She paused. For once she had the grace to blush, as well she should have with the accusation she made. "But there's no need for spending your reserves on frippery for me. I didn't marry you for your money."

He snorted, wounded. If only she knew. Money was the one thing he'd plenty of, and could offer her. The agency's clients usually paid all his expenses, living and otherwise. As a bachelor, he kept no house, had no wife to send the money home to. Consequently, his salary accumulated in the bank. And, though no financial genius, he'd invested in several ventures that had paid off handsomely. A few frocks, he owed her that much, just to assuage his guilt. As for the ring, the Mine Owners' Association had paid for that. Part of the expense of keeping his cover. "Frippery, is that what you call a new dress? One with material thick enough so you can't see through it?"

She flushed again. "There's no need to insult me. I was trying to be delicate." She made a move to stand, but he caught her wrist and pulled her back.

"Delicate, aye, lass?" He grabbed her chin and pulled her face around, forcing her gaze to meet his. "I'm wounded." A snippet of conversation from his days riding with McCullough came back to him. "I can't let you think I'm the kind of man who'd take a wife he couldn't support, who'd live off her. I may not be working that you can see, but I am being paid. And I've got me an interest in a fine store in Pennsylvania. My partner runs it, sending me my share of the profits monthly. I've got money to live on, money to support both of us. And if I say I'm buying you a new frock, then I am, with my own money, not yours. And you've no say about it."

"Oh, I don't?" She was choking down a smirk, surely she was.

"No, and as for this notion of yours that you're working to support us, let me clear something up for you. I'm open-minded enough to let you work right now, only because your job gets us a place to live. Not that I couldn't afford to pay for our own place. I just haven't seen one in this one horse mining town that's fit for you."

Her eyes misted over for just a minute, then she started to laugh, and he with her. "Anything you say, Ian McCullough."

He pulled her over into him, bringing his lips onto hers with a noisy crunch of the aging bedsprings. A loud pounding on the door interrupted them.

"Hey, McCullough. You're not at it again, are you? Let her go," one of their fellow tenants yelled through the door, laughter in his tone. "We're hungry and needing our breakfast." More raucous laughter floated into the room. Keely pulled away from him.

"See what you've done?" She slipped on her shoes and stood, making for the door. She moved a little tenderly.

"You should've let me draw you that bath."

She shot him a look and disappeared into the hall, slamming the door behind her.

Later, when he came down to breakfast, the men greeted him with hoots and leers. The two old gold prospectors, whose names he always had trouble keeping straight, gave him long, serious looks. But the young McNalley wasted no time with pretenses. "Miss Byrne's looking a little tired and maybe a might saddle sore today. Didn't you let her get no rest, you awful beast?"

All present laughed. That would have been fine with Dietz if McNalley would've stopped there, but then he addressed himself directly to Keely. "How was he, Miss Byrne, did he satisfy you?"

"It's Mrs. McCullough to you now, boy," Dietz said.

McNalley smiled back at him. "Yeah, isn't that what I was implying by my question?" McNalley's lewd tone angered Dietz. "But she still hasn't answered my question. Let me rephrase it. How's she like being Mrs. McCullough?"

"She won't be answering that question."

"Afraid of the answer, McCullough?" McNalley edged dangerously close to fighting. Dietz eyed him steadily.

Gem was nothing more than a dog pile. Too many men, all of them fighting for supremacy, all wanting to be pack leader. Dietz had no intention of abdicating McCullough's well-known reputation for toughness to the young pup in front of him. Smooth as glass he drew his Colt's 45 and aimed it at McNalley. The kid paled visibly.

"Keep up this talk and the two of us will have to be stepping into the alley." Dietz caught Keely's horrified look, but she neither spoke nor made a move to stop him. Good woman. She'd just have to trust him a moment. "Mrs. McCullough is a fine woman." Dietz caressed the words, giving them a meaning beyond the innocent. Several chuckles echoed around the room. "And fine women don't go talking about such things, questioned or not. There'll be no more ribald remarks or questions, made to or in front of Mrs. McCullough." Dietz smiled. "Now if you'd asked me, I'd have said she had no complaints."

The boys, including McNalley, started hooting as the tension broke. Dietz holstered the Colt and slapped McNalley on the back. "Give the boy his breakfast, Keely. Thinking dirty thoughts tends to make a man hungry." He leaned in close to McNalley. "We got to get you a whore, lad. We do."

Keely smiled at Dietz when he looked back at her. She set a plate of eggs and ham in front of McNalley, then one in front of him, leaning low and close to him as she reached from behind. He wanted to grab her and drag her back upstairs right then. She pulled back.

"Mr. Allison stopped by this morning with a message for you from Mr. Waters. He wants to meet with you at the union hall at ten."

"At ten?"

"Yes." She smiled. "We've got us a little time between breakfast and then." Her meaning was clear enough. Damn, without her suggesting things, he might have been able to resist her. He sighed raggedly. She seemed determined to make a father of him yet.

Dietz found Waters in his private office, puffing on a large, aromatic cigar as he looked over a stack of correspondence. Waters looked up from his work when he heard Dietz's footsteps.

"You're wearing an ear-to-ear grin, McCullough, if I do say so. Have a nice evening last night?"

Am I really beaming like a fool, or is that just what everyone tells a bridegroom the day after?

"Seems I'm getting that from everyone today." Dietz winked. "To answer your question—I did, and a fine morning, too."

Waters kicked out the chair across the desk from him for Dietz. "Have a seat."

Dietz dropped into the chair. "You're developing a habit of sending for me straight off in the morning."

The returning look Waters gave him made him feel like a plant growing under a cloche—warm, cornered, and under scrutiny. Waters riffled through his papers, found what he was looking for, and shoved it across the desk to Dietz, considerately turning it right side up for Dietz to read.

"What's this?" Dietz arched a brow.

"A background check I ordered on McCullough back when I first thought about hiring him. I wanted to make sure he really was our man. Big Sam just brought it over from the post office. Sometimes the post can be mighty slow around here. I'd given up on ever seeing this and hired McCullough anyway."

Dietz's heart skipped a beat, noting Waters had not said, *A background check on you, McCullough.* He drew the papers close to him with a steady hand, keeping his expression masked.

Did this new information reveal something that suddenly had caused Waters to doubt Dietz's identity? What else explained Waters' renewed scrutiny and cautious manner?

Dietz wondered if he'd have to make a quick exit. His holstered Colt's 45 felt heavy and useless, but the Derringer in his inside coat pocket could be reached surreptitiously. Two or three other miners milled around in the front offices. If Dietz fired at Waters, they'd hear and come running. Those men worried him. Given everything, he placed his odds of escape at fifty-fifty. Waters would end up with the worst end of the deal—dead. He smiled back at Waters.

Waters thumped on the papers before Dietz and sat back suddenly, apparently satisfied with his work.

Dietz fanned the information out in front of him. "McCullough. Physical description," he read from the sheets before him. "Six feet tall, one hundred seventy-five pounds, dark brown hair, blue eyes, medium build, physically fit." He gave Waters a brilliant smile. "Nice description of myself. Makes me sound nice and handsome. I don't see any discrepancies, do you?"

"Thirty-eight years old," Waters shot back. "You look a little young."

Hell, yes, Dietz thought. And with good reason. Dietz was only thirty. "I guess you're meaning that as a compliment. I don't take it as such necessarily myself, mind you. Some of us are cursed with youthful appearance."

"Cursed?"

Dietz laughed. "Other men don't like to follow boys."

Waters laughed outright, then slid open his desk drawer and withdrew a photograph. He held it with its back to Dietz, his gaze flitting between photo and Dietz, presumably testing Dietz to see if he squirmed. Dietz smiled confidently back at him. He'd been in tighter situations than this. Still, if that were a photograph of McCullough, he could be in trouble. "Something from my family album, I presume?"

Finally, Waters appeared satisfied. "Appears so." He pushed the photograph across to Dietz.

Dietz took it and held it up to inspect, spotting McCullough immediately. The grainy photograph had been taken some years back. McCullough stood in front of a building of some sort with four or five other men. He wore a felt mining hat slouched low over his eyes. Dietz laughed again, put on his own hat and adjusted it to look like the picture. "There's your problem, Waters. You should have just asked me. I'd have humored you."

"I recognize you in the photograph, McCullough."

Dietz pushed his hat back. Now was the time to seal all suspicion in its grave. Fortunately, McCullough had been a long-winded, self-important bastard who loved to talk about himself. Dietz passed the photograph back to Waters and sat back, trying to look casual, but still poised to reach for the Derringer.

McCullough's stories tumbled through his mind. Should he share some? A sudden memory of a scar on McCullough's shoulder came to him. "I suppose you've got a record of some of my finer moments there in front of you. You want to see my scars?" Dietz didn't wait for Waters to answer. He stripped off his coat, stealthily palming his Derringer, and unbuttoned his shirt, wincing a bit at his wound. He pulled his shirt off and pointed to scar he'd gotten in a knife brawl several years ago. It didn't look exactly like McCullough's, but Waters wouldn't know that.

"Put your shirt back on, McCullough." Waters smiled. Dietz could see he was convinced.

Dietz nodded as he buttoned his shirt back up. He paused to take in Waters' expression. Something still bothered Waters. "Something in that report you don't like?"

"Michael Byrne."

This time Dietz almost did lose his composure. "What about Byrne?"

Waters seemed to study him for a moment, measuring his words before speaking. "How shall I put this? Byrne confused me. He didn't seem like a student of yours."

Clearly Waters thought Dietz should know what he was trying to say, though Dietz had no idea. "How so?"

"In the months before his death Byrne became increasingly against using violence. Yesterday you seemed surprised when I told you that, but this report indicates clearly that you already knew about his actions."

This playacting a real person could kill him. He'd made too many mistakes already. "Oh, that." Stupid filler words to buy time. Dietz sighed, his mind dashed off at a clip looking for a believable lie. "Byrne and I had our disagreements. Last fall I sent him clear instructions on how to change the owners' minds about how they treated their workers. My directions weren't timid. Byrne wrote me back, letting me know what he thought of my ideas. Surprised the hell out of me. I kept wondering what had happened to him. Yesterday you surprised me yourself with your description of Mick. I didn't think he'd gone so far, though I should have assumed it.

"About a week before he died, he wrote me a letter asking me to consider breaking off my friendship with Keely. I suppose he told you about that?"

Waters shook his head.

Dietz smiled self-deprecatingly. "Not a confidant of his, I see."

"No," Waters said. He leaned back in his chair, seemingly relieved. Maybe Waters really did like him.

Dietz cleared his throat. "He didn't like my suggestions. Claimed I wasn't the man he remembered." Dietz sighed. "Years ago we used to be of like mind. Byrne had the rare combination of passion, courage, and conviction in him and we got along fine. Those days he'd do anything for the cause." Dietz paused, trying to appear as if remembering fond thoughts. "I don't think he went soft, just took a misguided, idealistic turn."

Waters seemed to consider a moment. "Maybe he did. Maybe he didn't. All I can say for sure is that he was fast becoming unpopular among the men." Waters paused again, looking thoughtful. "So why'd you come out and marry her?"

Dietz should have known the question was coming. "I never considered giving her up. Keely and I were in love, no matter how unconventional our courtship." In truth, Dietz had wondered the same thing himself, but he could never get McCullough to talk about it. McCullough hid something, some reason other than love and altruism. "Before I could respond to Byrne's request, Keely wired me about his death." Dietz acted sad and distant. He shook himself. "Then I knew I had to take care of her. I had to marry her. What kind of man would leave her alone? So I proposed. Despite our differences, I think Michael would have wanted it, had he known how things were to turn out."

"And you love her?" Could there be any doubt after yesterday's shotgun wedding? But Waters' question seemed to hold sinister overtones. What was going on here?

"I do."

Waters nodded as Dietz assessed him, feeling like he played a game of chess where the board went unseen. All things considered, Dietz decided to throw a move, give Waters something on him, see how Waters would use it. Dietz cleared his throat. "Keely doesn't know about Michael's request, you understand. I'd appreciate her not finding out. There's no reason to make her feel bad or give her room for doubt now." Dietz kept his tone even, the equivalent of a poker face.

"Naturally." Waters gave him a slow, nasty smile. Dietz had no doubt that Waters would use the information any way he needed to keep McCullough in line. Waters just verified Dietz's first impression of him. But what the hell? That little secret was nothing compared to the real secret he kept from Keely.

"Your confidences are safe with me," Waters said.

In a pig's eye, Dietz thought and smiled.

Waters spoke again. "And since you mention your wife, I feel compelled to give you a friendly word of advice. Keep her home where she belongs."

Dietz cocked a brow, seething inside. He could let Waters, or the Clan, or the union, or whoever Waters spoke for, push him only so far. Waters just smiled. Finally Dietz was forced to speak and set things straight. "That wasn't part of the deal yesterday. Let me clear something up for those involved. My wife has a mind of her own and a heart to match. She isn't going to give up her charity work as long as there's one person in this camp who needs her help."

Waters cut him off with a quick gesture. "Charity work's fine. I have no complaints on that account. I just don't want to see her at any more union functions."

Visions of the burning cabin came to mind. Dietz felt compelled to answer, and when he did, it came from the heart. "Nor do I."

Waters collected his papers from across the desk. "Good." Waters reached for the photograph sitting on the desk between them, breaking Dietz from his cold thoughts.

"Mind if I keep this one?" Dietz asked, reaching for the picture first. "To show Keely. She hasn't seen any of me from the old days."

Waters shrugged. "Fine." Evidently Waters wanted to demonstrate that he could be reasonable. "We do understand each other?"

"Yes. And since we're making promises to each other—tell your boys to keep their rocks to themselves. I don't need any more of their calling cards littering my home." Dietz threw the accusation out to gauge Waters' reaction.

"Rock?" Waters looked genuinely puzzled.

"As in the kind that came sailing through my window last night."

"I don't know anything about a rock." Waters actually sounded innocent, and maybe, a bit worried.

Dietz guessed his concern leaned more toward being uninformed and losing some control over someone than out of any fear for Dietz's safety. But if Waters knew nothing about it, what did it mean and who had thrown it?

"Probably just a prank," Waters said. "Now to more important matters. I've got an assignment for you."

CHAPTER TEN

Dietz left Waters' office disturbed, head buzzing and swelled with too many thoughts to sort properly. Despite his resolve to remain detached, his emotions raged. Waters had set him on a delicate balancing walk where the consequences of falling didn't bear contemplating. Waters still didn't completely trust him. So his loyalty must be tested. Again. Damn.

As Dietz walked past, Patterson stepped out of his store. Dietz locked step with him.

"Allison." Dietz greeted Patterson.

"McCullough." Patterson's eyes danced merrily. "How's the married boy this morning?"

"Well-sexed and feeling like shit."

Patterson laughed and cocked a speculative brow.
"Guilty conscience?"

Dietz shook his head. "It's all part of the job. One of
the side benefits." Though Dietz laughed off Patterson's chastisement, he felt guilty for deceiving Keely—
an emotion he didn't like and hadn't felt regarding the
job before. "Worse. I've just come from Waters' office."
Dietz snorted. "He's got a job for me."

"Is that so?"

"You already know about it?" Damn, Patterson. He
always knew everything.

"Waters is a suspicious man. He's been for testing
you all along." Patterson spit on the ground, making a
wet ring in the dusty road. "What's he want?"

"So you don't know?" Dietz smiled. "Want to
guess?" Dietz watched his feet as they walked, keeping
his face low so no one could read his words.

"If I were a betting man, I'd say Waters wants John
Monihan, the manager of the Gem mine, dead."

"Depending on the bet, you'd be a wealthy man."

They reached the end of town. Patterson stopped
walking.

"Is this common knowledge?" Dietz stared up into
the white pines covering the surrounding hills. A crow
arced overhead, lazily riding the wind as it bellowed its
raucous cry.

"Common enough. Monihan's been warned."

Dietz let out a sigh. Things weren't as bad as they
seemed. "Waters is a fool. He told me no one else knew
of the plan. I thought I was cornered. But if it's com-

mon knowledge, I can blame their nebulous spy for Joe's miraculous escape."

Patterson shrugged and laughed good-naturedly. "You're going to have to make the attempt."

"Yeah. But how? Waters is a fool. What does he think—that Monihan's going to come parading down the mountain for a drink in town at my request?" Dietz shook his head. "If Monihan has half a brain, nothing short of an earthquake is going to dislodge him from his stronghold. What am I supposed to do, storm the mine?"

Patterson slapped him on the back. "You'll think of something."

"Wonder what O'Brien thinks of Waters' games."

"Waters is a loose cannon. I doubt O'Brien would approve, but once something's done, it's done. And getting rid of Monihan is going to have popular approval, I can tell you that now."

"How much time you think I've got?" Dietz looked directly into Patterson's dark gaze. Patterson's eyes danced with amusement, like always, the cool-headed son of a bitch.

Patterson shrugged. "How much time you want? I'd say we've got two, three weeks before something big blows."

"Yeah." Dietz didn't like it, any of it. Patterson turned to leave. Dietz knew they shouldn't be appearing together in public too long or look too friendly, but Dietz couldn't let him leave without his curiosity being relieved. "What do you know about Michael Byrne's death?"

Patterson looked startled by the sudden turn in the conversation. "Nothing directly. But that's not what you're asking, is it?"

"Could it have been intentional?"

Patterson's expression became serious. "Anything's possible, but you're asking, is it probable? I'd have to say yes. No one saw anything. That's what they're all claiming. Officially, Byrne's death is listed as an accident. You suspect otherwise."

"It's only a theory. Any idea who would have done it?"

"None at all. And that's the problem, isn't it? Caving a tunnel in on a man isn't the style of any of the union thugs I know. A slug to the back—yeah. Still, it smells suspicious." Patterson smiled again and gave him another pat on the shoulder. "Cheer up, boy. The mines are closed. You don't have to be worrying about being buried alive yourself." Patterson started off again, then paused to ask a final question. "Need anything from Wallace?"

"No." But Dietz had other worries.

Keely stood reverently at the side of the bed in her room, purposefully avoiding looking at the broken window beyond, or the mess littering the floor on the other side. Remember the wonder of last night, Keely, she told herself. Forget the ugliness. Let it wash away.

In her right hand she held a broom poised for action, in the left a silent dustpan. She set the dustpan down and sentimentally ran her hand over the rumpled sheets. Oh, McCullough. She remembered violet eyes piercing her soul in the darkness, firm arms bracketing her, bracing him above her. She smiled at the memory of McCullough holding her and his intensity as they made love. She flipped back the top sheet. Her gaze landed on a rust brown stain in the center of the bed, muted by other evidence of their lovemaking. She leaned the broom against the night table and sighed as she stripped the bed. Silly, but she'd almost rather not wash these particular sheets, rather not destroy the proof of their coupling. But who kept such a trophy, and who had extra sheets to spare?

Oh, McCullough. Such pleasant memories, such drastic intrusions, Ian McCullough and the rock.

The room smelled of damp morning air, sweet and cool. A breeze blew in, ruffling the doily draped over the edge of the night table. Keely shivered, not wanting to look at the window, to see the fragmented remains, to remember the chill of the crash. Curses to whomever sent the rock sailing. Cold fingers of fear traced her back. Was the rock only a prank, a base form of charivari? If only she could believe that. But she remembered Michael and the threats only too well.

She took a deep breath, recoiling from her own thoughts. Old Joe's cabin red in flame against the night came to mind, bringing with it the smell of singed air and fear so real it were as if the air carried it from the blackened remains of the cabin up the hill. Mr. Waters didn't like her, nor she him. But the look he gave her that night spoke of more than distaste. It issued a warning. Well, Mr. Waters be cursed. He wasn't going to stop her from doing the work Michael had started.

The union was worthy and good. Good for the men, good for their families. Without it the owners would surely exploit them. After all, who were they but uneducated men with brawn and bravery enough to haul ore in damp, dark tunnels? Men foolhardy enough to play with dynamite for a living. The mining engineers and managers would always be well respected and well paid, but the men who did the work? Well, there would always be plenty enough of them willing to work for whatever petty price. At least that's how she imagined the owners thought.

The union on the other hand fought for fair pay and honest, decent treatment of its members. But it was more than a labor union. It was a fraternity, a brotherhood. The union held dances and sponsored social events. The union used dues to pay medical expenses for its members. A lump swelled in her throat. She remembered a cold winter day and a wooden marker on the hill under the pines. The union even paid for funerals. She swallowed. It had paid for Michael's, despite the feelings of some that with his talk of peaceful negotiation with the owners he had turned traitor. Without the union, Michael would have been buried without a funeral. She could not afford one. She wiped a tear away and tossed the sheets next to the door.

Last autumn a few violent men had infiltrated the union. Now they gained power fast and furious. She couldn't let them frighten her. Steeling herself, she walked around the bed and stared at the clutter on the floor. Shards of glass glittered in the sunlight, the broken edges reflecting brilliance like the facets of a diamond. In the center of the destruction lay a naked gray basalt rock, like any other that littered the surrounding hills. She half-expected to find a note wrapped around it, some definite warning. But it was bare, hideous and sinister only by virtue of its use.

She tread cautiously across the floor, broken glass crunching under her boots, and picked up the rock. Suddenly reviled, she stood and impulsively hurled it with as much strength as she possessed out the hole it had made in her window. She watched it fly through the air and disappear into the dense woods behind the building, satisfied only when she heard the thud of its landing. Her eye caught sight of footprints in the small, soggy, flat patch of ground between the house and the hill. Her gaze followed them from around the corner of the building, back around to her window, and then to where they disappeared up the hill.

She began to tremble, first with fear, then with anger. Whatever the rock meant, she wouldn't let it defeat her. She retrieved the broom and swept up. The dustpan trembled as she filled it, matching the meter of her tremulous thoughts. She loathed whoever had meant to ruin her wedding night. On her way out of the room, she picked up the sheets. She dumped them into the washtub to soak, emptied the glass into the garbage, and spun around to nearly collide with McCullough.

"Hello, lass."

"Oh, McCullough!" He smelled good. He looked good. She dropped the dustpan and fell into his arms.

"You've been cleaning up, I see. You should have left it to me."

She pulled away enough to look up at him. He watched her with an intense expression.

"You're upset," he said.

"Footprints," she said somewhat cryptically, but McCullough seemed to know what she meant.

"I know, lass. I tracked them up the hill to an empty whiskey bottle. After that, I lost them in the underbrush."

"So our vandal was just a drunk?"

He pulled her back against him and cradled her head against his chest. "Seems so."

McCullough didn't sound convinced. Though she wanted to know if Mr. Waters had said anything about the incident, she didn't press McCullough for information. Whatever he thought, he preferred to keep to himself, and she preferred not to think about. Not at this minute. Not while pressed against McCullough.

"What are you about this morning?" she asked.

"I thought I'd go upstairs to the room. I've got some thinking and planning to do. I'll fix the window later."

"The bed's not made." She didn't know what had made her say it. It seemed more than that she didn't want him thinking she wasn't a fit housekeeper.

"Isn't it, lass?" His eyes sparkled and his voice went thick. She blushed. "Seems a shame to waste an unmade bed."

"Aye, it does."

"What are we waiting for, Mrs. McCullough?"

"For you to lead the way."

Dietz acted the role of new husband too well, feeling the strong desire to repeatedly bed Keely. He didn't understand his powerful feelings. He was no virgin, nor had he ever been particularly deprived. And he knew full well the consequences of his actions. If he didn't restrain himself, he would get her with child, and soon. Yet, consumed with desire, he could not stop himself.

Naked, Keely rolled away from him, and sat and swung her legs over the side of the bed. Dietz propped up on an elbow and admired her shapely rump, the curve of her back, the smooth, unblemished skin of her shoulders. Keely did, indeed, believe in giving him an eyeful. She turned to look back at him over her shoulder. As she did so, the point of one breast peeked past the arm at her side. He always had loved breasts. Her smile sent him over the edge. Though he had exploded inside her just minutes before, he became aroused again and reached for her.

She laughed and slid out of his reach, coy thing. "I've work to do, McCullough."

"You do indeed."

She turned to face him, standing boldly before him. "Not that kind. Not again until the night. What will the men think of all the thumping going on in here in the middle of the day?"

"You don't want to know."

She stooped to look for her underthings in the jumble of discarded clothes on the floor. Her breasts bounced nicely as she did. She found her chemise, poised it over her head, then dropped it abruptly as something on the floor caught her attention. "Oh, I hadn't even noticed before. Your saddlebag spilled." Her frown turned to a laugh. "We must have bumped the table it rested on as we wrestled our clothes off." She giggled. "Funny what can distract one's attention so they don't notice things." She knelt. "I'll just straighten it up."

He couldn't let her see the photograph of McCullough he'd stuffed in the bag after leaving Waters. He hadn't wanted Waters showing the blasted thing all over town. He may have been able to fool Waters, but how many others would notice the differences between the two men? Dietz felt certain Keely would. Damn. Why hadn't he hidden the thing?

Dietz rolled out of bed, and had her by the hand, stopping her in seconds. Heart pounding, he shoved the paraphernalia back in as she watched him, curious, and bemused. He'd aroused her suspicions.

Then, because he couldn't think of anything to distract her, certainly nothing as pleasant, he caught her and made love to her again, right there on the floor. When they finished, he looked her in the eye. "I'm taking you to Spokane and soon, Mrs. McCullough, to buy you gowns that make you look as pretty dressed as naked."

She laughed. The sound, which should have made him happy, gave him only bittersweet joy.

"Waters told me to keep my wife at home." A look of concern flitted across Keely's face. Was she afraid of Waters? Did she suspect him of being involved with Michael's death? Or was she afraid he'd obey Waters?

Dietz hugged her close to reassure her. "What do you say we make a show of this trip, just to prove to Waters I have no intention of keeping such a fine woman home?"

She smiled at him, looking more at ease. "Aye."

"Keely." He suddenly needed to explain. "I told him I couldn't restrain you from your charity work. I have no intention of making you any kind of hostage."

"I love you, McCullough." She kissed him, cutting off the warning he meant to issue. He'd have to tell her later.

The next day McCullough made good on his promise. Keely found herself in the big city, heart of the Inland Empire, Spokane, Washington. Electric streetcars, emblazoned with the Washington Water Power name across the side, buzzed along the roads, chasing horses and carriages out of their way. In every way Spokane embodied the idea of a modern city.

Three years earlier most of the city had burned to the ground. Now, everything was rebuilt, new, modern, and clean. Electricity illuminated shop lights and powered the streetcars. The Washington Water Power Company provided all the electricity in town. Signs and advertisements boasted its state-of-the-art service. Just the year before the company had completed the Monroe Street Station, harnessing the mighty force of the Spokane Falls that tumbled through the heart of the city, damming the once free-flowing Spokane River.

Coming from Gem, where outhouses hung over the creek comprised the city sewage system, wearing a worn, out of fashion work gown, Keely felt like she had suddenly stepped out of the previous century. She hung on McCullough's arm as they strolled down the street, clinging to him, and admiring his composure and confidence as they walked toward the dress shop.

The train ride in had been pleasant, the speed it traveled exhilarating. Keely had never had much occasion to travel, not even the distance of ninety miles to the big city. She scarcely rode the train at all, and never farther than Wallace. The short distance and the grade between Gem and Wallace didn't allow the trains to reach peak speed. Keely had felt like she was flying as the rail car sailed and bumped and hummed over the rails on the ride in, especially seated next to McCullough, who flirted and told stories she could hardly believe about life back East and truly big cities. Staring at him, hearing him speak, chased all rational thought away until she was caught up in nothing but him.

Yet, McCullough seemed enigmatic. Something, some small fear about him resided in the back of her mind. Maybe it was only that she was too happy and could not let it be, or trust that it would last. She sighed. In McCullough, she could see nothing that Michael would have been unhappy with. But there had been a rift between them, a difference of opinion. What was it?

Yesterday, after their loving when she bent to pick up the spilled contents of the saddlebag, McCullough's reaction had compounded her small sense of uneasiness. She was no fool. He didn't want her to see something in that bag. Union business? Something she wouldn't like? Or merely something not her business? She had been tempted to rifle through his things, especially the bag, but honor held her back.

She looked to him and answered his smile as they strolled along. He was too handsome, too perfect, too worldly, too savvy, knew too perfectly what to say, almost an actor playing a role. Something about him didn't exactly match the man of the letters, and Michael's perceptions. But did it follow that personality perfectly exhibited itself in writing and the impression of others? Could it be that he was simply better in person? Silly fears. Why should she worry about being too content?

He'd taken her to dinner at a restaurant with white linen tablecloths and crystal glasses, and ordered her things too rich and sumptuous to enjoy every day. Then he took her on her first streetcar ride, and now to the dress shop. They ascended the steps. He smiled and held the door open for her. A bell tinkled overhead and a woman greeted them, offering her assistance.

"What may I help you with today?" The proprietress's voice carried the proper cultured, modulated tone to indicate respect. Deitz felt grateful that despite Keely's blatantly working class dress, the shopkeeper did not choose to act superior. Well, with the mining country so near, and fortunes being made every day, maybe outfitting such women was not uncommon.

Keely turned to him, obviously hesitant. Dietz loved her innocence, her sense of wonder. Dietz answered without hesitation. "We've come to purchase a new gown for my wife. We'll also need the required under-garments to get the proper look."

"Evening or day wear?"

The woman's question momentarily stumped him. What was appropriate for Keely? What would she have a chance of wearing? "Day. Something to wear to church and special occasions, and another simpler gown for everyday wear. For wearing while attending to household duties."

The woman smiled, her attention already focused on Keely. "Hmm. Small and trim as she is, with such a slender waist, I believe your wife will look beautiful in just about anything, sir. But I have a suggestion for the special occasion gown that I think you will like, but it is not ready-made. However, I have a pattern and draw-ing I can show you." The woman frowned barely per-ceptibly. "For the everyday dress, I think ready-made should suffice. We carry a fine selection. I'm confident we'll find one you like. I also have a large stock of un-dergarments and accouterments."

She showed them to a desk and leafed through a pattern book, finally finding the design she sought. She turned the book around to face them. Keely had re-mained mute, but when she saw the drawing her eyes grew round.

"I picture it made up in emerald green glacé." The woman reached for a swatch, and handed it to Keely.

The woman knew her business. Emerald had been the color Dietz had in mind for Keely all along.

"We'll cover it in black striped drapery net, and decorate the bottom of the skirt with emerald ribbon drawn through slashes in the drapery." The woman nodded, caught up in her designing. "Bertha frills, a standing collar, ribbon to accent the vee of the yoke at the waist, a rosette ribbon at the waist, leg-o'-mutton sleeves."

Keely looked overwhelmed. Dietz stared at the drawing. He didn't like the skirt. "I was imagining a flounced bell skirt."

The woman smiled. "You are quite right, sir, that flounces have been and are still in fashion. But I think the circular bell suites the design better and is more on the leading edge of fashion."

Dietz's mistress on his last mission had been quite a belle, wild over fashion. He had learned a thing or two from her in their brief time together. Enough to know a flounce from a train. But the nearly year's lapse in attention had put him out of date. He frowned. "I don't like the train."

The woman smiled again. "We can eliminate the train in favor of a simple round length."

Dietz suddenly felt Keely's gaze on him. He'd said too much, exhibited too much expertise. Damn, without realizing it, he'd slipped out of character and become himself. The realization shook him up. He'd never slipped so easily before. What about her overcame him so? Keely made him go blind to everything but her. McCullough would not be so knowledgeable about ladies' fashion. Now, he could do nothing but ignore Keely's confused look and plunge on. "Do you like it?"

"It's beautiful, but—"

"It's yours." He placed the order and made the arrangements to have the dress shipped.

CHAPTER ELEVEN

Dietz decided they should spend the night in Spokane, rather than Coeur d'Alene as he originally had intended. The trip meant business as much as a temporary reprieve from the tense mining country. Business he had not yet accomplished. He wanted to set up a small bank account for Keely. Damn, but his conscience bothered him over his deception and he intended to set a little something aside for her for after he left.

Then he needed to wire the mine owners his latest information and mail a report to the Chicago office. And he had arranged a meeting with the owners' Spokane attorney, W.T. Skoll. But much as he hated to, he had to get rid of Keely first. Fortunately, she looked tired and overwhelmed by the city. He would take her to the Rockport Hotel, get her settled, and excuse himself to run errands.

Keely strolled next to him as they left the dressmaker's shop, her hand resting in the crook of his arm as he carried their packages. He smiled at her, wondering if he could trust her. Would she repeat the details of their visit to her friend Lacy? Would she innocently reveal facts that could incriminate him? So far the visit had been purely innocent, but would the absence he was about to insist on anger her, or arouse any suspicion?

"You look tired, lass."

"I am. The day has been wonderful. But I am looking forward to catching the train to Coeur d'Alene."

He gave her a full-out grin. "You'll have to look forward to it tomorrow."

She gave him a confused look.

"Would you mind a change of plans?" He tried to look pleading. "I know we planned to spend the night in a hotel on the lake, but—" He paused, unsure how to phrase his deceit. "I have some business best attended to here. I got a recommendation for an excellent hotel in town. It's not on the river, but it has opulence in its favor."

Keely looked uncertain. "Business?"

"Business. Things you're best off not knowing about." That, at least, was true. Though tempted, he didn't elaborate. Lies about loose ends back East, an acquaintance he should look up, or labor leaders he should meet all bounced through his mind. But he refused to voice them. The less said, the fewer lies and details given, the better. "I'm sorry, Keely. But you know who I am. I never stop working. I was hoping you wouldn't mind a rest in the hotel while I take care of things. Then later we can have a nice meal together."

She smiled, but it looked forced. "Certainly."

The interior of Rockport Hotel took Keely's breath away. More beautiful and finer than any building she had ever seen, it carried her senses to a place she could not have imagined really existed. Rich mahogany paneling lined walls dotted with oil paintings so large they could have passed for walls at the boardinghouse, and all were framed in gold gild. The stair rails gleamed dark in deeply polished mahogany. Polished doorknobs dotted the doors along the hall like rows of gold buttons. On slick, buffed wood floors plush jewel-toned carpets greeted the feet, but looked too fine to actually tread on.

The rectangular building opened to a two-story center atrium. Standing just inside the entry from the reception desk, Keely stared up two stories to the frescoed ceiling. On the second floor, rooms lined each wall. An exposed hallway ran past the rooms, protected by a filigreed rail. The building stood taller than just two stories. Keely guessed the guestrooms lay on the upper floors. She should have protested staying in such an obviously expensive setting. She turned to McCullough, who seemed to read her thoughts.

"One night, Keely," he said. "A week's wages for a night. At any price it's cheap to give you one night of excess. One night to remember." His smile beguiled her. His tender words, the sentiment behind them, overwhelmed her. How blessed she was to have him.

She smiled and laughed. "I've married a spendthrift for sure, Ian McCullough."

"Yes, you have. But one with good cause." His answering laugh matched hers, but his words unintentionally brought reality back. "Some people imagine they've got all the time in the world for saving, but none for spending. There's time enough in our lives to be frugal, time enough when the danger is past. But who knows what the future holds? Maybe this is all the time we have. Maybe only now is ours."

His tone sounded light, and the smile didn't break from his face, but his words sent a shiver of fear through her. Were things more dangerous than she imagined? Did he think he'd be killed? No, he couldn't. She tried to push the unsettling thought away. Fear gripped her, not allowing her to ask the question whose answer she feared most.

A porter arrived to carry their bags to their room. Keely took McCullough's arm and followed the porter mutely. Suddenly the opulent surroundings faded away, lost to the terror of her thoughts. When they had settled into their room, she finally asked, because she could not vanquish the fear. "You won't leave me, McCullough?" He looked suddenly alert, wary.

"Leave?"

"I mean die." She paused. "You think that violence will erupt, and your life will be, maybe already is, in danger." She took his arm again. "Am I right?"

"Yes, Keely."

She swallowed. She couldn't ask more, and he didn't seem inclined to volunteer anything. "What kind of business are you off to now?"

He gave her an unreadable look. "Legal business, Keely. Tying up loose ends." He gave her a light kiss on the cheek and picked up his hat. "Don't worry yourself, Keely. I intend to be careful, and do what I can to prevent any violence." His tone became soft and tender, reassuring. "Put the dark thoughts away and get some rest."

After he left, Keely sat on the magnificent four-poster bed and tried to obey him. But there were times that success required more than intent. She pondered his mysterious business, finally settling on a thought that made sense—McCullough went to have a will made. That explained the reason for his earlier subterfuge—he hadn't wanted to worry her. She saw that clearly and was deeply touched, and just as deeply frightened. She didn't want to lose him, not ever.

Dietz stopped by the bank and then went directly to Dr. William T. Sutterfield's office, who, hopefully unknown to any union man who might be following him, was a good friend of W.T. Skoll, attorney-at-law. Dr. Sutterfield's nurse ushered him into the doctor's office, giving the appearance of him coming in for a private consultation. Dietz hoped only that it didn't get out that he was in poor health.

W.T.'s assistant, J.D. Netherman stepped into the office some minutes later. He greeted Dietz with the correct code word and sat down in the doctor's chair opposite him.

"Where's Skoll?" Seeing Skoll's assistant surprised Dietz.

"A court case kept him away. What have you got for us?" Husky, powerfully built, thickly mustached, and clear-eyed, Netherman looked everything but lawyerly.

"Waters has tasked me with murdering John Monihan." Dietz delivered his message deadpan, watching Netherman's reaction. Netherman didn't appear surprised. He looked bored.

"Monihan's been threatened before."

"Yeah, but not seriously." Dietz flicked a piece of lint off his sleeve. "The boys in Gem are a suspicious lot of bastards. They've got themselves a spy and are off on their own witch-hunt to find him. How many men they find guilty and ruin won't matter to them, as long as they find the right man eventually. Thirst for vengeance runs high. There's talk of bringing a man in from Montana to sniff the traitor out.

"Point is, I haven't been there long enough for them to suspect of the original spying. But they're testing everyone. I'm going to have to make the attempt on Joe. If not, I might as well waltz out of town right now. It's your client's call." Would the clients call him off the job now? Dietz hoped the hell not.

Netherman sat silently, apparently considering Dietz's words. "You have a plan?"

"Sat up half the night figuring one out." Netherman appeared a wary accomplice. And Dietz was no fonder or trusting of Netherman than the lawyer seemed of Dietz.

"Want to give it to me?"

"Not particularly, but I guess I have to." Dietz stood and stretched. A day of train travel and shopping had made him stiff and restless. "We held a union meeting late last night. The membership voted to approve the latest plan to shut down the mines.

"They want to flood the Tiger and Poorman Mine, and the lower works of the Gem. The way I see it, we can use that situation to our advantage..."

Keely waited for McCullough to return well past the usual supper hour before deciding she had better get herself something to eat before the hotel restaurant closed. Fret, worry, and hunger made her irritable. What kept him? Surely he wouldn't be out drinking late again? Not here in a town where he had no drinking buddies? But what business could have kept him so late? Surely a law office would be closed by now?

She sat alone at a small linen bedecked table, reviewing the day as she ate the last of the least expensive meal on the menu. At least she had thought to bring a small bit of her own money. Still, half a day's wage for one meal? Worse still, she barely tasted it. Worry numbed her senses.

Something wasn't right about McCullough. She couldn't recover from her suspicion. Her thoughts flashed back to the dressmaker's shop. How had he known so much about fashion? An ugly fear welled up inside her. In the two years that they corresponded, he had never mentioned courting any other woman. But what if he had? Some fashionable woman who cared enough about such things to make him take an interest in them? Someone very different from herself. How could she compete with such a woman, especially when McCullough seemed so obviously to want Keely to dress that way? Keely sighed.

He was her husband, but she wanted more than that. She wanted him to love her the way she did him, with ridiculous, overwhelming intensity, until nothing else mattered, and every thought except ones of her seemed trivial and a waste of time. He said he loved her, but did he? Did he really?

His inattention to her this night upset and worried her. How dare he leave her alone in the strange, large city? Did he care so little? At home, even last night, when he'd stayed out drinking, she could forgive. It was what all men did. But couldn't he stay with her here?

She paid her bill and went back to the room. She had barely returned when the door opened and McCullough came in wearing, much to her satisfaction, a suitably sheepish grin.

"Sorry, business kept me late."

"I see." She walked over to him and took an intentionally obvious breath. She could detect no alcohol on his breath. The subtle aroma of bay rum and leather greeted her. She frowned, confused. If he hadn't been out drinking, and he didn't smell of another woman, where had he been?

He casually set his hat on the night table. "Have you eaten?"

"Just."

"Good." He seemed relieved.

"Are you going to tell me where you've been?"

"I can't, Keely. You know that." His violet blue eyes looked cool and impassive when he spoke. He wouldn't tell her, no matter how hard she pressed. Of that she was certain.

"Must there be secrets between man and wife?"

"You know the answer to that, Keely. You've never asked me to reveal the things I did, the way I worked, before."

"No, you're right. But now we're married—"

"What does that change? Did you lie to me when you told me you trusted me and didn't need to know details? Or was that only subterfuge?"

He had her. She spoke in a resigned tone. "No."

"Keely McCullough, what has made you so insecure?"

"You, McCullough." Her answer seemed to surprise him.

"Me?"

"I never thought I'd love you like I do. Be jealous of things as insubstantial as secrets. I want to be with you every minute. I want to know everything about you."

"Do you? Then be with me now, lass." He pulled her into his arms, and swept her into a kiss.

At his touch, Keely felt herself falling into an emotional abyss so dark, so consuming, and so pleasurable, it felt like falling into cool, shaded water on a hot day.

But water could drown. The irrational thought caught her by surprise, popping into her mind from nowhere.

Then let me drown in him, her answering thought volleyed. *Yes, let me drown.*

Samuels' store sat next to Patterson's combination store and boardinghouse. Dietz reluctantly turned in. He would have preferred patronizing Patterson's. Why not help fill the pockets of a fellow detective? Not that Dietz imagined Patterson needed money. Recently widowed, Patterson had no wife to spend his salary, no home to keep. Being single had its advantages. The agency paid well. And Patterson was making money playing store on top of it all. What a strange life they led. The odd thought struck Dietz—was he still single? He didn't know anymore.

Dietz's restlessness drew him out this afternoon, running errands for Keely to keep from going mad. The last two days had been quiet. Too quiet. Like the eye of a storm. Tense. Still. Humid and sticky with tension. Dietz was getting fidgety. Adrenaline filled him as he waited to play his next move. But he had to wait for the union to make its attack on the Tiger and Poorman. And for now they were playing good boys. Damn, he hated being on someone else's schedule.

Samuels' place smelled of dust and sweat, stale. Samuels was nowhere in sight, but his assistant Big Frank called out to him as Dietz stepped into the darkness from the bright day outside.

"McCullough." Big Frank nodded. "Glad you stopped by. You got yourself a letter. Came this morning in the mailbag."

"A letter?" Why hadn't he thought that someone would write to McCullough? After all, short of him, who knew McCullough was dead? Dietz hadn't exactly advertised the fact.

"Don't seem so surprised, McCullough. You got yourself a few friends back East, I suppose." Big Frank wiped his meaty hands on the soiled apron he wore and stepped from behind the store counter to the mail counter. He pawed around a bit before handing Dietz an envelope addressed in a bold, masculine hand. Dietz took it without comment and stuffed into his pocket, measuring Big Frank's attitude. The man seemed almost smug. Well, there would be time later to see if the letter had been tampered with, to see if any justification lay behind the smirk.

Big Frank stepped back behind the store counter. "What brings you today?"

"Keely sent me after dried onions. She ran out, and the ones in her garden won't be ready for a few more weeks."

"Ain't that the way with onions. We got some in the cellar I can sell you." Big Frank chuckled. "So it's come to this already. Out running errands for the missus."

Dietz snorted. "There's nothing happening in this forsaken town. It's either help the wife or sit on my hands."

"I thought you were supposed to be cooking up plans." Big Frank sounded almost accusing.

"Oh, I am. But I have to wait for the big boys to say jump before I act."

"Waters is planning something big. Soon. Don't you worry." Big Frank's eyes gleamed wickedly. These men enjoyed violence. "How many onions you going to want?"

Five minutes later, Dietz dumped the onions on the kitchen counter without running into Keely and disappeared out back, up the hill out of sight where he could read McCullough's letter without getting caught. He studied the postmark. Pennsylvania. Then scanned the envelope. Sure enough, the union boys, or maybe just Samuels and Big Frank acting alone, had opened and resealed the letter. Time to find out what Big Frank found amusing.

"Well, McCullough. Let's see what's been going on in your absence," Dietz said aloud to the trees and spread the letter out on his lap.

McCullough,

You lucky son of a bitch, Maggie has decided to drop the assault charges. Well, for a nominal fee, which you can feel free to repay me at any time. So does she forgive for love or money?

She looked a fright after you took your fists to her the last time. But I suppose you know that. Not that I can say I blame you. Maggie has always been an aggravating woman. And I've always said the two of you together were like an unstable explosive. So I suppose you have to let off a head of steam from time to time just to keep from killing her. But she looks better now, and she's missing you. I suppose she'd take you back should you come home now. And since the law doesn't want you anymore, you can. The whole matter was kept hushed up, the scandal secret. You lucky dog, what do you do to your mistresses to keep them pining after you? Myself, I think they should give up.

So have you actually married the young wench, Mick's sister? Is she as pretty as he claimed? The respectable wife you've been wanting in your bid for respectability? The young, sympathetic thing to get the vote in your bid for election? Ah, McCullough, I keep picturing it, but it isn't easy.

If she's as innocent as Mick claimed, then you should have no problem stepping out behind her back. I don't suppose Maggie minds sharing. She never has before.

Write and let me know how it goes.

Wilcox

Dietz tossed the letter aside. *Damn the bastard! That explains McCullough's benevolence in taking on the care of Michael's sister. Political aspirations, charity case for a wife to appeal to the voters.*

Dietz balled his fists as dark, mercurial thoughts slipped through his mind. Hideous images of McCullough touching his Keely. Coward, philanderer, woman beater, anarchist, murderer. The man had loved violence on every level.

Guilt had not particularly plagued Dietz since killing McCullough. He'd already been fully aware of McCullough's character, or so he had thought. Dietz inhaled deeply. Any sorry ass coward who drew a gun and intended to shoot a man in the back deserved what he got. And self-defense was self-defense. But now

Dietz thanked God that providence had intervened and he had lived while McCullough had died. To think of McCullough abusing Keely—

He cut the thought short and reached for the letter, intending to shred and burn it. But he stopped suddenly and folded the letter, returning it to his pocket. Who knew? Maybe there would come a day when it would be important to prove McCullough's character. He hoped not.

Waters smiled across the room at Samuels. Gaffney, who moments earlier had lounged insouciantly in the chair by the door, now sat straight-backed. A vicious look gilded his face. Fine, good. The boy had always been sweet on Keely Byrne. His anger over the revelations Samuels had shared from the letter to McCullough might come in handy someday, should McCullough become too powerful. Let Gaffney take care of him. For now, McCullough was exactly the kind of man the union needed.

"Good work, Samuels," Waters said.

Samuels smiled. "I came right away."

Waters shoved a cigar across the desk to him to show his appreciation. "Smoke?"

"Thank you."

Gaffney continued to stew. Might as well release the boy. He looked as if he could use a little action to cool off. "Gaffney, why don't you take the afternoon off? Go have some fun?"

"Yes sir." Gaffney strode into the sunshine and the furious heat of early summer afternoon. He liked heat.

It matched his temperament. *Damn that McCullough. If he lays a hand on Keely—* Gaffney didn't bother trying to calm himself. Thoughts whipped through him too quickly, anger boiled too hotly for any attempt at peace.

Sweat collected in Gaffney's palms. He wiped them against his pant legs, trying to push away the ugly nausea that thoughts of killing, and memories of Michael brought. He'd killed Michael to get Keely. He would kill McCullough to save her. He had to, he owed Michael that. But how to do it?

CHAPTER TWELVE

"How was your time in Spokane?" Lacy gave Keely a knowing look as she wiped her floured hands on a kitchen towel. Keely watched her friend thump and knead the bread dough on the table before her. Lacy's kitchen felt cool and comfortable this afternoon, a pleasant contrast to the boardinghouse, which seemed to soak up the heat.

Lacy laughed. "You should see your face, Keely. You're positively glowing. I take it your man isn't holding back anymore, is he?"

"Oh, Lacy, if he is, I'm not." Keely's gaze swept the room, taking in the improvements obviously made by the plodding Kyle Vandergaard. Mended chairs, a window that finally latched again, a milk pail in the corner, and ample food on the table all spoke of him. Lacy seemed, if not exactly happy, then content. For a brief moment Keely envied Lacy her domestic contentment. But would she trade passion for it? Would she wish McCullough less secretive, less strong and committed to cause?

Lacy smiled. "You love him."

"It's that obvious?"

Lacy dumped her dough into a bowl to rise and covered it with a clean towel. "Should it be a secret?"

"No."

"Something bothering you?"

"Oh, Lacy, I love that man so much it scares me. If something happened to him..."

"Why should something happen to him?"

Keely traced patterns with her finger in the flour dust on the table in front of her. Should she burden Lacy with her fears? "Do you have to ask? Something is afoot. Something dark and sinister, so secret that McCullough cannot even hint of it to me. Don't tell me you haven't noticed the quiet these last few days. What is it that holds the men at bay? Boredom chases them to the bordellos, bars, and gambling halls. They're in none of those places now. Why? Because they're planning something. They've got something to occupy themselves now, something more fun than drinking and women." Keely took a deep breath and without thinking stood and began pacing.

"The union's changed since the jackals from Montana and elsewhere took it over. Gone are the principles and sense of honor. The men that fill the highest offices in the Gem Union these days—" Keely shook her head. "Outlaws and criminals, men without ethics or morals. Men who love violence and the power fear gives them.

"Michael realized it and tried to fight it." Keely shuddered involuntarily. "McCullough's right in the middle of it. He's like Michael. He'll do the right thing, no matter the cost. I used to think that's what I wanted. I used to believe McCullough would be my avenging angel come to take retribution for Michael's death. Come to make the owners pay. I never thought we'd be fighting our own. I never imagined that what I wanted could jeopardize all my dreams, my heart."

"Sit, Keely. You're pacing."

"Sorry." Keely walked to the chair but couldn't force herself to sit. Instead, she gripped the back of the chair. "I'm worried about McCullough. He doesn't think I notice, but I see the tension in his face. He's trying to protect me from his struggles, like Michael did." Keely pulled the chair out and sat.

"What's wrong with that?"

"What's wrong! If he insists on keeping to himself, how can I help him?"

"By just being there." Lacy spoke with authority. "Sometimes that's all there is—being there."

"No. There has to be more I can do. You and I have both lost too much to the mines. I can't sit by and lose McCullough, too." Keely sighed. "You can bet the union isn't planning a peaceful demonstration. Much as Michael and now McCullough try, they can't shield me from what goes on in town—the beatings, the vandalism done to the mines, the evictions. The men have

been out on strike now for close to four months. *Peace*
has not worked. There will be violence and it will be
horrific, a real uprising.

"McCullough promises me daily that he'll try to stop
it. And I know he means to be the voice of reason. But
this thing is bigger than all of us, and if McCullough
means to be in the middle of it, as he no doubt does,
then I will be there, too."

"Let the men handle things, Keely."

Keely stared at Lacy, knowing her talk had frightened her. Lacy's house sat at the edge of camp, and she
had children to protect. Kyle might work for the dairy,
but when terror reigned, would the men remember and
leave the Vandergaards alone? Somehow Keely feared
the scope of things would be too big, that no one would
be safe. "I didn't mean to frighten you, Lacy." She
forced a smile. "You have Kyle to protect you now."
She stretched her arms out, encompassing the room.
"Look what a fine job he's done fixing the place up."

Lacy smiled. Maybe she was warming to Kyle.

"Are you happy?" Keely asked.

"Happy enough. Kyle's handy with a set of tools and
good with the children."

"And you, too."

Lacy laughed. "Maybe. He's awful fond of me. Kyle
isn't like your McCullough. He wears everything he
feels and thinks right out there on his face."

"Good for you, Lace." Keely thought about
McCullough and the deep secret she knew he carried. If
only he would confide in her.

"I suppose you've heard about the new family camping out by the woods."

"New family?"

"So you haven't. Woman and three bitty kids camping in a tent. Their name's McKenna. Her man had been working in Montana, but lost his job and came to the Valley looking for work. He hadn't heard they shut down months ago. Those poor folks ran out of money. He left them alone while he goes to find work. Breaks your heart." Lacy's voice cracked.

Keely supposed Lacy was remembering her own meager days of living hand to mouth.

"I do what I can," Lacy said. "But I'm not so far away from those days myself. Kyle has been so good, but I can't ask him to support another family, too. Is there something you can do?"

Keely bit her lip. Of course she hadn't known about the McKennas. Excepting the trip to Spokane, since Waters' warning McCullough kept her in town. But Lacy seldom asked for help. What could Keely do but accept?

Lunn Gaffney had been waiting for his chance at McCullough. Now, as Gaffney walked away from Waters' office, he smiled. Waters had called him in to brief him about McCullough's attempt on Monihan. Gaffney sneered. So McCullough thought he'd be going alone to meet Monihan. What kind of a fool did McCullough think Waters was? No, Waters would be there, tailing McCullough, Gaffney at his side.

Lunn stepped out of the building into the fresh sunshine outside. The air smelled heavy with the scent of recent rain. Lunn looked up to see the last of the rain clouds being chased away by the breeze. Rain, like clear glass beads, sparkled on the surrounding trees. Monihan would not be stupid enough to show up at the meeting unarmed. Lunn chuckled. McCullough, with his plan to smoke Monihan out of the mine, was smart. But not smart enough to outsmart Gaffney.

Waters wasn't clever enough either. Ever since Lunn had confessed to Waters his part in Michael's death, he'd held Lunn prisoner to his wishes. So Lunn had become Waters' hired thug and gun, assassin for the union. Tied to each other's secrets as they were, neither could squeal on the other, him and Waters. And though Gaffney didn't like the killing, he did it to protect himself. Now came payback time. Lunn was coming along as Waters' insurance, to shoot Monihan should McCullough fail to. So if Gaffney, out of professional eagerness, fired early and happened to miss Monihan, but hit McCullough, who could charge him with anything other than union spirit, if anyone other than Waters found out at all?

Yes, it was a good plan. Monihan would have to fire back. Waters was sure to assert that it was Monihan's bullet that hit McCullough. That would suit both their needs—protect Gaffney from murder charges, and feed the fire against the mine owners.

A sudden worry over Keely crept into his thoughts. Would she blame him? He thought a moment longer. Keely would never know the truth, just as she didn't know about Michael. Once McCullough was dead, Keely would be his. Who else could she turn to?

As he thought, Gaffney strode up the street and into the woods outside of town. He stopped suddenly under a skinny white pine. In a flash of inspiration, he shook the tree and was immediately showered with pine-scented rain. He shook himself like a dog and laughed, enjoying the earthy feel of cool rainwater on his skin.

Tomorrow, McCullough. Tomorrow.

The plan was deceptively simple, and that's what worried Dietz as he stood and tucked his Derringer into his pants pocket. The little gun was only good at close range, but easily concealed, it yielded the advantage of surprise. Today he intended to be fully armed. He picked up his Colt and spun the cylinder slowly, loading a bullet into each chamber. One shot in the Derringer, six in the Colt. Seven shots. He hoped not to have to fire a single one.

McCullough had supposedly sent Monihan a missive, asking him to meet McCullough in the clearing up Clark Road outside of town. McCullough allegedly baited Monihan by offering to give him information about a planned attack on the Gem and negotiate some kind of truce. Because McCullough had spared a scab's life his first day in town, the union boys hoped Monihan would trust him and come down to show his respect.

Of course, back when Dietz went to Spokane, he had warned Monihan that the whole event was a planned attack on his life, and that while Monihan was called away, the miners planned to flood the Gem. Monihan would not show up. An armed guard would be sent in his place. Yesterday, Dietz had gone to Waters late in the afternoon and requested a backup. Dietz wanted a witness to see that the scabs had ambushed him, as the play was to appear.

Dietz sighed. He would not have attempted the risky operation except that he saw an opportunity to pass along valuable information to the mine owners. Around camp the hunt for the spy had intensified. Heavy suspicion fell on Patterson. Just recently the Butte Union had sent a spy breaker named Dallas out. As such, Patterson had been unable to reach the Wallace post office on any reliable schedule. And Dietz was not having much better luck.

According to Dietz's own plan, the horsemen would surround him. He would appear to fight off the men, while secretly handing off a message. He would break free and hide in the forest while the scabs rode off. Dietz's backup would be hiding in the woods effectively unarmed. Earlier Dietz had filled his gun with duds. He could fire to his heart's content, but with a weak load of gunpowder, the bullets weren't going anywhere.

Dietz took a deep breath. The plan seemed solid, but still a foreboding fear lurked, creeping from the corners of Dietz's mind to front and center. Dietz shook it off.

"Breakfast, McCullough." Keely's voice floated up the stairs from below. Damn, when had the mere sound of her voice gained the power to overwhelm him?

"Coming," he called back. Moments later he ambled down the stairs to the aromatic smell of coffee and cinnamon rolls. Flushed from working over the oven, Keely looked like fresh bread herself—warm, moist, and ready for the taking. Dietz smiled to himself, remembering the same glow on her face in bed, after their lovemaking. He ignored his urges, and forced his thoughts back on business.

She held a plate burdened with cinnamon rolls and eggs out to him as he walked up to her. "Sweet, like you, lass." He took the plate and bent to whisper in her ear. "Save a little energy for me later. Make we can cook something up."

Keely laughed. As Dietz pulled his chair up to the table he noticed a basket filled with food sitting on the kitchen counter. Keely's charity work. "Are you going visiting today?" Dietz nodded toward the basket.

She was busy dishing out breakfast to another boarder. She didn't answer. He finished his breakfast and rose to leave, pausing to take Keely by the elbow and bring her around for a kiss.

"Where you off to, McCullough?" she asked.

"Union business." He stared at her as she smiled up at him. "Stay home today, lass. It's not a good day to be out and about." She looked doubtful. "Promise." He squeezed her arm.

"I've a few things to do."

Stubborn woman. "Stay about town then."

She smiled back at him.

Keely sighed as she watched McCullough leave. Something was up today, something that made

McCullough nervous. She plunked into a chair at the table and picked at a roll in front of her.

After leaving Lacy's yesterday, she'd stopped by to see the McKennas. Poor, desperate people. She'd given Mrs. McKenna all the money Keely had on her, a whopping thirty-five cents and made her promise to buy the children a meal. Keely had made her own promise—to stop by today and bring them a basket of food.

McCullough was worried enough to ask her to stay in. Something he'd never done before. But the McKennas were starving to death bit by bit. How could she explain a day's delay to those hungry children? She had to go. Surely whatever the union had planned for the day would take place by the mines. The McKennas camped on Clark Road, far away from any danger. She hadn't actually promised McCullough a thing. Besides, she would be careful, and he would never know.

Dietz and his backup, Selter, hid beside the road, concealed by a dense spread of oceanspray and popberry bushes with white berries still green on the vine. Dietz cocked his head, listening for approaching hoof beats.

"Remember," Dietz warned. "When they get here I go out alone. You're not to fire under any circumstance unless I signal for help. Got it?"

Selter was young and inexperienced, and to Dietz's knowledge not prone to violence, the perfect accomplice for this mission. The boy's gun trembled as he practiced aiming at the road.

"Point that thing down toward the ground. We don't want any accidents," Dietz said. Impatience overwhelmed him. Selter kowtowed, obviously in awe of McCullough. Dietz doubted the boy actually had the nerve to fire, but there were no certainties in life.

Leaves rattled behind them. Dietz swiveled around and scanned the area. No breeze, no animals or humans in sight. Still, Dietz couldn't get past his sense of foreboding and the feeling that someone watched him. Had Waters followed him after all? Dietz thought he'd made himself clear. Waters was to stay away. Dietz frowned. If Waters were out there, he was a damned good tracker.

Dietz felt his pocket, checking for the message he intended to hand off. If anyone caught him with it, he was dead. He heard riders approaching. The sound spurred a burst of energy in him and a heightened sense of his surroundings. Whether Waters lurked out there or not, it was time to put on a show. Dietz turned to Selter. "Stay down."

The pounding of horse hooves grew louder.

"Sounds like more than one horse," Selter whispered.

"Damnation," Dietz muttered.

The riders came into view and stopped at the appointed place. Beside him Selter tensed.

"McCullough, we know you're out there. Monihan sent us." The scab who spoke looked nervous, but his voice did not waver. "Step out and present yourself before we spray the bushes."

"I have to go out. Hold your fire until I signal you,"
Dietz said to Selter. Muttering curses, Dietz slid forward out of the bushes and into the road.

"Where's Monihan?"

"Drop your weapon," the scab leader commanded.
Dietz tossed his Colt to the ground.

"Monihan?"

"He doesn't trust you," the lead scab said. "Before he
comes out he wants some proof that your intentions are
honorable."

"Look, all I want is for the strike to end and the men
to go back to work." Dietz stood perfectly still in the
middle of the road. "I can't give my information to anyone but Monihan."

"Give him a good faith offering. If he likes it he'll
come down and meet you for the rest."

"Why should I trust you?"

"What choice do you have?"

Dietz handed the scab the message he'd written out.
"That's only part."

Lunn crouched in the bushes next to Waters, shaking with rage. Damn that Monihan for welching on his
word. What was he supposed to do now? Well, to hell
with it. Taking out a few scabs might be compensation,
at least in Waters' mind. As McCullough stepped forward toward the scab, Lunn took aim at his back.

A sudden crunch of a twig caught Dietz's attention
just as he handed the message off. He turned toward
the sound. His heart stopped. Keely stepped from the

bushes, humming, an empty basket on her arm. For a moment, time stopped. Dietz caught the surprised look on her face, feeling it would be burned into his memory for all time. Almost instantaneous with seeing her, he saw a gun barrel sticking out of the bushes behind them, away from where Selter hid. Damn, someone meant to shoot him in the back, but Keely blocked the path.

He dove for Keely, sending her sprawling. He heard the rush of her breath as he fell on her, knocking the wind from her. Gunfire cracked the still air. The scabs rode off, camouflaged by the wake of dust at their backs.

"Damn it, lass. I told you to stay home," Dietz said when the fear pounding in him resided enough for him to speak.

He should have said something else, something kind. But she'd scared him, stepping out of the woods like that. He looked down at her as tears welled and wet her cheeks. Her soft rounded breasts heaved beneath him as she gasped to get her breath back. He saw the cold fear in her eyes, and the hurt that clouded them. Damn the lust pumping through him and the overwhelming desire to protect her. He was falling in love with her, cruelly, futilely in love.

"I thought I told you to keep your wench at home, McCullough. Now look what she's done." Waters stood over them, his voice venomous.

Without thinking Dietz pushed himself up off Keely and faced Waters. "You arrogant son of a bitch. I told you to let me handle this. Was taking pot shots at scabs more important than getting the job done? I had things under control."

"The hell you did, McCullough. I told you to kill Monihan, not give him information."

Dietz threw a punch and knocked Waters flat before he thought of the consequences. "No one calls me a traitor. *No one*." Dietz stood over the bastard, waiting for him to get up, itching to take another swing at him.

"McCullough!" Keely yelled from behind him. "Stop!"

Dietz turned to face her and her accusing look.

Shit! She heard what Waters said about McCullough killing Monihan.

"Keely—"

"No, McCullough. We don't fight our own." She turned to Waters. "I'm sorry, Mr. Waters. McCullough warned me to stay home, but I ignored his wishes." Dust streaked her hair, face, and clothes, but fire lit her eyes. She dusted herself off, picked up her basket, and walked away from the men down Clark Road toward home.

Dietz watched her go. Damn if he'd go after her.

Selter stepped from the bushes looking shaken and pale.

Dietz glared at Waters. "You ruined the operation and damn near killed my wife." Anger pulsed in Dietz's ears as he pointed to himself. "I'm the expert in terrorism and undercover work. I'm through taking orders from you. From now I make my own plans—who to kill and when."

Dietz expected a fight, some sort of recrimination from Waters. Instead, admiration shone in Waters' eyes. Frustrated, Dietz turned, ready to retrieve his Colt's 45 and head back to town and a stiff drink.

Waters' laugh stopped him midstep. "I like your priorities, McCullough. Business, then wife. Fine, go make up with her now. Comfort her. Come see me in my office tomorrow. We have exciting plans to make."

Lunn slumped, concealed in the bushes downhill from the road, where he had stumbled and fallen after nearly shooting Keely. Where had she come from? Why had she been there? If McCullough hadn't pushed her out of the way...

Damn McCullough. She'd probably followed him there.

Lunn's breath came raggedly, like his lungs fought breathing. He tried to piece together the last few minutes, but they were blurred, impossibly intertwined, distorted. Had he pulled the trigger before Keely appeared, or had her appearance startled him into shooting? Could McCullough have been fast enough to beat a bullet? Gaffney would never forget the surprised look on Keely's face as McCullough lunged for her.

Lunn again tried to recall the sequence of events. He had aimed at McCullough. Keely had stepped into the road from nowhere. He had sat rooted in place for a minute, fearing the worst, watching McCullough sprawled over Keely. Then McCullough had pushed up on his arms over Keely, and Lunn could see her chest heaving. She was all right. In that instant he hated himself for what he'd almost done. But he hated McCullough more for his intimate posture over Keely.

Suddenly worried that Keely would see him, Lunn had run like a frightened deer down the hill. Miraculously, Waters had stepped from the bushes and taken the blame, letting Lunn escape undetected. What would Waters want from him now?

Waters' laugh floated down to him, carried on the wind. Moments later Waters crashed through the underbrush, calling for him.

"Here." Gaffney waved to him.

Waters spotted him and came to him, plunking down beside him. "They've gone. All of them, even Selter. No one knows you were with me."

Lunn nodded. Waters wanted something.

"Were you shooting at the scabs or McCullough?" Waters asked.

Waters was too clever. When Gaffney turned to face him, Waters was laughing and his eyes shone hot with excitement.

"I know how you feel. You hate him. But I want him alive. Did you see him step from the bushes to face those damned scabs?" Waters laughed again.

Lunn bristled at the admiration in Waters' voice.

"The man is fearless. We need *more* men like him. When he's cooled down, we'll let him into the inner circle. And you," Waters pointed at Lunn, "leave him alone."

Dietz found Keely in their room at the boardinghouse, sitting on the bed with her knees pressed to her chest, cheek pressed to knees. Tears salted her cheeks. Dietz's anger fell away. He wanted to comfort her, but wasn't sure she wouldn't turn him away. She didn't even look at him as he shut the door behind him.

"I hate Monihan," she said flatly.

Dietz cleared his throat, but couldn't speak.

"He was on duty the day Michael died. He wouldn't send for the doctor. He let Michael die."

"I know," Dietz said.

She gave him a one-eyed look. "I heard what you meant to do out there." She raised her head to look at him straight on. "I wish he would die, but I don't want you killing for me, McCullough."

Dietz almost believed he'd heard wrong. Keely thought this was about Michael and her? He realized then how far apart he and Keely really were. McCullough could love her and she could love him. But John Dietz worked for the other side. She could never love *him*.

He plunked down on the bed next to her and stared straight ahead at the wall, no longer angry, but still hurting. "You took Waters' side and walked away from me."

She reached out and stroked his cheek with the back of her hand. "I'm sorry. I did what I did because I can't afford to have Waters any angrier with us than he already is. He's dangerous, McCullough." She continued stroking. He sat, mesmerized by her touch. "And I meant what I said about not fighting each other. Divided, we'll never beat the owners."

His hurt ran so deep that he barely heard her words. "Keely, I don't easily forgive being abandoned. Ever since my mother—" He cut himself off, suddenly worried he had committed an unrecoverable slip. He'd forgotten and become Dietz again. Keely looked at him curiously. "I don't remember now. How much have I told you about my childhood?"

"Nothing," she said.

"I never told you."

"No."

"Did Michael tell you anything about it?"

She shook her head. Dietz sighed. Fortunately, Dietz remembered that McCullough's family had been similar to his—two brothers, two sisters. McCullough and one brother being the oldest, conveniently like Dietz and his. "My father died the year I turned five," he began slowly. "The influenza. I was the only one with him in the room when he passed on." He shivered. "No matter how much time passes, the image doesn't fade. To this day, I don't know where my mother was at the time." He took a breath. "Probably doesn't matter. He left behind five of us kids ranging in age from babyhood to seven. Me, I was second in line.

"Make a long story short—Mother thought she couldn't raise us all. The miners' union paid for a funeral, and took up a donation for us. They even offered to support Mother until she could marry again. There were enough men around wanting wives, even widows with children. And Mother was very beautiful." He paused, remembering a Texas cattle ranch on the plains, and his mother, all beauty and aloofness. He also remembered his grandfather, uncles, and neighboring cattlemen all offering to run the ranch for her so she could keep her children. He remembered equally well the day she turned her two oldest, ages seven and five, out.

"She wouldn't hear of it. She turned me and my brother out on our own."

Keely gasped.

Dietz still remembered the long walk down the wagon track drive, the complete feeling of loneliness, and uncertainty, of not belonging anywhere.

"What did you do? How did you survive?"

He didn't like remembering. "Slept in the streets. Lived with neighbors kind enough to take us in when it got cold. Got jobs in the mines." Slept in haylofts. Bounced between uncles and neighbors. Became cowboys.

Keely turned his face toward hers and kissed him gently on the mouth with lips as moist and soft as a baby's. "I love you, McCullough." She kissed him again, equally softly. "I'll never desert you, I promise."

She couldn't know what keeping her promise would cost her, but it didn't matter anyway, he wouldn't hold her to it. When she found out the truth—

He reached for her shirtwaist and pulled it loose from her skirt, snaking his hands beneath it, trying for a touch of bare skin.

Keely slid her hands down his chest, gently massaging the buttons out of their holes, stroking his chest.

When his shirt hung open, she pulled away, stood and undressed.

He matched her pace, peeling his own clothes off in tempo to her striptease.

Let them look, Michael had told her long ago, Dietz remembered her saying, and let him look she did. He could barely keep from gawking at her when she was fully dressed, but naked she was irresistible—pale, unblemished skin, soft curves, pert breasts, and a slender waist.

He pulled her into his embrace and pressed her against him.

She held tight, pulling him onto the bed. "Make love to me now, McCullough. Wild and hard so there's only us."

They bucked together on the bed while the backboard tapped an irreverent staccato against the wall and the world melted away. When it was over, they lay tangled in each other until he tried to pull away.

"Don't. Not yet." She traced the path of the trickle of sweat that dripped down his chest. "I like feeling the tingle of your sweat on my body. I feel like every pore, everything I own is open for you."

"I love you, Keely." He, *John Dietz,* loved her. But she'd never realize the difference. "You scared the shit out of me today, Keely. A second's difference in the timing—"

"I know. I'm sorry. Next time I'll listen to you. I *promise.*" She traced his chest lightly with her fingers and sighed. "But, oh, McCullough, we're such a team. Together, we'll beat the mine owners. Then we'll settle down and raise us a family, children who will have both parents to love them."

Some team. *He* loved Keely Byrne, but *she* loved Ian McCullough.

CHAPTER THIRTEEN

Dietz, fresh from Keely's bed, stepped out of the boardinghouse into the sunshine. Music tinkled on the breeze from every saloon from Dutch Henry's on down the street. Men whooped and hollered, staggered and strutted, drunk or on their way, from every gambling hall and drinking establishment in town. Damn, while he'd lingered in bed with Keely, listening to her explain about the McKennas, the union had flooded the Tiger and Poorman, and if Monihan hadn't been sufficiently prepared, the Gem Mine. Nothing else explained the euphoria. Gone were the tension and sense of purpose of the last several days. The men celebrated. For himself, Dietz felt relieved not to have had to partake of an action against his employers.

Dietz squinted into the sun. Time grew short, very short indeed. Soon, he would have to send Keely away to Spokane for protection. Once the men went to war, no one would be safe.

Originally, Dietz had meant for McCullough to stay after the violence and say a proper goodbye to Keely. But he now saw the danger and futility of that plan. He would send Keely away, and when she got back McCullough would be gone, ostensibly to avoid the authorities which would certainly swoop down on all the union leaders. Were they so cocksure as to think the government would let them get away? He laughed inwardly. Fools. The mine owners had money, power, prestige, and friends in high places. Not to mention that the United States government didn't take kindly to civil insurrection.

Yes, shortly after Keely returned to the Valley, he would send word and McCullough would be dead. *For good this time.* Dietz shuddered in the heat of the midday sun as he thought of hurting Keely, of her grieving and then marrying some else, of ceasing to love him.

He walked up the street and forced his way into Dutch's through the crowd tumbling into the street.

Inside, Dutch's was dark and hazy with smoke. Peters, a shift boss at the Gem when the union wasn't striking, whacked Dietz on the back. "Old boy, where were ya this morning? We missed ya at the doings." Peters slurred his words and his breath stank of whiskey.

"Out on a special mission. You flooded the Tiger and Poorman today. Anyone hurt?" Dietz asked without preamble.

Peters waved at him and shook his head. "Not a stinking man."

"Better luck next time." Dietz moved on, eavesdropping on the crowd as he went, picking up snippets. Something felt wrong. The men's happiness had a brittle edge and anger he hadn't expected. Phrases like "barbarian" and "spy in our midst" were repeated too often.

Dietz found Samuels and Big Frank at the bar bent over a newspaper, cursing. Dietz ordered a shot of rum before addressing them. "Looks like mighty entertaining reading, lads."

Samuels shot him a look. "This came in the mail today." He spun the newspaper around for Dietz to see and tapped his finger on an article.

The Coeur d'Alene Barbarian. The mine owners' rag? Dietz masked his expression as he read Patterson's latest report printed in full detail. Damn. "Looks like we got a spy among us. But we've suspected that before."

"Yeah." Samuels tapped the paper again for emphasis. "But everything in this article points to the traitor being in the Gem Union." Samuels shook his head disgustedly. "One of our own."

"Looks like it," Dietz said noncommittally, but his thoughts rested on Keely and Patterson. He would have to send her away sooner than he thought. As for Patterson, sooner or later suspicion would fall on him. Dietz would need to be there to cover his backside.

Keely hummed as she cooked dinner for the men. They'd be needing food in their stomachs to help sober them up, though like as not, all they would be wanting was coffee. Something had happened. Whatever the men had been planning had been accomplished. The miners sounded like raucous crows as they partied in the streets. With hope, the action would be enough to induce the mine owners to settle this business. The Fourth of July was just days away. Maybe there would be another reason to celebrate this year. She would pack a picnic. She began chopping an onion.

Her thoughts passed lightly over the current business. She had her own reasons for wanting the strike settled. She put the knife down and felt her stomach. No babe grew there yet. But, oh, she hoped there would be soon—when this business was finished. Then she and McCullough would have children of their own and love them and care for them like neither of them had been. McCullough had surprised her with his vulnerability. She would never have guessed about his past. It explained so much—his reluctance to talk about it, his independence.

She picked the knife back up and began chopping again, thinking of his mother. Wretched woman! Was she still alive? McCullough hadn't said. No matter. McCullough belonged to Keely now and she meant to love him until all the scars of his past ceased being red and ugly and faded to thin white lines so faint that they didn't show or matter anymore. She loved that man. Nothing, nothing could ever change that.

Keely unwrapped the towel from her freshly baked cake and set it on the blanket beneath her as she reached for the knife and plates. The picnic did not seem to be distracting McCullough from his worries as she had hoped, nor she from hers. Flooding the mines had done nothing to resolve the continuing conflict, nothing but further anger the owners who now vowed to extract restitution for the damage and prosecute the perpetrators. The tension in the Valley hung between them unspoken and heavy, made thicker by the worry that McCullough had been involved and would eventually be caught and taken from her, at least for a time.

She continued her preparations, pulling from her basket a small bowl of delicate wild strawberries and handing them to McCullough.

He popped one in his mouth and smiled. "When did you pick these—dawn?"

She cut him a slice of cake and set it beside him. "I did."

He shook his head. "You shouldn't have. It must have taken you hours." He eyed the bowl of tiny fruits, each strawberry no bigger than a good-sized blueberry.

"Almost. I know of a good patch." She smiled at him. "Strawberries for the Fourth of July are a must, you know. There's nothing so sweet as a wild strawberry, and they only come once a year. The rest of the year one must be content with eating them in jam." So much to say, such inane conversation. She watched him eat his cake, wishing away the worry lines etching his face these last days, but they persisted. Finally, she had to speak.

"What's bothering you, McCullough? The union problems?"

His answering gaze, dark with intensity, frightened her. "I don't mean to frighten you, but you know things have gone too far to settle peacefully." He paused, took her hand in his and squeezed it gently. "I can't stop it. I can no longer pretend that I can."

A hawk cried out overhead, momentarily diverting his attention. He released her hand and looked up, watching it, his expression wistful, as if he wished he could fly away with it. Didn't they all?

"I love you, Keely," he said suddenly. "*I* love you."

She wondered at the force with which he spoke, at his repeating it. Her heart would have danced, but she felt something ominous behind the words, almost a warning.

"I would never intentionally hurt you. Not if I could help it." He took her hand again and pressed it between his. "You have to believe me. You must remember that, no matter what happens. *Promise*." He did not ask, he commanded.

"Of course." His words touched something deep and sentimental inside her, moved her almost to tears.

Suddenly he laughed, but it didn't sound joyful. Derisive was the word that came to mind. "If only you knew the implication of your promise. You may regret it."

"*Never*, McCullough." Emotion shook her voice, making it raspy and breathless.

He looked as if he might kiss her. She certainly wanted him to, but he backed away.

"I want you to understand that in the next few days, or weeks, I will appear to be doing things you disagree with. But believe me, it will be necessary. You'll have to trust me. Will you?"

She would have promised him anything, and she did. Of course she trusted McCullough.

He let out a pent-up breath. "Good." He stood, extended her his hand, and pulled her to her feet. "The first thing I'm going to do is buy you a train ticket out of the Valley, to Spokane. You should be safe there—"

"No!"

"Keely, you promised." He took her chin in his hand and turned her face toward his. "Your safety is the most important thing in the world to me. I have to protect you the only way I can. I'll set you up in the Rockport. When this thing is over, you can come home."

She didn't know why she noticed, but he didn't mention sending for her. How would she know when to come home? It seemed a minor point. She let it slide, fighting to think of something to make him change his mind and let her stay. "I'll go graciously, but only when the danger becomes immediate. You give the word then and I'll fly leaving. I promise." Her voice broke. "I want to be with you as long as I can."

He wore an unreadable expression, looking as if he fought to maintain a poker face. "All right, lass. I'll trust you on this one."

She couldn't believe she had succeeded so easily. He pulled her into a kiss and then back down onto the blanket where he pushed up her skirts and made love to her cushioned by a mattress of pine needles and leaves while a hawk circled overhead, riding a thermal. She laughed to herself. She, too, was flying, inside, where it counted most.

"Ian!" she screamed to the hawk and the white pines as she soared to a new height, to the pinnacle. Moments later he rolled off her. She adjusted her skirts, and gasped for breath, silently cursing the corset that restricted her lungs. McCullough's eyes shone brightly. His look devoured. He laughed, and this time he sounded happy.

"You're flushed, lass."

"And winded."

"Did I do that to you?"

"You and my corset." She wriggled her skirt down and adjusted her shirtwaist.

"Do you like fireworks, lass?"

"That's later tonight."

He laughed again. Such a lovely sound. Then he pulled her to him and kissed her again. "Oh, I do love you, Keely."

"I love you, too, McCullough."

They finished their picnic and made their way back to town arm in arm. How lovely to look so innocent, like all they had done was picnic, to share such a secret. They were nearly home, standing on the boardwalk down the street from the boardinghouse when Keely heard horse riders approaching. From the tempo of the hoof beats they rode fast and furiously. She looked up in time to see them at the edge of town. McCullough must have seen them at the same instant.

"What the—" he said.

American flags hung from every building. Streamers looped between businesses. Suddenly the riders drew their guns. Keely realized their intent. But before she could scream or duck, they began shooting, riding up the street, taking deliberate aim, and filling each flag full of holes. McCullough pulled her back into the store they stood in before and pushed her to the ground.

As suddenly as it began, it ended. The drumming hooves receded into silence.

"There are your fireworks," McCullough said.

She couldn't speak. A question formed on her lips, but could not escape.

McCullough pulled her to her feet, reading her mind. "Not yet. It's not time to go yet."

"Just a warning." Waters laughed, the same odd, grating guffawing Dietz had come to hate. Dietz supposed it was meant to be self-deprecating.

"It was damned stupid. The owners have had enough warning to last a lifetime. Nothing, short of war, has, or will, change their minds. It only made us look bad." Tim O'Brien, president of the Central Union spoke as he fidgeted with his shirtsleeves. The room was hot and close and laced with tension palpable enough to run your fingers through.

They packed into Waters' tiny office like cigars in a box, all rank, smelling of sweat, dust, and leather. Perspiration beaded on Waters' forehead, from heat or stress, Dietz could only guess. In all probability Waters didn't like being upbraided by the boss, someone who he considered his inferior in all respects. Besides Dietz, Waters, and O'Brien, Patterson, the judge, and Gaffney were present. They waited for the guest of honor to arrive, the reason for the meeting.

"Shooting up the emblem of our nation, on its birthday for cripes sake, doesn't sit well with people, good cause or no. Have you seen the headline splashed in all of the newspapers? *Union men desecrate flags!*" O'Brien snorted. "Some way to generate sympathy."

A knock on the office door interrupted O'Brien's tirade. A short, banty Irishman walked in wearing a grin Dietz couldn't describe as anything but sinister.

"Ah, the man has arrived." Waters stood to greet the stranger. The men parted to let the newcomer through. "Come in, come in." Waters effused over the new arrival. "How was the ride?"

"Hot and dusty."

Waters laughed and slapped the man on the back. "Gentlemen, meet Dallas, our spy catcher." He looked overly pleased with himself. "The Butte Union sent us their best."

Dallas laughed, evidently reveling in the praise and attention. Dietz inventoried the expressions of his fellow inmates of the tight, stale room. No one looked as pleased or impressed as Waters. O'Brien looked openly skeptical. Patterson's face was a mask. Dietz's own heart beat double-time. Besides being too close to Thompson's Falls for Dietz's tastes, he'd been through Butte with McCullough. Would the fellow recognize him? Dietz couldn't remember ever seeing Dallas before, and certainly he would remember a one-eyed man? But there had been so many towns, so many varied men, Dietz could not be positive.

Waters made introductions around the room in pace with Dietz's inventory. Dallas bobbed his head, and shook hands as his gaze traversed the room. When Dietz's turn came, and Dallas' one eye looked into his, Dietz saw no recognition. His pulse slowed. Dietz did not believe the little Irish rooster could be such a good actor as to conceal a former acquaintance. Surprised recognition was not easy to suppress. Dallas's gaze drifted quickly over Dietz to Patterson, and lasted a moment longer than necessary.

"This is Allison," Waters said.

Dietz saw the look and suppressed a shudder. Patterson was under suspicion, but true to form, Patterson didn't flinch, or sweat any more than the heat required. He stood with his posture easy and his smile calm. *Such a collected son of a bitch.*

"You see, O'Brien," Waters said. "Suspicion of a spy has fallen on the Gem Union. But we took immediate action. We'll find him, and soon, before the big plan goes into effect."

The meeting lasted only minutes longer. Patterson and Dietz left together. It might not have been prudent, but Dietz felt compelled to speak with his fellow

detective. He ambled alongside him as Patterson headed back to his store.

"So what do you think of our spy catcher?" Dietz
asked nonchalantly.

"He's a one-eyed, two-legged, Irish hyena if ever
there was one." Patterson laughed.

"He suspects you, you know that."

"Half the town suspects me, boy."

"Suspicion flies like the crows around here, but
mostly it's unfounded and irrational. Dallas is different.
Dallas is dangerous. He's just ignorant, plodding, prying, and bullying enough to prove something."

Patterson laughed again. "You warning me to keep
my nose clean?"

"Naw, I'm a mother hen. I'm worrying over you. Do
you have an escape plan?"

They'd reached the front of Patterson's store. Patterson stopped. "Thought maybe I'd just cut me a hole
in the floor and disappear."

Dietz frowned. "If you need me, I'm here."

Patterson shook his head; the tiniest smile toyed
with his lips. "Something happens to me and I have to
leave, you check with Mrs. Shipley. She'll know as
much as anyone about what I'm up to. Meantime, we
watch each other's backs." Patterson paused. "You
come through Butte on your way here?"

Dietz nodded.

"Then you've got as much reason as I do to be careful."

CHAPTER FOURTEEN

The heat in the kitchen felt oppressive, too hot for any reasonable comfort at all. Keely wished for relief, but short of a dip upstream in Canyon Creek, which being mountain fed always felt cool, nothing could be done. She couldn't wade in town—too many prying, lascivious male eyes, too polluted with privy waste. And since the incident, she dared not wander anywhere. McCullough gave her free reign, though she felt him watching her, sensed his protectiveness. Her own fears kept her prisoner. Her worry didn't center on herself, but McCullough. Another slip up by her would endanger him.

She looked out the window to the hot, dry hills. Even the white pines seemed to droop, weary in the heat. Dust covered the leaves of the underbrush like a

sense of evil had floured the town. Keely shuddered in
the heat and turned her thoughts elsewhere. Oh, for a
sliver of ice! But the ice in the cellar had melted a
month ago. There would be none until winter. The
iceman from Wallace dared not come into town. Even
train traffic had slowed to a near stop now that trouble
seemed imminent. Those who could chose to avoid it.
In Gem there was no escape. Fear lurked everywhere,
in every corner and shadow. In every face she saw either fear or anticipation, depending on the personality
and the situation.

Through it all she chose to concentrate on her private joy in being McCullough's wife, to hope for the
future. Even in those thoughts there was not complete
satisfaction. McCullough looked worried and distracted. He indicated at every turn that his time was short.
His manner confused her. He lived wildly, made love to
her with abandon, drank, laughed, bought her things.
He commented on the sunsets and told her private
thoughts. He never struck her as fearful, or afraid, just
certain. Certain that their time together grew short. It
scared her beyond reason, yet she could in no way stop
herself from enjoying every minute with him, and wondering.

She finished punching down a loaf of bread she'd
been making, and slapped it into the buttered pan,
dreading the thought of firing up the oven. Just then
Joe Murphy swung in through the door, looking wild
and winded and pale with fright.

"Where's McCullough?" he asked without preamble.

"He's in the back room, resting."

Murphy pushed past before she could stop him, almost before she'd finished speaking. He barged in on McCullough even as she tugged on Murphy's arm in an attempt to stop him.

"Keel?" McCullough said sleepily, then saw Murphy. "Murphy, what the—" McCullough sat up.

Keely loved the sight of him when he woke. Startled awake, hungover from too late a night of partying and lovemaking, his jaw firm and covered with stubble. Even in the worst case, McCullough never looked puffy-eyed or bleary with sleep like most people. He always woke instantly, always immediately alert. His gaze fell on her. She gave him an apologetic shrug. Man, how she loved those violet eyes of his.

Murphy followed McCullough's gaze and scowled at her. "I got to talk to you alone, McCullough."

"You can't burst in on my husband and then send me away, Mr. Murphy. You say what you have to in front of me," Keely said.

"It's union business, ma'am." Murphy seemed suddenly to remember his manners.

"My brother died because he was a union man, and I'm every bit as loyal as him." Keely refused to back down.

This time McCullough shrugged. Good, he was letting her stay.

"Shit," Murphy said.

McCullough sat up. Keely tossed him the shirt thrown over the chair next to her and he pulled it on. Then he stood and pulled on a pair of pants as casually as he would pull on a pair of gloves. "What's bothering you, Murphy?"

Murphy looked around furtively, as if he expected the walls to eavesdrop. When he spoke his voice barely qualified as a whisper. "I've just come from warning Allison. That damned Dallas has been in town inside three days and he's claiming he knows who our spy is."

"Good." McCullough finished buttoning his shirt, the last of his perfectly muscled chest disappeared and Keely hoped she'd be able to concentrate better now. "You going to keep us in suspense?" McCullough asked.

"That jackass. He thinks it's Allison. Our own recording secretary!" Murphy's voice pitched shrilly. He swallowed like he meant to gulp his panicked words back down. "It's ridiculous. But they've called a special meeting of the union." He swallowed again, almost for emphasis. "They mean to kill him tonight. I warned him to leave."

McCullough speared him with a look. "It's your habit to warn spies?"

Murphy stammered. "He swore he's innocent, and I believe him. He refuses to leave town, says he won't be a coward, that he must clear his good name."

McCullough nodded. "If he's innocent, he has nothing to worry about—"

"Innocent, or no, they want blood. They're going to kill someone. Look, I've noticed you and Allison together. I figured you're friends. Warn him, warn him to leave."

McCullough's face went blank, as if he'd pulled on a mask. Keely held her breath, praying he would stay out of the trouble. As much as she liked Mr. Allison—

"If Allison's made up his mind, he's made up his mind. You couldn't stop him, neither can I. Like I said, if he's innocent, he has nothing to worry about. If not, he knows the consequences. He swore a Molly Maguire oath, same as we all did, pledging his allegiance to the union, under penalty of death for betraying his brothers. If he *is* the spy, he deserves to die."

Keely found her ice in McCullough's voice and the steely set of his face and eyes. Suddenly she felt like she did when submerged in the frigid waters of Canyon Creek on a hot day, chilled and gasping for breath, reaching for any warmth as she came to the surface.

McCullough turned to look at her. "Keely, are you all right?"

"Fine." How she spoke, she didn't know, but her response came out breathy and barely believable.

"You'll be at the meeting tonight?" Murphy said.

McCullough nodded.

"Good. See you there." Murphy turned on his heel and left as abruptly as he had arrived.

Keely stepped into McCullough and collapsed against him, listening to the reassuring drumbeat of his heart.

"Must you go?" She didn't need to ask. She knew the answer. She felt him nod. "Will they kill Mr. Allison?"

"If they have to."

"He's a nice man." Why couldn't she think of something better to say? "Will the trial be fair?"

He pulled her closer in response.

The icy, gasping feeling returned. "Be careful, McCullough. Be careful. I love you." Would the trouble never end?

That night the miners packed the union hall.

Everyone seems to know Dallas intends to unveil the spy, Dietz thought. He sat in the back near the door, calculating the odds of escaping unharmed. The Derringer rested in his coat pocket. He fingered the cold metallic Colt's 45 at his side. Hundreds of men filled the room, most of them armed. If they convicted Patterson of being the spy, Dietz would have to defend him. He couldn't let the mob lynch a fellow agent. But the odds of his own escape were practically nil.

He could shoot into the crowd and create some confusion. To date no one suspected McCullough of spying. With hope, he could distract enough men so Patterson could sneak out while Dietz broke for the door. It was a long shot. He hoped that tonight Patterson lived up to his cool-headed reputation. Could he possibly lie himself out of this one? Dietz had no idea. He'd been unable to meet with Patterson and make plans. He knew only what Murphy had told him. Patterson must have had some plan.

Patterson sat onstage with President Waters, Eaton, Judge Brown, and Dallas.

Waters called the meeting to order. Patterson, in his role as recording secretary, then stood and read the minutes of the last meeting. If he trembled inwardly with fear, he didn't show it. Nothing gave him away, not a tremble, a stutter, a wayward gaze, or a bead of perspiration. Patterson sat and Dallas got up to make a speech. Suddenly silence echoed off the walls, and reverberated in Dietz's ears in time with his own frantic heartbeat. Time for the games to begin. Thoughts of Keely pounded through his mind. It was too soon. He didn't want to leave yet, not without being certain that Keely would be safe. He willed Patterson to remain calm, to show the wily spirit he was renowned for.

"Brothers!" Dallas shouted.

He thinks he's running a revival meeting, Dietz thought, only without the hope of God-fearing results.

"You have allowed a spy in your ranks and he now sits within reach of my hand," Dallas continued.

Such drama. Dietz was reminded of the Last Supper in the Bible. Christ offering Judas the bread and then bidding him on his way. So this is the way Dallas chose to play it. What an actor, an orator, Dallas the hyena was. If he offered Patterson a sop of bread, Dietz would have to shoot on principle.

"He will never leave this hall alive." Dallas punctuated his speech with podium pounding and hand waving. "His fate is doomed. You know your duty when it comes to dealing with traitors to our noble cause for the up-building of true manhood."

The room thundered with applause. Patterson clapped as wildly as any. Dietz put his hands together, imitating Patterson. What did he have planned? Waters pounded his gavel on the podium, calling for order. He called for a ten-minute recess. The union boys surrounded Patterson and pulled him off the stage.

Dietz, keenly aware of the weapons he harbored, pushed through the crowd toward him. Every exit crawled with union boys, jumpy, excited, out-for-blood men with too much idle time and too little to occupy it. A good killing might liven things up. Dietz had no doubt that with this incident, the union leaders hoped to incite the boys into real war. Give them a taste of blood and they would want more. A cause, every man needed a cause, and an enemy.

Waters saw Dietz coming and motioned for the crowd to let him through. "McCullough, you're just in time for the trial."

Poker face, Dietz reminded himself. *Poker face.* Now's the time to earn those big bucks they pay you. Dietz couldn't remember ever having been this nervous on the job before, and he'd been in situations as tight. Usually excitement and adrenaline overcame him. Nothing compared to the heady rush of a good job, a tight squeeze, and a fine escape. But Keely made all the difference. He had a reason to live, a reason to keep his cover a while longer, if only to protect her. Damn, this nervousness could foul him up. He forced himself to concentrate. There had to be a way out.

"We've got you now," Dallas said, still on the stage, glowering down at Patterson. Like a cat, he leaped agilely down.

Patterson stepped up. "What's the matter, gentlemen? You seem puzzled."

Dallas held up the union's book of minutes and screamed at Patterson. "There's a leaf cut out of this book. We want an explanation."

"Waters ordered me to do it." Patterson stood supremely still, acting calm and almost confused.

That's it, Patterson, Dietz thought. That's why Patterson was almost legendary in his own time. What an audacious accusation to make. Dietz hoped it stuck.

Waters cursed. "Liar!"

"You'll remember back a while when we voted to flood the Tiger and Poorman?" Patterson drawled, Texas style, his old cowboy days evident in his lazy speech. "I wrote down the full facts of our resolution and read it at the next meeting. After that, Waters ordered me to cut it out and burn it, as nothing of that sort should be on record in case the book fell into enemy hands."

Every face turned toward Waters. Dietz thought the slimy bastard might deny it. Clever Patterson. Dietz remembered the incident well enough. Patterson had not burned the page. He'd had Dietz mail it to their contact in St. Paul.

Waters nodded. "He speaks the truth."

Dallas looked ready to explode. He wouldn't be letting up on Patterson. Waters called the meeting back to order and made a conservative little speech. "Men, it is my recommendation that we sit on this matter a while longer, that we do nothing tonight. The time is coming, and will soon be at hand, when we will act and move on to greater things."

The men cheered. Dallas scowled. Dietz's heart settled back down to its normal trot. He had time, but not long.

Back at the boardinghouse Keely fell into his arms. "Mr. Allison?" He didn't have to ask to know what she meant.

"Found innocent."

"Thank goodness."

"Like I said, Keely, an innocent man has nothing to fear." But a guilty one? He had to get Keely out of town. But could he bear it, knowing he would never see her again?

"Oh, McCullough, the terror. The town was too quiet, and then the union hall would just shake with applause." She paused. "Though it was still light outside, I closed the blinds. I, I couldn't face a lynching. I found myself waiting for gunfire. I don't know what I expected. Could I have had so little faith?" Her eyes misted up. "You have more faith in the union than I do. Oh, I don't deserve you." She pressed into him again.

Holding her like that created torture pure and simple. His heart stretched tight on an emotional rack with no escape. Every word she spoke only convinced him further of their differences. He was no union man. He was a union buster.

"Keely," he said. "I have something I have to show you." Her gaze met his, completely trusting. He led her upstairs to his room. *Separate rooms, separate lives*, he thought. If only he'd kept it that way. But they didn't sleep apart, and he no longer lived apart from her, in his heart or elsewhere.

He stifled a sigh. He had needed this room. He had convinced Keely by claiming that he needed an office, some place private to think. That was certainly true, but he also needed a place to hide his secrets. He pulled his saddlebag from beneath the bed, then seated Keely on the bed while he opened the bag. He handed her a bank account ledger. "That's yours. I set it up for you when we went to Spokane. Do you remember? I was late that night. I stayed out taking care of business. You were angry—"

"I remember." She looked about to cry.

"It doesn't matter now." He kneeled at her feet, next to his bag on the floor. "There's enough money there to see you through for quite a while." A lifetime? He hoped she'd at least get a good start on it. "If something happens to me, you use it. Do you understand?"

"Oh, McCullough." A tear slid down her cheek.

He reached up and brushed it away, fighting a damned lump in his own throat. "My will's on deposit there as well, for safekeeping. I saw a lawyer that day." He couldn't face her sad eyes. He fumbled in his bag for the final item longer than he needed to. He pulled the drawstring bag out and set it in her lap. "Gold pieces. Eagles and half eagles. A small fortune that. Had to sell one of my best horses on the way here." He tried to sound light. Actually, he'd sold McCullough's only horse. Well, it was one truth at least.

Keely didn't laugh. "Why? Why now? Why are you so certain?" Her voice broke with emotion and grief that Dietz could barely face.

He hadn't meant to, but he was hurting her, and only more lay ahead. "Did I say I was certain? I'm just preparing."

"You don't have to and you're not!" She ran her fingers through his hair. "What makes you think you're going to leave me?"

Damn, her choice of words was fatal. Did she have to hit so close to the truth? "Ever have a premonition?"

"Never!" She was too adamant.

"I have. Sometimes a man knows things and can't say how." The truth, but gilded. He felt ashamed of himself. She started to sob. He pushed off the floor and sat beside her on the bed, taking her in his arms. "Hide the money someplace safe."

Two days slid by. Keely felt herself being hurtled toward some unalterable destiny. On one occasion she said as much to McCullough. He laughed and said she'd been influenced by her Irish superstitions; would she be looking for little people next?

"You're Irish, too, you and your premonitions!" she had shouted back.

He masked his expression again. "Half," he said. "Fortunately my Scottish side has better sense."

She'd been angry, but she realized now fear had driven it. They had made up and made love in the wild, reckless manner they'd become accustomed to.

Standing in the kitchen, remembering, she felt caged. Like the small wild bunny she'd caught as a girl, she wanted to throw herself against the walls, to rail at a fate that robbed her of what should have been the most joy of her life. She had not left the boardinghouse in over a day, not even to set foot on the front porch. Filled with drunk, angry men, the streets reeked of danger and alcohol. Lust, for anything, women or violence, shone in the eyes of the miners. Keely didn't dare leave her sanctuary, her prison.

She had been staring sightlessly out her window, but suddenly a man seated on a crate outside the post office caught her attention. She'd noticed that man following Mr. Allison all morning. Blast these miners. They proved Mr. Allison innocent, couldn't they leave him alone?

Mr. Allison emerged from the post office, whistling and heading back toward his store. Keely had had enough. She meant to warn him. She stepped outside, happy to be outdoors, happy that indignation had set her free. "Mr. Allison!"

He stopped, turned, and smiled at her. "Don't mind my impertinence, Mrs. McCullough, but it isn't safe for a lady to be out on the streets." He laughed in a gentle, kindly manner. "For anyone."

"I don't disagree, but I need coffee. I hope you have some stocked. With all the drinking going on, there's been a lot of coffee drinking, trying to overcome the effects of excess."

Mr. Allison held the door open for her. "Let's ask Mrs. Shipley what she's got."

Kate Shipley, the only other person in the store, stood behind the counter, looking out the window behind them with a concerned expression. Her little five-year-old boy played near her, running and darting between the barrels of dry goods. Keely grabbed Mr. Allison's arm and leaned in to speak to him.

"Mr. Allison. I know all about the accusations made against you earlier in the week. I also know you were exonerated. I must tell you how relieved I am. I couldn't believe you would be so low as to be a spy, a hideous private detective!" She paused, feeling Mrs. Shipley's gaze on them. "That's why I feel I must warn you. There's a man sitting on a box in front of the post office. He's been following you for the last day."

Mr. Allison looked in the opposite direction of what Keely expected, toward Mrs. Shipley, and frowned. Mrs. Shipley's gaze fixed on the post office.

"He has," Kate Shipley said. "I've been waiting for you to return so I could warn you myself."

"Either of you ladies recognize him?"

Keely shook her head. So did Kate. Mr. Allison turned, and made like he wanted to examine something on display in the store window, but his gaze focused on the man outside. Keely watched him closely, but no recognition flickered. A puzzle—why would someone be following a nice man like Mr. Allison? He smiled warmly and turned back to the ladies. "Must be a case of mistaken identity." He led Keely from the window. "Do you still want that coffee, or was that just an excuse?"

"Both. Please put the coffee on the boardinghouse account for me, Mrs. Shipley." While Mrs. Shipley wrapped up the purchase, Keely took the opportunity to speak with Mr. Allison. "Do you believe in premonitions, Mr. Allison?"

"No, can't say as I do. Why do you ask?"

No one seemed to, no one but McCullough. "McCullough does. He has this notion that something is going to happen to him, something to take him from me."

Mr. Allison gave her an oddly sympathetic look. "Does he now? Well, I wouldn't worry. So far as I know, he isn't a prophet."

"But he's been making provisions for me in case..." She couldn't finish.

"Likely he's just being cautious. Taking a wife will do that to a man. Just be glad he loves you enough to care about your future." Mr. Allison's hard expression sat at odds with his sentimental words. As so often lately, Keely felt like she witnessed a play where everyone had roles but her.

"Times are dangerous. You heed your husband's warnings, Mrs. McCullough."

"I will, Mr. Allison. And you watch out for yourself, too."

Panic pulsed through Dietz's veins, ripe and biting. Sweat dripped from his forehead, not from fear, from fighting. He wiped the salty sweat away with the back of his hand, then tenderly felt his jaw, his mouth. The rusty taste of blood met his tongue. He took a blow to the mouth. No teeth broken, just a fat, split lip. Didn't the scab understand it was a mock fight? Evidently not.

The scab lay just downhill from him, doubled over with pain, concealed in the underbrush out back of town, uphill as close to the Gem as Dietz could manage. Dietz saw him clearly. With luck, the union crowd cheering at his back, the bunch of jackals, couldn't see a thing.

Dietz cursed under his breath, then whispered heavily. "I'm going to create a distraction. Then you run like hell for the mine."

Dietz staggered back to the road and the waiting union boys, shaking his head, clutching his ribs as he emerged from the heavily forested hill. One good deed done. One scab who might live, provided the boy made it back to the Gem.

Shit. Half a dozen scabs beaten nearly to death in an afternoon. And Dietz had to walk in on this fight on his way back to town. The panic coursing through him had little to do with the scab. Patterson had been fingered as a private detective. Dietz needed to get through the brawling and get back to warn him.

"McCullough!"

Dietz didn't recognize the voice.

"I lost the coward in the brush."

A volley of curses erupted as the union men crowded around him. "Shall we go after him?"

"You boys do what you want. I'm going home to nurse my wounds before the big meeting." Dietz looked around at the faces rimming the circle around him.

"Yeah, you bet." "Good idea." And similar sentiments echoed around him. The boy would be safe, for the moment.

Dietz stopped by Dutch's on his way home and begged a basin of water and a towel off Dutch. Dietz didn't need Keely fussing over him. Dutch seemed to understand. Back at the boardinghouse, looking reasonably normal, Dietz begged off from Keely's attentions and questions, claiming he needed a rest.

The General Assembly of the union would meet later in the evening, like always on their regular night. They were going to kill Patterson there. On Dietz's way past Keely to the bedroom, she grabbed his arm and told Dietz about the man following Patterson.

"Not to worry, lass. I'm sure it's nothing."

Keely saw his mouth then. He knew by her expression. Cold water hadn't been able to totally quash the swelling and bruising of his lip.

"McCullough?"

"I was in a fight, lass. Jumped by a scab but not seriously hurt. You should have seen him."

She reached out and gently stroked his face. "I'm sorry."

He winced. "They're fighting all over town. It's been a banner day for fat lips and black eyes. Stay in the house where you're reasonably safe, lass. Promise me."

As soon as Keely stopped fussing over him and left him to rest, Dietz sneaked out the back window of the boardinghouse, circled behind in the woods, met up with the road and crawled through the empty culvert under the street. He crept back of the buildings and crawled through the board Patterson kept intentionally loose in the high, tight privacy fence he had constructed around the back of his store. Dietz felt like a kid playing an obnoxious game of hide-and-seek. Moments later he let himself into Patterson's store and found Patterson in his rooms.

When Dietz pushed the door open, he met Patterson drawing a bead on him in the sight of his Colt's 45. "Didn't your mama teach you to knock?"

"Knocking is a little too obvious. My mama didn't teach me a damned thing. She threw me out at age five."

Patterson dropped the gun to his side. "You're looking pretty today."

"I've been fighting scabs and saving scabs. What mixed lives we lead." Time ticked too short for niceties. "Let's get down to business. I sneaked out of the house and need to get back before Keely misses me. I know you know that you're being followed. Keely told me," Dietz said. "Your tail has been consorting with Dallas." Patterson didn't appear surprised. "His name is Black Jack—"

"He's from Nevada," Patterson interrupted. "Where he blew up the Prinz and Pelling Mine when I was on assignment there. We heard he skipped to Africa. I guess he's back. I've been wondering all afternoon if he recognized me or if I just looked familiar. I guess now I know."

"He's union. A regular member," Dietz said.

"Yeh."

"You have to get out of town, Patterson. He recognized you and told the union brass. They'll kill you for certain this time."

"I'm not leaving, Dietz. Not until the operation's over and I've done what I'm paid to do." Patterson smiled. "Don't expect there's much chance of me escaping anyway. Billy Flynn was here earlier. I always liked

Billy. I used to room with his brother-in-law John Day. Well, I'm rambling. I've known what you're telling me all afternoon.

"Billy came over drunk as they come and crying like a baby, telling me how he hated to go back on union principles and warn a traitor, but he couldn't believe I was one. Billy confirmed what you're saying. I asked Billy why they suspected me again, especially considering I just proved my innocence yesterday. He claims he was sworn to secrecy, but that someone recognized me as a private detective. It had to be Black Jack."

"You're not going to be foolish enough to come to the meeting, are you?"

"No, I won't be going. You'll have to be our eyes and ears, Dietz."

Dietz, still standing, shifted from foot to foot. "You have an escape plan?"

Patterson shook his head in the negative. "I'll have to get to the mine."

"Shit, Patterson. Cross Canyon Creek, climb to the wide-open rail bed, and then hoof it up the hill to the mine? The trip's filled with dangers. And how do you plan to get as far as the creek? I had a deuce of a time sneaking over here myself. The back of your fence is clear, but they've got scouts. You know they'll be surrounding your place soon. You need to get out now."

"No, boy. I need to play a calm hand."

"And I need to get home before Keely misses me." Dietz turned toward the door. "You go anywhere, let Mrs. Shipley know. I'll follow when I can. Do what I can." Patterson nodded. Dietz turned and left.

Minutes after Keely left McCullough's room, she returned with a cold compress for his lip. The bed was
empty. She hadn't heard the back door open and close.
Perplexed, she glanced up in time to see McCullough
sneaking off back into the woods. Where was he going?
Why had he lied to her, wanted to get rid of her? Did-
n't he trust her? Fears, worries, anger all welled up at
once. Could he have union business so important?

She went back into the kitchen to check on the pies
she was baking in the oppressive heat and spent fifteen
minutes stewing. She would show him. She meant to
return to the room and wait for him. She would catch
him sure and certain. But when she returned and
opened the bedroom door, she found him back in bed,
sleeping, his breathing soft and steady, his expression
relaxed. She sat on the bed next to him and brushed
the hair from his face.

What's going on, McCullough?

CHAPTER FIFTEEN

Dietz's watch read eight forty-five. The union meeting had started at eight. At eight thirty, half an hour after Patterson should have shown up, Waters dispatched a committee of three men to Patterson's store to see what kept him. Of course, Dietz knew what kept him, a sense of self-preservation. Dietz guessed every man in the hall knew as much.

Anticipation laced the crowd, which buzzed and murmured as they awaited the committee's return. Frankly, Dietz had been glad he had not been appointed to face Patterson. Suddenly the men went silent. The committee walked in empty-handed and conferred with Waters. When Waters said nothing, the crowd started humming again, men whispering to their neighbors, speculation buzzing like flies.

Dietz hoped Patterson was unharmed and heading uphill to the Gem Mine and relative safety. There seemed to be no absolutely safe refuge anywhere. Finally, the guard from the door walked up to Waters and handed him a folded piece of paper.

"Men, we have our answer." Waters adjusted his glasses and began reading. After scanning the page in silence, he looked toward the crowded hall. "Mr. Allison sends us his resignation," he said with great pomp over the angry cries from the crowd. The air crackled with hatred and bloodlust.

Waters banged his gavel for order and continued. "Mr. Allison regrets that he can no longer hold the post of recording secretary. He also cannot continue being a member of the miners' union, when we have been planning to knife him in the dark, under the false impression that he is a private detective, one of the lowest and most degrading professions a mortal man could follow. He says, and I quote, 'to be accused of such a black crime is more than I can stand.'"

Nice theatrics, Patterson, Dietz thought.

The reaction of the crowd was mixed, but most men appeared disappointed. There would be no lynching tonight. With the main entertainment for the evening postponed, Waters adjourned the meeting. "Men," Waters said. "I have to call the meeting to a close, but let's not waste the night. Throw open the doors and let's have us our dance!" He banged the gavel. "Meeting adjourned!"

Shit, a dance. All Dietz wanted to do was go home and crawl into Keely's arms. But he couldn't miss gathering the important information sure to be floating around the wagging tongues of the eager, angry miners. What did they have planned for Patterson?

Several fellows jumped up on the stage with fiddles and guitars in hand. The guards threw the doors of the hall open. Women, mostly girls from the bordello down in Wallace, tumbled in along with a tide of men from other camps.

Maybe it wasn't smart to come, Keely thought as she stood in the dark street outside the union hall with several dozen women. Some she recognized as miner's wives, dressed in worn dresses, looking faded and poor and eager for fun, something to make the tension recede into the background, if only for the night. Most of the rest, the gaudy, painted ones who wore gowns too bright and too short, were working girls, obvious whores from the bordellos in Wallace. Keely stood apart from them, both pitying and repulsed.

Though signs advertising it had been posted earlier in the day, McCullough had not invited her to the dance. Whether out of possessiveness or protectiveness, she did not know. But she didn't intend to miss the fun. She had never danced with McCullough, not once. This might be her last chance. For a while, she amended superstitiously, as if a slip of a thought could seal a fate. For a while.

She wore the new dress that McCullough had ordered her from Spokane, the one made of emerald green glacé and covered with black-striped drapery net. An evening breeze, moist with dew, blew lightly,

ruffling the hem of her gown and dancing across the
bare flesh revealed by the low cut. Suddenly, the doors
to the union hall flew open. Joe Riley, who guarded the
door, grinned at the ladies, bowed comically, and with a
sweep of his arm gestured them into the hall.

Keely half-expected McCullough to be waiting for
her, arm extended in welcome. Whatever romantic notions she harbored, she could not find him as her gaze
swept the room. The band tuned up and broke into a
lively rendition of *Johnny Get Your Gun* and the room
burst into a swirling mass of dancers. Keely frowned.
Where is McCullough?

Beer and whiskey flowed into the room. With every
passing moment, every drink consumed, the room
buzzed louder with male voices punctuated with female
laughter. The whores plied their trade with abandon,
dancing, flirting, and cooing to the all too lonely men.
Who could blame them? Dietz reasoned that business
must be slow so many months after the shutdown. Most
of the miners spent, gambled, drank, and whored reck-
lessly at first. But hard times caught up to them, and
now most were broke or nearly. Like anyone, the girls
needed to eat, needed to work and stay occupied. Who
knew, maybe they were as lonely as the men were. At a
quarter a dance, at least they stood to earn a little cash
tonight.

One of the painted ladies caught his gaze and beckoned to him. Attractive in a hard, used up, jaded way,
she could not compare to Keely. He smiled back but
made no move on her. Another Dietz, months ago,

might have been tempted, but today he wanted no one but Keely. Over the whore's shoulder, framed in the window behind her, Dietz caught sight of a familiar silhouette. Patterson? What was he doing here?

Dietz pulled a quarter from his pocket and headed for the door. As he brushed past the whore he handed her the coin. She reached for his arm, trying to pull him into the crowd of lively dancers.

"No, thanks, darling. Give yourself a rest with my compliments."

She pouted. "But I like dancing with handsome men."

He shook his head.

"If dancing doesn't suit you, I can give you something more."

"Give or sell?" He laughed when she frowned. "Either case I'm not interested." He brushed past her, wound through the crowd, and stepped into the crisp night air and the shadows where Patterson spoke with a leading member of the Mullen Union, Kelly Kerrey.

"What are these rumors I hear of trouble?" Patterson asked. As Dietz joined the two, Patterson nodded to him. "Kerrey, you know McCullough?

Kerrey extended his hand for a shake. "I do. Good to see you."

"The same." Dietz noticed that Patterson kept his hand at his side, near his trusty firearm the Colt's 45. "What's this I overheard about trouble?"

"Blood will flow here in the next few days," Kerrey said. "I can't give an exact date. The union bosses are keeping a lid on it. We all have to be ready for our marching orders at a moment's notice."

"Sure," Patterson said. "Haven't we been ready?"

Kerrey laughed. "For what's coming up? I don't know. It will be a regular uprising against the scabs and owners. Rumor has it that the riots in Homestead back East a few days ago will look like a skirmish compared to the war that's being planned here."

Dietz went cold. Time was up. He had to get Keely out, if it wasn't already too late.

"And you boys will be right at the heart of the action," Kerrey continued. "You ought to be proud. All the neighboring unions have been ordered to concentrate their forces and arms here in Gem."

"So we're expected to play host to a party when we don't know the date?" Dietz spoke casually. Kerrey slapped him on the back.

"Heard gossip that it's billed to come off tomorrow night." Kerrey stared toward the dancing in the hall, looking enticed. "But like I said, the Central Union executive committee is keeping it quiet." Kerrey's eyes lit up as he fixed his sights over Dietz into the union hall behind him. "Whoa, now there's a tasty morsel and she's smiling at me. I can't be wasting time with you boys."

Dietz turned to look back over his shoulder into the hall just as Keely stepped out. "McCullough?"

"Keely?" Wearing the new special occasion gown he'd had made for her in Spokane; she took Dietz's breath away. Curses to him for letting her get under his skin, for always being on his mind. Now he had to be man enough to leave her.

"Thank goodness I found you." She came up and took Dietz's arm. "I was beginning to fear for my safety. I thought the men would dance me to death. Without you to protect me I've been pinched, felt up, and propositioned as no decent lady should be."

"My heart breaks. This woman belongs to you?" Kerrey asked.

"My wife," Dietz said.

"My apologies, ma'am. I had hoped your smiles were for me. Now I see I was mistaken. But if you all will excuse me, I may still be able to find a partner." Kerrey tipped his hat and departed, slapping Dietz on the back as he went. Kerrey looked momentarily confused as he looked around to bid Patterson goodbye.

Patterson had disappeared into the crowd when Keely walked up. *Damn.* Dietz would have to catch him later. They had plans to make.

"What are you doing here, Keely?" He tried in vain to keep the emotion from his voice. Could she tell how she affected him? Could she see in him the hurt he was about to inflict on her?

"Looking for you."

Her light green eyes bore into him, piercing him with their love and lust. He wanted her forever. One more night would never be enough. "How much did you hear?"

She held his gaze, but stubborn woman didn't answer.

"You're leaving tomorrow. First thing, as soon as I can get you to Wallace."

She didn't argue. "Will you dance with me first?"

"One dance, lass. Then I'm taking you home. I'm not in a sharing mood tonight. If we stay at the hall, I'm sure to be obliged to give you up for a dance or two."

Keely took his hand and pulled him into the hall. As they stepped into the light from the darkness, he noticed how young and innocent she looked, how beautiful. A good ten years separated them. Suddenly, he felt every one. Every year that took him from the optimism of youth, the invincibility. Every experience that guided him toward cynicism. He'd seen too much, done too much, hurt and been hurt too many times.

She led him out to the dance floor. The band struck up a lively tune. With Keely in his arms, they danced a lively two-step, alone in an overwhelming crush of people. Her face flushed, her eyes shone brightly, her laugh tinkled and floated above the buzz of the crowd. Her breasts bounced enticingly. Heat and exercise sparkled on her skin.

Footsteps tapped the floor in a happy, exuberant cadence. Dancing brought back a familiar, exciting rush. Forget the guilt for one night, Dietz. For this last night. His laugh matched hers. He smiled to encourage her, letting the dangers of the job, the apex of fear and survival instinct push him over the edge into a high that came only when danger beckoned. He lived for risking his life; he just hadn't counted on losing his heart.

"You dance well." He leaned into her, shouting above the music. You bounce very well, too.

She mouthed a reply that he could not hear over the music. They pounded round the room again. The music stopped, but to hell with it, he didn't want to stop dancing. He continued whirling Keely around the floor.

"McCullough, everyone's watching."

"Let them." He guided her toward the door. "Make way. Let us through."

The crowd parted.

Dietz was keenly aware of the way men's gazes followed his wife as he led her toward the door. She was his, and he meant for every man to know it. Just as they reached the doorjamb he pulled her against him and kissed her. Not quickly, but deeply, slowly, languorously, with his tongue obviously in her mouth. He rocked her against him in a kind of dirty dancing most of the lonely miners could only dream about. Let them see his stamp on her. Let them remember how she had belonged to him when they came to court her. Let them remember that no matter what happened or how they were separated, she would only belong to him.

He pulled away from her before he lost complete control. The crowd cheered. He held her hand in one hand and with the other saluted the crowd. Then he pulled her, laughing, into the street, tugging her along at a pace that forced her into a short, choppy run.

"We gave them a quite a show, McCullough."

"Aye, lass. I wanted them to see for themselves who has privileges with you and who doesn't."

"You think they know now?"

They reached the boardwalk in front of the boardinghouse. She stumbled as he pulled her up the step. He caught her and pulled her to him, nuzzling her neck. "If they don't they will now. Was dancing with me what you hoped for?"

"Everything and more." She breathed heavily. Her chest heaved as she caught her breath. He fixed his gaze on those fabulous breasts of hers, rising and fall-ing, sparkling, soft. He kissed her, traveling the length of her neck, kissing the tops of her breast. "Sweet, lass, sweet."

"McCullough, if you've got more of that in mind, we'd better go inside." She sounded happy, flirtatious. That's what he loved about her. She didn't chide. She wasn't priggish or unnecessarily prudish. She had a way of never pushing him away, of always pulling him in.

"Not private enough her for you, lass?"

"Not tonight. Too many men pouring into town. I don't mind the men seeing how I feel about you, but I don't want them seeing all my assets."

"Your monthlies?"

"Over."

A more perfect statement he could not imagine. He should have been dismayed. Now there was no graceful escape, no excuse to stop. She did not carry his child. She would not, unless he gave her an opportunity. He should have walked away, gone back to the action as he intended, made sure he left her with no burden. She looked up at him with those pale green eyes. How could he ever resist her? Selfish bastard that he was, why would he ever want to?

He pushed the door open, swept her into his arms and carried her back to their room. A pale sliver of moonlight slid in through the window, slanting across the bed. Just inside the bedroom door, he set her down. Then he reached for her and cupped her breasts, drawing them to his lips for a kiss, running his tongue between the cleavage. Salty, earthy, alive, he loved the taste of her. Reluctantly, he released her and moved toward the window. "I'd better draw the curtains." The thud of a dress hitting the floor stopped him short.

"Tell me what you're doing, Keel."

"I just took my dress off."

"So I heard. You want the curtains closed or not?"

"I'm unbuttoning my shoes."

He smiled. Though his back was turned to her, he imagined very clearly her slender fingers running nimbly the length of the shoes. Thump. Thump. Then a subtle rustling of skirts, a swish as they hit the floor.

"Underskirts," she said. "The ones with lace inserts we got in Spokane."

How did she make her voice sound like silk, sweet and breathy enough to take his away? She was silent a moment. He had a notion to turn around, but liked the game she played too well. "Lass?"

"Just wiggling out of my corset cover."

"Wiggling, eh? I'd like to see that."

She ignored him. "I like the idea of being spotlighted by moonlight. There's nothing back there behind the house but an old hillside. You mind it watching?"

His heart hammered amid his ribs, pounding out a rhythm, drilling inside him like a sledgehammer against a pin in a mineshaft. But he needed to be drilling Keely. "I mind nothing as long as you don't."

She laughed. "Garters, silk stockings long and soft, bustle."

He heard the thud and made a mental inventory. "That leaves, what, a corset and a pair of drawers?"

"I'm unfastening the corset, a hook at a time now."

He spun around. "Now don't do that, lass. That's my job." He'd seen whores, rich women, and others, in every imaginable ensemble of lingerie created, but not one ever looked as good as Keely did wearing plain cotton drawers and a corset.

"I believe that we're unevenly matched now, lass. Turn around while I even the score." She turned slowly, looking in the moonlight like a pale, white angel—his angel, love personified.

He ached for her now, but he would not rush this night, this last time. He always made love to Keely to a wild, reckless tempo, always trying to shut out himself, always trying to forget McCullough's shadow, the ghost he'd become. Not the real McCullough, he was no threat at all, never had been, but the McCullough Dietz had created, the man Keely believed she loved. Tonight he intended to take it slow, to make love to her as himself, John Dietz, that she might, when she remembered, remember him as the best. But it was not for her alone. Keely had shown him who he was—not actor, not chameleon, but a man who loved her. He intended this night, for himself, to make love to her as that man.

He pulled off his boots and set them by the bed, then shed his shirt and other clothes. He stood barefoot, wearing only his pants as he came up behind her, circled her in his embrace, and nuzzled her neck. She smelled of lavender. "Flowers, Keely?"

"Lavender on the bedside table, from the garden."

He hadn't noticed, but now that she mentioned them, a lump rose up in his throat. How was he going to live without her and her flowers? Would a garden ever be as sweet? "On you, lass. I smell lavender."

She giggled. "I tucked a nosegay into my corset."

She had no perfume. How had he been so negligent? "When this is over, I'll buy you all the toilet water a girl could want." He made an empty promise. Once a liar, always one, but so help him, if he could, he would have. He pulled her to the bed and onto his lap, facing away from him, stroking her from behind. Soft scents, soft skin, soft curves.

She wrapped her legs and bare feet around his calves, spread her legs, and settled in on him. "Keely," he whispered, stroking her thighs. She made him forget his technique, his carefully crafted lovemaking process. All he had to do with Keely was follow his senses, touch her, play her body. Loving her felt as natural as breathing, as easy as eating sweets. No one had to teach him this.

"The corset, McCullough."

"Not yet, lass." Making love in a corset was like a knight making love in armor, but for the moment, he liked the breathless quality it gave her. A woman cinched tightly could never breathe properly.

He rocked her on his lap, against him as he rubbed her thighs and touched between her legs, staring over her shoulder at her bouncing breasts. He loved little things about her—the shadow of her breasts, the curve of her hip, all the rounded contours of her body, the way she quivered when she got excited.

"Ian."

He hated that name, but tonight he would not let it spoil things. He unlaced the corset and unmolded it from her body, tossing it carelessly away, reaching for the touch of her under the lace vest she wore beneath the corset. Her breath came in a gasp. He pulled the small spray of lavender from its resting place between her breasts, imagining himself nestled there. He could no longer stand the ache. He stood her in front of him and shimmied out of his remaining clothes, watching her do the same. Then he pulled her on top of him and thrust upward.

They rolled on the bed. He rocked into her, undulating slowly, reining back until he could stand it no more.

When it was over, he rolled from her, watching her in the moonlight, realizing there had been only two in the bed.

"Oh, McCullough, look at me." Her voice trembled with joy. "My legs are still quivering from the force of it."

He loved her forthrightness. Other women, even whores, didn't speak of their pleasure. But his Keely did.

"Sometimes, after it's over, like tonight, I can still feel you in me, your fullness." She traced his chest with her fingers. "I hate when the feeling goes away. I'd gladly walk like a cowboy the rest of my days, legs straddled, feeling full up with you, if only the feeling would stay."

She would not forget him. The thought hit him full force. He had never been so thankful. If he could never forget her, neither could she forget him. He knew it would never be the same with another woman. Lust was just lust, and the act the act. Afterwards mattered most, when the person you were with made all the difference. What he felt for Keely went beyond the physical. Knowing the emptiness to come, he should have been ashamed of his gratefulness that he left his imprint in her. But he felt no guilt now, only fulfillment.

She lifted her face to his. He kissed her mouth, then her neck, then her breasts. "Lavender will always remind me of you, Keely. I promise." He sat up, hearing for the first time since they'd come home the ruckus outside in the streets. He had work to do. "I've got to go. I've got business to attend to."

She nodded. "Will you be back tonight?"

"I don't know." He really didn't. He hoped so. "I love you, Keely. I do." He stood and dressed, feeling her watchful gaze upon him.

CHAPTER SIXTEEN

Dietz slipped into his own room, grabbed his Winchester rifle, and filled his pockets with ammunition. Someone had to warn Monihan at the Gem mine about the coming attack. With Patterson under tight surveillance, he'd inherited the job. He sneaked out the back door of the boarding house, skirted town by way of the woods out back, slipped into the culvert again and wound up behind Patterson's store in a timbered swamp near the bank of Canyon Creek. A movement out in the water, underneath the overhanging trees caught his attention. Dietz froze.

A man waded through the creek in front of him, holding a rifle over his head, looking like a captured prisoner surrendering. Patterson? Dietz called out to him softly, a whisper on the breeze. The man froze, turned, looked at him, waved him on. Patterson sure enough.

"What are you doing out here?" And why were they *both* risking their necks to get to the Gem, Dietz felt like asking.

"Don't go getting annoyed with me, boy. I have to warn Monihan—"

"What do you think I'm doing?"

"You obviously didn't see my little incident at Dutch Henry's." Patterson pressed on, wading farther out into the creek. Dietz moved with him. The creek water felt like ice, so cold through his boots that his toes ached. He'd be glad enough to reach shore.

"What happened?"

"The union boys have got two of Monihan's men over at Dutch's, getting them drunker than skunks."

"What are scabs doing out and about town?" Blasted, foolhardy scabs. They made Dietz peevish. Because of their foolishness, tonight both he and Patterson risked their necks. "You'd think since Mr. French's visit this morning the boys at the mine would have sense enough to stay home. If the union thugs are brazen enough to make an attempt on the Secretary of the Mine Owners' Union in broad daylight, what's to stop them from messing with a few insignificant scabs after dark?" Dietz had little patience with men who took needless risks.

"French came on a fool's mission. Guess he felt it necessary to make an attempt to settle things peacefully. He should have known better." Patterson paused and looked up at the stars through the rustling leaves of the bushes overhead. Evidently satisfied that they hadn't been detected, he continued on.

"Should have." Dietz kept his voice low. "Back to the point—there's nothing illegal about getting a couple of scabs drunk, so what brings you out?" All this talking made him nervous. The night air carried sound better than any medium he knew. He didn't want to be blasted in the water like a sitting duck, but Patterson seemed intent on telling a story.

"One of the union boys told me they're going to kill those two. That's the point of getting them juiced up. I went up to Dutch's to warn those two boys, but they wouldn't listen. One of them is as big as a bear, too big for sense. He claims he can defend himself." Patterson sighed. "That may be true sober one on one, but the union boys don't play fair. I'm off to warn Monihan." Patterson paused. "The Gem seems the safest place for me, all things considered. Now that you know I'm out, you can go back."

Patterson's speech placated Dietz somewhat. "Could." He kept pace with Patterson, who laughed quietly.

They reached the edge of the creek. The open bank provided no cover. Down stream union guards stood duty on the bridge. Dietz dropped to his belly to avoid detection. He and Patterson crawled combat style, side by side, in silence. Ahead, cover loomed dense, dark, and enticing.

Every scratch, every slither, every clink of their gun belts seemed to echo around him, magnified by his fear of detection. Dietz scratched his elbows on the rocks and branches protruding from the bank. Muck caked his shirt and his elbows ached by the time they snaked across the banks to the railroad bed. Shit—gravel.

Dietz slid over the metal tracks on his stomach. Even so gravel crunched beneath his boot toes, loud and ugly. Voices floated down to him from the bridge, laughing, boasting. Fortunately the union boys, caught up in their own tales, overlooked him.

Patterson reached the woods. "Run!"

Dietz pushed up and sprinted toward the mine entrance.

They found John Monihan, Mine Superintendent, in his office. He didn't seem surprised to see them. "Trouble?" Monihan spoke calmly, but worry lines were etched around his eyes and mouth.

"Looks like you're expecting some," Dietz said.

"Union boys streaming into town, guards on the bridge between here and there, what's a man supposed to think?" Monihan pointed out his window.

"We came to warn you," Dietz said. "Word we got is the union has something big scheduled for tomorrow. But we don't know specifics, just that it will be bigger than what happened in Pennsylvania earlier."

"You should have saved yourself a trip," Monihan said dryly.

"That isn't all," Patterson spoke up. "They're planning to murder two of your boys tonight. They've got them over at Dutch Henry's." As Monihan swore under his breath, Patterson related his story. "I went to Dutch's to try and warn them, but while I was seated at the saloon I saw a crowd gathering, watching me. Earlier someone recognized me as a private detective and told the union brass. I resigned my post today.

"Anyway, before I could convince your boys of the danger, Old Shoemaker came up to me and told me to duck my nut out of there, which, though I hate being bossed around, I did. The one fellow of yours, the big one, seemed to think he could handle them, but I tell you, he's wrong."

Just then a knock sounded at the door. One of Monihan's guards poked his head in. "Boss, the constable is here. He's got Big Pete with him. He looks bad." Even in the dim light, the guard's face looked pale, and his voice shook.

The constable's voice rang out from the distance. "Put him in his boss's office, boys." His tone sounded almost gleeful, the bastard.

"We can't let them find you here," Patterson said to Dietz, and shoved him under Monihan's desk. Crammed into the tight cubbyhole with a chair at his back, Dietz cursed silently. Patterson and Monihan stepped around in front of the desk to block any view of him. Moments later, Dietz heard the constable and his cronies enter the room. A thud sounded as they dumped Big Pete onto the floor unceremoniously. Dietz's heart thudded wildly for a second when Monihan left the desk to bend over Big Pete. Fortunately, the constable didn't deign to bend over and join Monihan in inspecting Big Pete's wounds further. If he had, he would have seen Dietz huddled beneath the desk. All Dietz got was a fine view of the constable's boots.

"He needs a doctor," the constable said. "Good luck getting him to one. He's a heavy son of a bitch."

Monihan mumbled something to the constable that Dietz couldn't quite make out. Thanks? That hardly seemed appropriate given the constable's attitude. But then, the constable was one of Judge Brown's henchmen. Maybe this represented a good will gesture, or just the prisoner's last meal, Dietz thought wryly. The constable walked to the door and without further comment, took his boys and left, slamming the door shut behind him.

Patterson motioned Dietz to come out from beneath the desk. An instant later Dietz got his first view of Big Pete. Monihan had rolled his coat up and tucked it under Big Pete's head like a pillow. Someone else threw a coat over him. The room began to fill with curious scabs and Thiel guards who had seen the constable bring Big Pete in.

"He hardly looks human, except for his shape," Patterson said slowly, his tone solemn. "They've beat him almost to jelly."

As he looked at Big Pete, anger erupted inside Dietz and he swore under his breath. "What kind of an animal—"

Monihan was bending over Big Pete, taking inventory. "Jaw's broke, and only God knows how many ribs. He needs a doctor and fast." Monihan looked up at the men surrounding him in the room. "We can't move him again. Someone needs to go for the doctor."

Dietz didn't hesitate. "I'll go."

Patterson frowned at him. "You can't," Patterson said. "It'll blow your cover. You don't think the doctor will tell?"

Silence echoed off the walls. Finally one guard spoke up. "The road to town is going to be heavily guarded. Going for the doc is a suicide mission."

"The man will die," Monihan retorted. The men all looked sheepish, but none spoke up.

A man's courage is best tested under pressure, Dietz thought. He wasn't afraid of going.

"I'll do it," Patterson said. "The union boys want a piece of my hide already. They can have it sooner if it will save your man."

One other guard volunteered to go with Patterson. Patterson grabbed his gear and looked to Dietz. "Get back to town, boy. I'll walk you to the road."

Every muscle ached as Dietz slipped off his boots and tiptoed into Keely's bedroom. He set the boots by the door. He should have bathed, but he had no energy for it. Would Keely notice that the smell of swamp, sweat, and mud replaced alcohol tonight? Would she care or question it?

Keely didn't stir as he prowled around stripping off his filthy clothes. The realization jolted him with guilt. A wife shouldn't have to get so comfortable with her husband's late night carousing that she didn't even wake when he came home. Moonlight shone in an arc around her, highlighting her fair complexion. Her features relaxed in sleep, worries forgotten for the moment. She should look like that all the time, he thought—beautiful, safe.

Keely deserved more than the lying, imitation bastard of a husband he was. How could he have done this to her? Why did his conscience always attack him when fatigue weighed him down? A few more days and he would leave and make things right. As right as he could.

He slid into bed and curled up behind her, threw his arm over her. She stirred and snuggled into him, pushing her tight little bottom up against him. He might have started something if he hadn't been so tired. Instead, he settled in, content. He was going to miss this. How would he live without it?

The heat made Dietz grumpy as he stood in the sun and barked orders at his platoon of men like a military sergeant. He'd been drilling them since early morning, marching them up and down the street in a mock military parade, waiting for the orders from the Central Union bosses to move out. Move out and do what? The union bosses must have put the fear of the devil into those in the know. No one was singing. Frustrated that he couldn't glean any useful information, Dietz ordered his men to keep moving.

That the union bosses didn't even trust McCullough, renowned union terrorist, irked Dietz. That they assigned him the menial task of drilling the men angered him further. But at least it gave him an opportunity to keep an eye on Patterson's store. Guards surrounded it, posted by the union.

Dietz knew Patterson had returned to Gem and holed up in the store. He'd seen him come off the train this morning, toting a Winchester rifle and strutting bold as brass down the street. Had he been to see Mr. French? Had he warned him? Patterson never faltered where courage counted. Shortly after that Dietz had seen a contingency of union boys go into the store. That set him on edge. Dietz kept marching his boys back and forth in front of the store, trying to figure how many union fellows he could take out if it came to that to help Patterson, waiting for an ominous round of fire. Neither occurred. A few minutes after the union boys arrived, they left. Bill Black, a known desperado, had given Dietz the thumbs up as they left the building.

"Good job, McCullough. That little show ought to have scared that damned spy sure enough."

Dietz had nodded. "You let him live?"

Black's returning laughter echoed eerily off the buildings. "Son of a bitch asked the same question. I told him same as I'll tell you—the time isn't right." Black shook his head, amused, and laughed again.

"You let me know," Dietz said, speaking before his silent men. "I want in on it."

Black nodded. "Sure, you and everybody else." He descended the steps from the store into the street and looked Dietz levelly in the eye. "Tell you what, McCullough. Because of your reputation, I'll let you in on the action." He clapped Dietz on the shoulder. "But it won't be for a bit. He isn't going anywhere. The fool says he's planning on staying until we carry him out a corpse." Black chuckled. "Looks like he's going to get his wish." Black walked off, pausing to call back over his shoulder. "Whip those boys into shape, McCullough. There'll be fireworks soon, and we'll need every man."

Throughout the remainder of the day, Dietz kept looking for an angle, a way to help Patterson escape. All the while his uneasiness grew. He pulled back from his thoughts and noticed that the men looked worn out and edgy. Dietz called for them to break ranks and take a rest. Just as he did, Conrad, one of Brown's henchmen, came riding down the street up to Dietz.

"How's the drilling going?" he called out.

"Fine." Dietz reached for his canteen and took a sip of water. "What brings you out?"

The men gathered around, expecting news. Conrad leaned down and whispered to him. "Let the men get some rest. I came to tell you that we'll be blowing up the Frisco Mill just before daybreak. Pass the word along."

"You're awful casual about the plan. You aren't worried about the owners getting word?"

"Nah. We'll be blockading the town. No one will be coming or going. How's the word to get to them?" Conrad winked and rode off.

Dietz's heart stood still for a bare second, and then thumped wildly into action. Keely—he had to get her out of town now, immediately, before it was too late. He dismissed the men and ran across the street into the boarding house. Keely stood over the stove cooking something that smelled good.

"Shut the stove off, Keely." Dietz spoke without preamble.

She turned and looked blankly at him, then quizzically. He went to her and taking her by the elbow, pulled her away. "Get your bags. I'm taking you to Wallace. Now."

Understanding washed over her expression. "When?" She stepped back to the stove, pulling the pans off and turning it off.

"Tomorrow, before daybreak. Keel, they're going to be setting up a blockade this afternoon. We have to go."

She nodded understanding and wordlessly turned toward the hall.

He followed her into the bedroom. Damn, how was he going to stand losing her?

She pulled her satchel from beneath the bed.

"Make sure you have everything—the money, clothes..." His voice cracked.

She faced away from him as she nodded and struggled with a large trunk. As he stepped to her aid, she turned, looked up at him with tears in her eyes, and threw herself into his arms.

"Keely." Damn, why did he have to be so inept?

"McCullough—"

He pressed his fingers to her lips. "I'll take care. I'll be all right—everything will be." He'd never told a bigger lie. Nothing would ever be right again without her.

She pressed her cheek against his chest.

He lost control. He had to have her one last time. He began unbuttoning her blouse.

"McCullough—"

"Don't say anything, Keely. Grunt and scream and moan if you like, but don't call my name." He undressed her urgently, wanting to see her in full one last time. Then he shrugged off his pants and underthings and carried her to the bed. Just this once, he didn't want to hear McCullough's name yelled in passion.

He made love to her urgently, thrusting wildly, both of them bucking until the headboard bounced and pounded the wall. The sounds of men outside in the streets marching and drilling faded away. Until they were both breathless and sparkling with exertion. Until he knew that part of him would die without her. Finally, completion washed over him, cleansing like cool stream water. No matter his duplicity with her, no matter the wrong he had done Keely, he loved her with a part of himself that he hadn't known existed. A part of him pure and unjaded, and vulnerable. She would never know, but he had given her that part of himself—his love, something he had never given before, and doubted he would again.

He rolled from her, the urgent need to get her to safety returning. He kissed her neck and pulled her to her feet.

They dressed silently, hurriedly.

When they finished, he spoke unnecessarily, "To Wallace."

Everything seemed inadequate. There were no words. No words.

Keely stood in the doorway of the Hotel Wallace and watched McCullough walk away, down the street to the train depot, back to Gem. His shoulders set, back straight, he looked proud and determined, confident.

She kept picturing his face, hearing his words as he wished her goodbye. *I love you, Keely. I love you.*

Why had he looked suddenly haggard? He seemed desperate for her to understand, and yet, his fears had never been founded. She knew he loved her. She had always known, from the first moment she laid eyes on him.

Was there something more he wasn't telling her? Blast him! He was half Irish. With their little people and pots of gold, Irish folk looked notoriously superstitious. But McCullough had never seemed so. She attributed it to his pragmatic Scots half. But now, she more than sensed, she knew he had told her goodbye, not for now, forever. She shivered in the heat. Had he a premonition of his own death? She believed in intuition. She'd felt it when Michael died. She felt a dread now, a sense of something amiss or about to go afoul.

She tried to force aside her own superstitious nature, and willed him to turn back and give her one last look before he departed from sight. But her thoughts brought no action. Determination drove him. He didn't mean to look back, but what did he see ahead?

A voice shook her from her thoughts. "That your man walking away?"

She hadn't noticed the stranger approach. She nodded mutely.

"I saw you two at the train station."

McCullough disappeared around a corner. She turned her gaze to the stranger, trying to place him, remember him. But truth be told, she couldn't remember anything past McCullough. The man next to her wore a sympathetic expression and looked kindly enough, non-threatening.

"Thoughtful man," the stranger said. "He tried to get you out of the Valley to safety, didn't he?"

Keely's hollow laugh came out more of a snort. "Is there such a thing as safety? Does a safe place exist?" She turned and walked into the hotel lobby.

The man followed her. "There's safer places right now than the Valley, miss."

"Judging from the crowd at the station, and the unavailability of trains, it would appear most people think so. I couldn't get a train out until tomorrow morning."

"That so. Smart men are seeing the wives and children out of the Valley." The man paused. "You look like you could use a friendly ear and a little something to perk you up. Could I buy you a cup of coffee, Miss—"

He waited for her to give her name. His tone held no flirtation, and there seemed to be nothing untoward, nothing other than kindness behind his words, but she felt no need for companionship just now.

"Mrs. McCullough. Thank you for your offer, but no thank you."

The man's expression lit up. He smiled in apparent recognition. "Would your man happen to be Ian McCullough?"

"Yes. Do you know him?"

"Not well, but I thought your husband looked familiar. Just couldn't place him without a name. I'm a member of the Butte City Miners' Union. They sent me over to help out the boys here.

"I met McCullough when he came through Montana. Your husband's reputation preceded him. Will he be involved in the big doings expected?"

The man's tone remained friendly and pleasant, but something about him made her wary. "My husband doesn't share his business with me, sir."

The man cleared his throat; embarrassment crept into his expression. "I didn't mean to be prying, ma'am. But I can see you're worried, and I just thought to set your mind at ease. I'm heading up to Gem, and I just thought that I might be able to look out for him for you. You don't happen to know where he'll be, do you, so that I can look him up?"

"No." Something about the man's persistence worried her. She walked away abruptly. Fortunately, he didn't follow.

Dietz didn't sleep at all that night, didn't even try. He had sneaked up to warn Monihan about the coming attack and then returned to Gem where he hung out at Daxon's saloon drinking with his union buddies, pressing for more information, for anything that would be useful later in convicting these thugs.

He couldn't see any way to avert the coming violence. Monihan, with fewer than one hundred men, couldn't stop the hordes of angry union men bent on revenge. Throughout the night the town had swelled with over a thousand of them. Dietz had run into Patterson up at the Gem Mine where Patterson stayed, helping keep watch, while Dietz went back to town to glean what news he could.

Dietz's head pounded. Too damned much alcohol. He needed something to eat. He excused himself. Facing the empty boardinghouse would mean facing life without Keely. He couldn't do it. He went to the Nelson Hotel. The French chef there knew how to cook a good breakfast. He had just settled into a booth when Tom Whalen shouted from outside. "Watch me shoot that damned nose off!"

A shot rang out. One of the waitresses screamed. The French chef came out of the kitchen, still holding a stack of wood, as if he'd just come from the woodpile. "Jim over at White & Bender's store poked his head out to see what was what and those fools shot at him!"

Dietz was McCullough now. He smiled warmly, amused. "Did they hit him?"

"Just missed." The chef retreated to the kitchen, shaking his head.

The shot's a blasted signal, a call to action, Dietz thought. Just as the waitress took his order, Patterson crawled in the side window, looking like a man on the run.

Dietz flashed him a calm, cocky smile. "If you're thinking of running, Mr. Allison, you had better think again. We've got guards everywhere. Why don't you just head on back home and wait until we're ready to deal with you?"

"To hell with you, McCullough." Patterson headed for the kitchen and the back door.

Dietz followed.

The French chef stopped Patterson short. "They've got fifty guards posted out there waiting to ambush you, Mr. Allison."

"I just came through there ten minutes ago. There weren't more than three." Patterson poked his head out and ducked back in.

Dietz casually drew his Colt and pointed it at Patterson. "I told you to get on home."

Before Patterson could move a lone man came up the boardwalk from the swamp out back, in shirtsleeves and unarmed.

"Ivory Bean," the French chef said.

Dietz cursed inwardly. Bean was a Thiel guard from up at the Gem Mine. What fool's errand brought him to town?

"I come in peace. The scab who got himself beat up the other day is dying. He needs medicine—"

The reverberation of a shot cracked the air. From out back, in the shade of the overhanging trees in the swamp, Dietz spotted a quick glimpse of Lunn Gaffney holding a gun aimed at Bean's back.

Bean fell face forward onto the boardwalk. A solemn red stain soaked his shirt. Shots whizzed through the air. No one moved to help Bean. There wasn't any point—he was dead.

CHAPTER SEVENTEEN

Women and children packed the Wallace train station. Tired, frightened, frustrated, and hopeful, they sought passage out of the Silver Valley. Eerily, and in sharp contrast to the norm, hardly a man made an appearance. Keely watched the ticket window as she waited on the platform to board her train to Spokane. McCullough had been wise to purchase her ticket the night before. She should be grateful for it, but she wasn't. Instead, she kept moving toward the back of the platform.

A young woman with a baby on her hip begged the cashier at the ticket window for a ticket, any ticket, to anywhere. Keely couldn't drag her gaze away from them, or the harried clerk who kept shaking his head. *No. Nothing. No.* At last the cashier gave up, stepped back from the window and pulled down his shade. The woman, tears standing in her eyes, stepped away, trying to coo to her baby, but she looked more like she needed comforting herself.

She should be on that train, Keely thought. *A mother's life, and that of her child, is worth more than mine.*

The train pulled up and braked with a great snort of steam. No incoming passengers departed. No one wanted *into* the Valley. The conductor set the steps up into the entrance. The crowd Keely stood in rushed forward, propelling her with them.

She shouldn't be here. If she left the Valley she'd never see McCullough again. A small voice seemed to speak in her mind saying, *Leave. Go to him. Save him.*

Suddenly, she knew her fate was wrapped around his, so intertwined it couldn't be separated. Come what may, she was going to be with him. She turned on her heel and fought her way upstream out of the crowd.

At the edge of the depot lobby, she found the young woman and handed her the ticket. "Go. Take your child to safety."

The woman hesitated only an instant. When the train gave another roar of steam, she murmured her thanks, snatched the ticket from Keely's outstretched hand, and ran for the train, baby and bags bouncing around her.

Two souls saved, Keely thought. Without looking back at the departing train, she ran for the street. She had to find a way to get back to Gem and past the blockade. As if sent by fate, Joe Poynton, recording secretary for the Central Union, rode up the street. She ran out into his path, waving and calling.

"Mrs. McCullough. You're like to get yourself killed jumping out in front of a man like that!"

His reprimand didn't set her back at all. "Are you heading to Gem?"

"I am, and in a hurry." He appeared agitated and put out with her.

"Then you're taking me back with you."

"No, ma'am. It isn't safe."

"I'm going one way or another. I'll be far safer with you than anyone else. The boys will be sure to let you through the blockade. If you don't want my blood on your hands, you'll give me a hand up." She stayed firmly planted in his path.

He motioned for her to come round and extended his hand. "But be quick about it."

For an instant Dietz, the French chef, Patterson, and the waitress were all too stunned to react. Shots buzzed through the air like angry bees around a hive. No one dared go out after Bean's body. Patterson got his senses back and sneaked back through the window over to his own building. How the hell Patterson meant to escape now, Dietz couldn't fathom, but he had to get moving himself. McCullough was expected at the bridge to post his men to defend the town from scabs and prevent any reinforcements from reaching the mine.

"Looks like I've been called to action," Dietz said, tipped his head to the waitress, and headed for the bridge.

Lunn headed the men that held the blockade. Keely saw him as they rode up. Lunn kept his gun trained on them. Mr. Poynton rode unflinching into the face of all those gun barrels, keeping Keely shielded and out of sight behind him.

"Halt!" Lunn called out. "Or we fire."

"Drop the guns, Gaffney," Mr. Poynton retorted. "It's Poynton and Mrs. McCullough."

"Keely?" Lunn's gun fell as he called his men off.

Poynton rode through the lines.

Lunn waited to help her off the horse. "Keely," he said again softly. "What are you doing here? I thought you fled to safety."

She didn't feel like explaining. "I had to come back."

Lunn turned to Mr. Poynton, who waved him over and asked for a briefing. The two men walked a short distance away from her, and though she strained to hear, she caught very few words.

Lunn whispered something to Mr. Poynton, who in turn looked shocked and then angry. Lunn said, "I'll tell her. I'll take her home."

Mr. Poynton replied. "I'm counting on you, Lunn. Take care of things."

Lunn nodded. Mr. Poynton slapped him on the back and went for his horse. Lunn came to her, looking uncertain. Displeasure colored his expression as he took her arm and roughly pulled her away. "You shouldn't have come back."

He seemed more put out than concerned. His whole attitude baffled her. "I'll take you to Lacy's. Her house is on the edge of town. It shouldn't see much action."

Keely shook off his grip. "You'll take me nowhere. I'm going home."

A thunderous roar cut off further words. The sound hurled down the Valley, deafening aftershocks echoing in its wake. The ground shook. Seconds later another blast sounded, silencing her screams. When realization hit her, she kept thinking the same thoughts over and over again. *Oh, dear God, they've blown up the mines. Please help us.*

There was no return for the boys now, no salvation. They had crossed the line. When the law took over again, they would be punished. *Michael, how right you were!* How many lives had the men ruined with their rash and inexcusable violence?

Lunn pulled her into a crushing embrace. He was one of them—one who would be destroyed. Him and McCullough.

As silence settled in an irrational wave of apprehension crashed over Keely. "McCullough!"

Lunn shook her. His eyes shone almost wickedly. "You can't save him now. You shouldn't have come, Keely. McCullough is a dead man."

"No! Liar!" She rebelled, though his words made no sense.

Lunn grabbed her in a grip so intense it frightened her, and pulled her face into his. "Listen to me, Keely. I don't know how else to tell you this. McCullough *is* dead."

"No, how can you know?" Panic coursed through her. Was she too late?

"You don't understand," Lunn said, forcing her to look at him as she struggled to pull away. "McCullough has been dead for months now."

She stared at him, dazed.

"The man you know as McCullough is a fake, a private detective, the man who killed McCullough in Thompson's Falls in May."

She stared at him. How could even Lunn make up such a lie?

The explosion shook the bridge. Timbers creaked and swayed. Horses whinnied and reared. Dietz's men scrambled to get a grip on the rails, or ran to shore, anything for stability. In the distance a tall pillar of smoke eased into the sky over the Frisco Mill, lazily curling heavenward into the blue. As the men realized the big plan had come off curses turned to whoops of excitement.

Damn, they've done it. Dietz stared off into the distance. Just a few more days to hang on and the mission would be over. Then Dietz could ride off to another assignment, one far away from Keely, one where he could forget.

A young man near him seemed unmoved with joy, more contemplative, almost regretful. When Dietz stared at him the fellow grimaced and shrugged. "I wish they hadn't of done it. There had to be another way. We're all in trouble now. You can't just go dyna-miting mines and shooting folks up without paying some kind of price." The young man nodded toward his compatriots. "They haven't realized it yet, but we're all going to pay for this."

The boy was right. If the Governor had any sense at all he'd declare a state of civil unrest and call in the state militia. Dietz began making calculations, trying to figure out how to save Patterson and stay under cov-er long enough to make sure none of the union bosses escaped before they paid the price.

It took nearly half an hour to calm the horses and get his men back in place. By that time kegs of whiskey and beer were being rolled from saloons into the street. The men drank and caroused and abandoned rank, leaving Dietz and a few loyal men to patrol the bridge.

A lone rider emerged from the woods on the far side of the creek and drew to a halt at the end of the bridge. Fear rode down Dietz's spine, raising gooseflesh as it went. Images making rapid connections flashed through his mind—the horseman, a job Dietz had done for the railroad in Wyoming. Dan McBride. How had he gotten out of jail?

"Dietz, or should I say McCullough, nice to see you again," McBride called out. Malice danced in his eyes.

Dietz posed casually as his heart pounded furiously in his ears. The bastard knew who he really was. Who had he told? His cover was blown for sure.

"McBride." Did McBride intend to drop Dietz here on the bridge?

McBride made no move for his firearm.

As Dietz leaned against the bridge rail, he surreptitiously palmed his Derringer. McBride stood in range of the tiny pistol. Dietz refused to go down without a fight.

"I'm flattered, Dietz. I imagine you've put a lot of men away. Thought you wouldn't remember me. What a coincidence this is." McBride pulled on the reins to steady his antsy horse. His voice dripped irony and innuendo. "I thought I took care of you last May when I told McCullough who his real companion was. Appears you got one up on him. Don't guess you'll get away this time." McBride paused for emphasis. "You know I'm a regular union member in Butte. It's a nice little town for a fugitive to live respectable. Been sent here to help Dallas find his spy."

Another mystery solved, Dietz thought. So McBride had seen him and warned McCullough.

"We've got our spy," Dietz played along. What did McBride have in mind? Why didn't he shout out Dietz's identity? Sweat trickled down the back of Dietz's neck, from the hot sun, and the cold anticipation of a flight for life.

"I'll say we have." McBride's smile oozed wickedness. "I guess I'll be seeing you at the hanging." McBride tipped his hat and clucked to his horse as he prepared to cross the bridge into town. As he passed Dietz, he leaned over to whisper to him. "Saw your wife in Wallace. Pretty little piece of baggage. She told me you were McCullough. Reckon she'll be a highly sought after widow." He winked and sauntered on by.

Dietz watched him go. A public execution, so that's what McBride was thinking of. Wait for the men to get all worked up and drunk and then entertain them with a hanging. The arrogant— McBride held so much confidence he didn't even worry about Dietz escaping.

Thank goodness Keely was safely on her way to Spokane. By the time she found out who Dietz was, he'd be long gone. Damn, a wave of guilt consumed him. She would be ruined here in the Valley. Would the people believe that she was the innocent she was, or would they condemn her with him? What would become of her? She would hate him once she found out. He supposed he deserved it, but he didn't know how he would live with the knowledge.

A vision of him swinging at the end of a rope came to mind. They would make him suffer first, that much he knew. And later, mutilate him. He had no intention of letting that happen. He would go down fighting, taking with him as many men as he could. He looked up the hill toward the Gem Mine. He had to find a way to get reinforcements to help Patterson.

Lunn walked away from the boardinghouse seething. He didn't care what that bastard McBride had said or planned. Poynton had given him orders to capture and kill that spy McCullough. He meant to kill him. But it had to be done privately, where Keely would neither see it nor suspect his involvement in it.

He kept picturing her face just after he'd told her— crushed, dazed. He hated that detective for what he'd done, and he would make him pay. Then Keely would be his, forever.

He turned to look back one last time at Keely's doorstep. She'd called him a liar. She'd stomped and shouted and cried and ordered him away. But why shoot the messenger? If only Poynton had done the work instead, but he thought it would be easier coming from someone she knew. Well, Keely wallowed in shock right now, but when she calmed down and realized the truth, she would be eternally grateful to him and run to him for protection. With him at her side, no one would dare harm her or accuse her of any involvement in the detective's duplicity. For himself, Lunn had witnessed her shock firsthand. Genuine shock.

For now he had to find the detective. If all had gone as Poynton commanded, the fake McCullough wouldn't know he had been found out. Sooner or later he'd be back in town, drinking and carrying on and when he did—

Keely stumbled to McCullough's room upstairs, tripping on her skirts, her vision blurred by tears. She'd called Lunn a liar because she had to lash out somehow. But Lunn could not be so vicious. He had to be mistaken—he had to be! But even as she tried to convince herself, fear gnawed at her. He could be right. It explained so much.

She reached the door to McCullough's room and flung it open. She staggered in and went directly to the bed and pulled McCullough's saddlebags from beneath it. Her hand trembled as she traced the engraved *Mc* adorning them.

Please, let Lunn be wrong.

The initials calmed her, gave her hope. How could an imposter become McCullough so completely without planning it? Could someone have had time?

Still on her knees by the bed, she opened the bag, feeling like Pandora, wanting to know, and not. Wanting the world to be like it had been and being afraid the contents of those bags would forever alter it.

She dumped the contents onto the floor. Her letters to McCullough—good. Articles of clothing—nothing unusual. A packet of documents. She untied them and slowly leafed through them, her heart pounding louder with each beat.

McCabe. Who's McCabe?

Letters of introduction, personal papers, all made out to McCabe. A leather wallet, money inside, and a return address for Collin McCabe. A photograph.

She picked up the photograph of a group of men, squinting as she tried to recognize any of them and having no luck. She turned it over. Scribbling on the back identified the men pictured. Ian McCullough. She began trembling, quaking with every part of her being. Then she knew. The man in the picture identified as McCullough was *not* her husband. Lunn had not lied, had not been mistaken.

Her breath came fast and furious, so fast she felt as though she could not breathe.

Dietz calmly dismissed his men to join in the merriment and crossed the bridge to the mine side of the creek. He couldn't be certain who knew he was a private detective, and who didn't, but given a strong enough bravado, he could bluff his way into the woods. Given any luck, he could sneak to the mine and relative safety from there.

He'd just crossed to the edge of the forest when someone hailed him. "McCullough, what are you doing out here alone?" The man, Roberts, was one of his union drinking buddies.

"Patrolling for scabs." Dietz smiled. "Wouldn't want any of them to sneak away."

"Sure enough not!" The man guffawed. "But I thought you'd be heading back to town."

"Why's that?" Dietz tried to sound amused and lighthearted.

"Just saw Lunn Gaffney escorting your wife back into town and she looked mighty upset. She was a yelling and a screaming at him something fierce. Crying, too."

Dietz's heart plummeted into his stomach. Keely was back. His surprise must have shown. Roberts mumbled something about being sorry and backed away. What did Roberts think, that he'd just revealed an affair between them to Dietz?

Keely was back, how? Why? And Gaffney had been with her? Dietz glanced up toward the mine and freedom and back toward town. The Dietz of old wouldn't have given a damn about anyone but himself and the mission. But the man he was now couldn't leave Keely to the union dogs.

Keely wasn't in her bedroom. Dietz ran back through the kitchen and mounted the stairs two at a time. Where was she? They had to get out before the word of his identity spread. The door to his room stood half open. The boardinghouse stood eerily quiet, only the raucous sounds of the party in the street split the silence. Dietz forced himself to the doorway. When he pushed it open it swung silently forward.

She sat on the floor in a puddle of skirts, head bent, back to him, clutching his saddlebags to her chest, the contents spilled around her. She knew. For an eternal instant he stood there. How could he face her hurt, her hate? It took all his effort of will to speak. "Keely."

She straightened her shoulders and turned to face him. Tears streaked her cheeks. What had he done? What a cocky, arrogant son of a bitch he'd been playing with her heart like that, thinking he could get away with it. Nothing he'd ever done had knotted such guilt, such self-loathing. And nothing, not even his mother sending him away, abandoning him, had left such a void in his soul.

"Who are you?" She spoke softly, enunciating each word distinctly. Round-eyed with shock and betrayal, she looked hollow.

Dietz stepped toward her. "There's no time to explain now. I don't know how many of them know who I am, but enough to put me in danger, and you, because of your association with me. We have to be—"

"McCabe?" She traced the inscription on his saddlebag.

The name caught him off guard. He'd used the alias so long ago. "Dietz. John Dietz." He took another step and extended his hand to help her up.

She shrunk back from him. "No." She shook her head. "Whoever you are, I don't know you. Leave me alone. Save yourself if you can."

Damn her! He grabbed her, pulled her to her feet, and shook her. "I'm not leaving you, do you understand? I can't leave you to them. I don't know what they'll think of you, what they'll do to you."

Inches separated their faces. A spark leapt into her eyes as she suddenly wrenched herself away from him. "Damn you! What do you care? You've ruined me, taken everything I had. What does it matter what happens now?"

"Keely—"

"What was this to you, a game?" Her breath came in hard gasps as she spoke.

He had to find some way to calm her, but he had no time. He lunged for her and pulled her into his embrace.

"I hate you. I'll always hate you."

"Twist the knife, Keely. Go ahead. You might not understand what I did, but believe me I had good reason. Someday I'll explain—"

"You'll never be able to explain killing McCullough."

Her words hit him so directly he nearly let go of her. Angry at his own reaction and vulnerability, he cinched his arms tighter around her. "McCullough was a class one bastard. You don't believe me, read through the papers under the mattress, the letters he received here in Idaho.

"He tried to shoot me in the back. I returned fire in self-defense. As for you, McCullough meant to use you like a common whore and leave you when he tired of the sport. He was nothing but—"

"And you haven't?"

"Ah, shit." He swallowed hard. "I never *meant* to take his identity. I seized an opportunity. I saved you." No use explaining further. She'd never believe him.

He dragged her toward the door. She kicked and screamed and spit, but he pulled her from the room and down the stairs to the kitchen. How was he going to get her out of town with her fighting him?

"Listen to me, Keely. I never meant for you to find out. I planned to disappear for good and leave you your good name and reputation and a fat purse of money to live on. But, damn it all, you came back. If you'd stayed on the blasted train like I told you to—"

She stopped struggling. "Let. Me. Go."

He needed to gain her confidence so he released her.

"Let me take you to Spokane. I'll give you enough money to start over somewhere."

"Blast you, McCullough—" She caught her mistake and corrected it quickly. "John Dietz. I don't *want* to start over. I want my life back."

What could he do? What could he say? She asked for something he had no ability to give.

A man crossed in front of the window on the boardwalk outside. The door swung open. Dietz cursed. He'd let the woman distract him from business again. Lunn

Gaffney stood in the doorway wearing surprise plainly on his face.

Before Gaffney had a chance to react, Dietz drew his Colt and grabbed Keely, holding her hostage in front of him as he formed a plan. Maybe there was a way to escape *and* give Keely what she wanted.

He pointed the Colt into Keely's ribs. "Drop your weapon, Gaffney."

Keely squared her shoulders and thrust her head high. "He's bluffing, Lunn. He can't hurt me any more than he already has."

Damn the woman. She knew how to cut him.

A crowd formed behind Gaffney. Gaffney wavered.

"I'll do what it takes to survive. Go ahead and test me." Dietz pulled Keely toward the hall and the back door. "Drop the gun. Slide it over to me."

Gaffney dropped his gun. "We'll get you, traitor. And if you hurt her, I'll make sure you suffer before we kill you."

Dietz laughed. "Hollow promises." He squatted, picked up the gun, straightened, and took another step back. "Call off the union boys behind you."

Gaffney motioned them back.

"Here's the deal, Gaffney. I'm going to leave by the back door, taking Keely with me as a shield. Then I'm going to make my escape in the woods out back. You play nice and stay put, I'll leave her cozy and safe up the hill in the trees out back."

"I'm giving you less than five minutes. Then I'm coming after you." Gaffney squinted angrily at him.

"Better make it fifteen." Dietz dragged Keely down the hall to the back door, feeling every beat of her heart as it pulsed against his arm where he held her. He paused at the door. The back of the boardinghouse stretched wide and empty, but anyone could be hiding around the corner ready to ambush. He had to take the chance. He pulled Keely backward toward the hill and the cover of trees and underbrush. He'd reached the edge when Gaffney burst through the back door of the boardinghouse with a contingency of men backing him up.

"Drop her!" Gaffney trained the sights of a Winchester rifle on Dietz just above Keely's head too close for Dietz's comfort.

Dietz made a split decision. "I'm giving you your life back, lass."

He released Keely, pushing her forward down the hill, below Gaffney's line of fire.

She screamed as Dietz turned and ran for the woods as a shot cracked over his head.

CHAPTER EIGHTEEN

Dietz crashed through the woods in a jolting, heart pounding run, stumbling over underbrush and rough, uneven ground. Damn, he had no plan other than reaching the culvert and sneaking into Patterson's store. Beyond that, he held little hope for escape. But at least he wouldn't die alone. Crazy, jumbled thoughts ran through his mind as he slid down the hillside and ducked into the dry culvert beneath the street. Above him on the hillside brush cracked and men shouted as they pursued him.

He and Patterson could hole up in the store. Eventually the union would charge in. But he and Patterson should be able to take out several men before being killed. Die fighting. Dietz slithered on his belly in a snaky, desperate dance to reach the other side. If the union boys were smart, they'd be looking for him to try and join up with Patterson.

Dietz emerged from the other side of the tunnel. The path to Patterson's back fence was clear except for two passed out, dead drunk terrorists. Too much celebration. Dietz sneaked past them, removed Patterson's loose fence board, and sprinted the distance of the yard into the back of the store.

Mrs. Shipley stood just inside, clutching her boy to her. Both looked frightened and startled.

"Where's Allison?" Dietz asked without preamble.

"He isn't here." Mrs. Shipley pulled her boy closer.

"You can trust me. I'm not after him," Dietz said.

She didn't look as if she believed him and he couldn't blame her.

"Look, I came to stand by him. I know they're after him. They're after me, too."

She wavered, debating whether to believe him or not. He saw it in her face.

A roar of angry voices thundered up the street from outside. The union was coming for Patterson, hundreds of men prepared for a lynching.

"We must hurry." He glanced out the window as he pulled out his Derringer and held it out to her. "Take this and take the boy and lock yourself in your rooms. Tell them we held you hostage if you have to."

Something about his desperate tone and words must have convinced her he wasn't the enemy. She pushed the gun back at him. "He went under the house. Follow me, I'll show you."

She led him to her room and pointed to a chest in the corner. "Help me move this."

He didn't ask questions, just jumped to her assistance. They slid the chest a couple of feet, then Mrs. Shipley bent and removed a square of carpet, revealing a hole just big enough for a man to slide through.

"Go," she said. "I'll take care of the rest. God be with you."

He ducked into the hole and hit dusty, musty earth. An instant later the light from above disappeared as Mrs. Shipley replaced the carpet and the trunk.

"What took you so long?" Patterson drawled from the darkness.

Dietz started. "Shit, Patterson, what do you mean to do, kill me?"

Patterson laughed quietly. "Not me. What happened? How'd you end up here?"

"Dan McBride blew into town and recognized me." Dietz's eyes adjusted to the darkness. He and Patterson rested directly under the middle of the store. "You got a plan to get out of here?"

"See where there's a hole big enough to let us out and a path clear enough to give us a half-assed chance of reaching the Gem."

A mob of men shouting in unison, followed by the tramping of feet in the store overhead, prevented Dietz from replying. Dallas's voice drifted down, demanding Mrs. Shipley tell them where Patterson was. Dietz held his breath as Mrs. Shipley spoke. "I haven't seen him since last night."

"Liar. Miss Olson saw him sneak back here from the restaurant this morning. Where is he?"

"Why do you want him?"

Dietz admired Mrs. Shipley's calm and courage.

"He's a dirty private detective and we intend to burn him at the stake as a warning to others like him."

"Why didn't you kill him yesterday when you had a good chance?" Mrs. Shipley, bless her, sought to buy them time.

Dietz could almost hear Dallas sigh with exasperation. "Yesterday the time wasn't right, but it is now and we will find him so you might as well tell or it will go hard with you."

Dietz waited, silently praying that Dallas wouldn't hurt her or the little boy. Seconds ticked by. Her little boy bawled for all he was worth, not that Dietz could blame him. Had he been five, he would have been tempted to the same course of action. But Dietz worried that the boy would give away their whereabouts.

"Do your worst," Mrs. Shipley said. "I don't know where he is."

"We'll find the bastard. He's in the house."

Footsteps pounded out overhead, fanning out throughout the house. Dietz heard the back door slam shut. They were in the backyard.

Patterson motioned to him for them to be moving on. They crawled on their hands and knees, looking for an opening out. The only one was under the boardwalk, which was raised about a foot above the ground. Patterson dropped to his stomach and led the way, snaking to the east toward the union hall. Dietz dropped down and followed him.

Up ahead, Patterson moved slowly. Dietz assumed Patterson worried about being seen. Dietz sure did. Some of the cracks in the boardwalk overhead were as wide as an inch. He cursed the shoddy workmanship and weathered, shrunken boards as he ate dust and moved along. His mouth went dry—too dry to make spit, or mud of the dirt he breathed in. He cursed again. He must be more scared than he thought.

When Dietz cared to look up, soles of shoes swarmed over the walks as thickly as space permitted. Once in a while Dietz caught sight of someone's eyes or face and his heart stopped. But no one returned his look. Likely they didn't expect someone to be under the boardwalks. Fools.

The talk he heard as he inched along related to the explosion at the Frisco Mill and number of scabs who had been killed when the union blew it up with giant powder. The voices were angry and agitated and laced with bloodlust. Dietz had no desire to be their next victim.

Patterson stopped ahead of him. Dietz heard an Irish brogue speak out. "Faith and why don't they send that spalpeen out? I'm wanting to spit in his face, the dirty traitor."

Dietz restrained himself from laughing. *Go ahead. Spit in his face, fellow. He's right beneath you.*

Patterson started crawling again. Dietz moved with him. He figured they'd covered about two store lengths since leaving Patterson's. The crowd on the boardwalk had thinned considerably. Suddenly, Dietz recognized Gaffney's voice above him. Patterson kept moving, but Dietz heard Keely's voice and froze.

He looked up to see Gaffney hanging onto Keely's arm, a gun in his free hand. "I'm going to kill him, Keely. I promise you. And then I'm going to take care of you, don't you worry. It doesn't matter to me about him. It wasn't your fault."

Dietz had come to a halt at Keely's feet, just at the tip of her skirt. Another few inches and he'd have a fine view of all he used to own. Keely didn't answer Gaffney. Instead, she looked down, right into Dietz's eyes. Her cheeks were dusty and streaked with tears. When she saw him her eyes flew open and her mouth made a nice round oh.

It's all over now, Dietz thought as he waited for her to turn him in.

They stared at each other for an instant that seemed severely long and far too short. His heart thudded in his ears as he lay there waiting for her to get it over with, willing Patterson far away as he did.

Gaffney reached for Keely, tucked his hand under her chin and drew her face up to his. Jealousy thundered through Dietz as Gaffney kissed her. Keely stepped into Gaffney's embrace, covering Dietz with her skirts. Suddenly he had an eyeful of her, petticoats and all. Just as quickly, Keely deliberately scraped her boots on the sidewalk above, showering him with dust.

He blinked too late and cursed silently. His vision blurred, obscured with debris. His eyes watered and teared up. He blinked trying to clear his eyes, and cursed some more. The saying *Here's mud in your eye* had never seemed more appropriate. The cursed woman, what did she mean to do?

"I've got to go, Lunn." She broke away from Gaffney's kiss. "Go join the men. I'm going to take a walk over to Lacy's and make sure she and the children are all right."

"Are you sure, Keely?" Gaffney asked.

"I need another woman's comfort right now. That's all. And she could use my help."

"Sure." Lunn sounded unconvinced, almost hurt. "Take care now, Keely."

"You, too, Lunn. I need you." She stomped again on the boardwalk over Dietz's head. "Horrible, nasty bugs," she said as she ground her heel into the wood above him. Then she began walking very slowly.

Damn. She was helping him escape? He crawled along beneath her skirts, keeping pace with her. She didn't look down again, and he gave up looking up. Suddenly, it didn't seem respectful. He couldn't figure her out. She certainly hated him. Maybe she just didn't want any more bloodshed. He crawled another twenty-five feet or so to the opening beneath the saloon. Where the hell was Patterson?

Dietz came to an opening large enough to crawl through and get under the saloon. Here was his escape route. Keely had saved him. He glanced up once and tried to signal his thanks, but she ignored him and kept walking. Right out of his life.

Patterson waited for him beneath the saloon as Dietz rolled out from the boardwalk. Built on piles, the

saloon stood four feet off the ground, which felt suddenly spacious. Dietz had never been so grateful to be
able to get up on all fours. He was damned tired of
playing snake.

Patterson signaled for Dietz to follow him and they
took off for the far side of the saloon and the daylight
that peeked through. Slash, brush, mud, treetops and
stumps covered the ground, making the going hard. At
the far end of the saloon Patterson paused. They both
checked their weapons.

"I lost my gold watch chain," Patterson said, almost
incredulously. As if that was the worst thing that had
happened all day.

Dietz cocked a brow. "Want to go back and look for
it?"

"Hell, no!" Patterson sputtered and made like he was
trying to spit, but nothing came out. "Always heard a
man can't spit when he's scared. My mouth is dry as
cotton. Guess I'm scared with a capital S."

Dietz laughed. "You're just now getting scared?"
Dietz shook his head. "I lost my spit back there at your
store."

Patterson gave a returning laugh and slapped Dietz
on the shoulder. "Let's move out."

"I'm with you."

Three union men stood at the corner of the saloon,
looking back up Main Street at the crowd. Dietz stared
at their backs. Killing them would be easy. But he held
back. It felt too much like cold-blooded murder. Only
cowards fired from behind.

Dietz glanced due south. Fifty yards in the distance the high railroad grade blocked the view of the Gem Mine and relative safety. But scaling the high grade would place them between two fires. Chances were that the scabs would mistake them for the enemy and open fire on them. A little to the left of them a stream flowed through a culvert under the railroad grade.

Patterson must have been thinking the same thing. Dietz watched his trigger finger twitch.

Finally Patterson spoke. "We don't want our friends up at the mine shooting us. The creek's our best bet." Patterson pointed to the union guards. "If we have to, I think we can fool them into thinking we're out to take a few potshots at scabs," Patterson said. "You lead."

Dietz nodded. They started out at a slow run, stooped like hunters going after game. Though they were literally open-backed targets, they couldn't look back for fear the three guards would recognize their faces and shoot. Dietz hoped the guards weren't suspicious types, because he and Patterson looked as suspicious as hell. Dietz held his Colt over his head to keep it dry and plunged into the culvert, Patterson right behind him swearing. Dietz heard the crack of a rifle shot behind him.

Keely knew the instant he left the boardwalk, but she kept walking to the end of the saloon in case anyone had noticed him or her own odd, slow walk. Did he mean to escape out back of the saloon to the Gem Mine into the hills above? Her heart pounded in her ears trying to drown out her traitorous thoughts. *Run!*

She took a deep breath and dabbed at her moist eyes with the back of her hand, blinking to hold back tears. Why should she cry for him? Why would he want her to? Blast her weak self, but she couldn't stop herself, not completely. Part of her hated him, but part of her couldn't forget him, or stop wanting him, or believe his perfidy was real.

When she'd looked down and seen him staring at her from beneath the boardwalk, she'd been so surprised she'd nearly given him away. Yet when she'd looked into his impregnable eyes, so calm, no pleading, just staring, waiting for her to act, she couldn't, and that ate at her conscience. He had betrayed her; used her to work against everything she believed in. By turning him in she could have proven her loyalty to the union. But she kept picturing him as he'd looked such a short time ago in his room at the boardinghouse, begging her to escape with him. Just conscientious? But the expression in his eyes, his pleading tone—

Why did she still hold onto that slim thread of hope that he loved her? What perversity made her ache for him? Whatever his motives, she reasoned he had some honor. He *had* risked his life for hers.

Her thoughts returned to the boardwalk. Lunn making promises to avenge her honor, and the traitor looking up her skirts. She couldn't bear it. Anger had overwhelmed her. The intimacy of the detective's position infuriated her, reminding her of past liberties he'd taken. She'd kicked dust in his face so he could not look, to handicap him and assuage her own guilt over helping him. She'd even let Lunn kiss her. The sour taste of his kiss still sat on her lips.

A shot thundered out from behind the saloon. Keely screamed and began shaking so uncontrollably that she could barely stand. *The union men are shooting at him.* She heard their shouts and curses. *Oh, John Dietz, run.*

She lifted her skirts and ran across the street toward home. *If they've killed him, I don't want to see it.*

"Buzzed just past my head," Patterson said.

Dietz looked back to see the three guards, all Swedes and obviously drunk, taking aim at them. He and Patterson plunged ahead into the boxed culvert. Water edged up to his armpits, cold and angry. The force of the current nearly knocked him over. He cursed again as he reached for a timber to brace himself and moved ahead, grabbing from one upright timber to the next to steady himself against the raging water. They moved through the culvert, a distance of close to fifty feet, fighting the current the entire way. At last, panting, they came out beneath a house on the other side only to be greeted by a large Swedish woman who, looking surprised and confused to see them emerge, called out to Patterson.

"Mr. Allison what were you doing under my house with your friend there?"

"Prowling around for a little exercise, ma'am, and hunting for scabs. You be careful now. You got yourself a perfect hiding place under there. Wouldn't want you jumped."

"No, sir." She retreated back inside.

Dietz eyed the distance from the house to the mine. Another two hundred yards in the open separated them from the scab fort—high ricks of cordwood with portholes. They could still get shot full of holes. Patterson looked at him. Dietz shrugged and the two took off running. The guards at the fort stopped them about twenty feet away.

"Drop your guns and come with your hands up."

"We're friends," Dietz replied evenly.

"Don't make a damned bit of difference. If you don't drop those guns, your heads go off."

Dietz tossed his Colt onto the ground and Patterson his Winchester. When they got a little closer, one of the guards apparently recognized them. "Say, aren't you those detectives who come here the other night?"

"We are indeed," Patterson said tiredly.

"Well come on in, men, before the union bastards fill you with lead."

Keely huddled on her bed, knees pulled close to her chest, trying to ball herself up tightly enough to stop the shaking. They hadn't killed him. She'd heard angry men shouting in the streets for backups to stop the traitors. Somehow he'd escaped, at least for the time being. But how was he going to get out of the Valley with every road, every path blockaded? If they caught him—

She shuddered.

Even if he made it to the mine he wouldn't be safe. She'd heard Lunn talking about the union plans to storm it, killing anyone who stood in their way. And traitors, she added silently. She shut her eyes, trying to block out the hideous images of the day. The shootings, the blood, the hatred.

A knock at the door startled her. "Mrs. McCullough?" Big Frank called out.

So not everyone had heard. Had she ever really been Mrs. McCullough? Was she a widow now?

She forced herself to reply. "Yes, what do you want?"

"The doc sent me to fetch you. We've got us a lot of wounded men and the doc's needing a nurse."

She straightened and sat up slowly. "Tell him I'll be right over."

"I'll wait here and escort you over, ma'am. It isn't safe in the streets."

No, indeed, and it wasn't safe in her troubled mind, either. "I appreciate it, Big Frank. Just give me a moment to wash up and I'll be right out."

"I'll wait in the kitchen."

He shuffled away as she walked to the washbasin and rinsed her mouth out with soap, trying vainly to wash away Lunn's kiss. She didn't want any man's caresses, not ever again. No one's but *the traitor's.*

Such a pity, because she wouldn't be getting them. *McCullough is dead.*

Shortly after Dietz and Patterson arrived, a union man came up the hill waving a white rag as a flag of truce. He demanded that Monihan surrender the mine.

Monihan refused. Good man. Dietz had no desire to be turned over to the cutthroats who wanted his hide.

"Then we'll blow you to bloody hell!" the union man shouted back. "We'll give you another hour or so to think it over." He departed.

Dietz sat across from Monihan in his office.

Monihan stood at the window, looking out back up the hill. "They're sending squads of men up the mountain to the main tunnel." He sounded defeated.

Dietz feared he would give up.

Patterson sat next to Dietz and a fellow named Fred Carter. Fred sat with his leg propped up on a stool, his foot heavily bandaged where his heel had been shot off. He was the only scab to escape from the Frisco Mill and damned lucky at that. He'd run the distance of the railroad grade right out in the open with lead showering him.

"Looks like they're using the same plan they originally tried at the Frisco—capture the main tunnel and then send a tram down loaded with dynamite and a long fuse. It would have worked at the Frisco, but they made the fuse too short." Carter shook his head. "I still don't know how they finally managed to blow the thing up."

"Seems like the only thing to do is go up the mountain and tie a post across the tram tracks so that it will derail any tram they send down," Dietz said. "I'll go."

What did he have to lose? He'd already lost everything important to him. He pushed thoughts of Keely away. Alone again, with no one to give a hoot about his hide, wasn't that life?

"I'm going with you," Patterson said. "It'll take two men to lift the post and cover each other."

* * *

The doc had turned the back room at Daxon's Saloon into a hospital. It stank of whiskey, body odor, and blood. The injured men disgusted Keely almost as much as the injuries. Most of the injuries weren't caused by upholding the glorious cause, but by carousing and drunken brawling. Those directly related to the incident repelled Keely nearly as much. The violence, the violence. She'd lost so much to this cause—Michael, and now McCullough, both McCulloughs.

She steeled herself to washing wounds and applying clean linen bandages. Perspiration pooled in rings under her arms in the hot, sticky room. Flies hummed in the air, buzzing around. Looking for carrion? There was plenty of it here and a goodly dose of hatred, greed, and bloodlust to match.

The men capable of speaking bragged about killing and maiming scabs. Suddenly the cause meant nothing to her. She wished herself miles away from here, miles away from herself.

Two union men came in carrying a groaning man by his arms and legs between them. They dumped him on a table and left.

The doctor examined the new arrival and turned to Keely. "Leave that fellow and come bathe this man. He's got a slug in his shoulder we'll have to get out immediately."

Keely drew a fresh basin of water and went to the man's side.

"Let me know when he's ready." The doc walked off to another patient.

Filth covered the new arrival. Keely doubted he'd ever bathed. When she bent over him, his breath stank of alcohol. Blood plastered his shirt to his body. As she cut away the sleeve, he spoke to her. "I took a direct hit in the action, but I think I got me a scab."

"Did you now?"

He disgusted her. She removed his shirt and began sponging his shoulder, taking away the caked blood like she'd once done for McCullough. *Oh, McCullough.*

"Name's Riley." He slurred his words.

"Uh, huh. Hold still, Mr. Riley. This may a hurt a bit as I clean up your shoulder."

"I'm tough." But he winced when she dabbed at the open wound. He stared at her as she worked, looking like he was trying to place her. "You must be an angel of mercy."

"Hardly."

"You got a nice, gentle touch."

"So I've been told." She kept working.

"I'd sure like a little more of it, when I'm feeling better." He was staring at her chest and the open collar of her dress as she bent over him. Before she could reply, recognition lit his expression. "Wait a minute. I know who you are—you're the detective's whore. Maybe you'd like to be mine for a time." He reached with his good arm to touch the tip of her bust.

She took the cloth she was holding and pressed it into his wound with startling force. Riley yelped.

"Speak to me like that again and I'll make this pain pale in comparison to what I'll do to you. I'm nobody's whore, never have been. The traitor duped me same as everyone else."

The doc came over to her and, taking her by the shoulders, led her away. "I'll see to him now. You look like you could use a rest. Take a few minutes to compose yourself, then come see me and I'll give you a new assignment."

So it had begun. They didn't fully trust her. Maybe they never would. Had Dietz been right, had he given her back her life? Was it even possible?

She hugged herself and stepped out onto the back porch and stared up at the mountain.

Her anger at the detective hadn't convinced them of her innocence. But how could they suspect her torn feelings about him? She stared at the ground, past her skirt stained with men's blood. What was going to happen to her now?

CHAPTER NINETEEN

D ietz lashed his end of the pole to the tram tracks. "You about finished, Patterson?"

"Been done for hours, Dietz." Patterson stared at a man guarding the station over the mill.

"Something the matter?" Dietz stood and followed Patterson's line of sight.

"Can't be sure, but I'm pretty certain that fellow is a union spy. Keep your back covered as we make our way to the tunnel."

"Shit. We're in plain view of town. We'll need to cover more than our backs." All too aware of the town below, Dietz forced himself to keep from looking for the sway of Keely's colorful skirts, the swish of her walk.

Stay inside, Keely. Where it's safe.

They slid down the steep hillside to the tunnel. The dry cheatgrass made their path slick. Damn grass stuck in his socks. Everything irritated him, but why should-n't it?

At the tunnel Patterson pointed out another spy. "We'll report him to Monihan when we get back."

"Appears they've got more spies than we do. Makes a fellow feel awfully safe up here."

Patterson laughed. "Course they do. There's but two of us. As for safety, when have we ever been safe, my friend? And when have we ever wanted to be?"

"You got a point."

When they reached Monihan's office again, any op-timism Dietz might have felt melted away. Ed Kinney sat in Monihan's chair, holding a message he'd received over the wires.

Monihan didn't bother with any formalities. "Post in place?" He didn't wait for an answer. He must have as-sumed that since they'd come back whole everything went well. "Mr. Kinney brings word from the owners—to prevent any further damage to operations we're to surrender the mine."

"Operations be damned." Dietz pointed to the mine. "What about the lives involved here? You can't turn your men over to those cutthroats."

Monihan turned to Patterson. "What do you think, Patterson?"

"I agree with Dietz."

Monihan sighed, took a deep breath and blew it out again. Heavy worry lines etched his face. He shook his head. "I agree with you boys, but given the circumstances, what else can I do? I have to surrender and hope for the best."

"I'm sure as hell not surrendering."

Damn these men and their greed. Are material goods all that are important?

Dietz looked around the room, meeting each man's gaze directly. "I'm not surrendering alive. I'll fight it out alone if I have to."

Patterson stepped forward. "You won't have to. I'm going with you. I'm not turning myself over to them either. Anyone else with us?"

No one moved.

Finally Monihan spoke. "Ask the rest of the men. Then I'll give you and whoever else is going with you a fifteen-minute head start before surrendering."

They didn't find any other takers. Patterson and Dietz slipped through the heavy brush and timber up a side canyon to the southwest, finally finding a secluded place to rest.

"Let's wait and watch the surrender while we catch our breath," Patterson said. "No use missing the fun."

They watched as over a hundred scabs marched to the depot platform and surrendered their arms. A loud cheer shook the Valley, echoing up the canyon.

"Shit," Dietz said. His heart hammered inside his chest, banging away a primal rhythm of fear.

The union men lined the scabs up and inspected them, pausing to look each man directly in the face.

"How much do you want to bet that they're looking for us?" Dietz asked.

"Not a thing. I agree with you." Patterson stood and picked up his rifle. "Let's get moving."

Keely left the saloon when the scabs marched into town and surrendered. She stood in the crowd, elbow to elbow with the men. Finally she saw Mrs. Shipley and worked her way through the crowd to join her.

Keely pressed her hands together, trying to hide the shaking. She scanned the faces of the men on the platform, afraid she might find *him* among them. The union might let most of the scabs go, but they'd kill Mr. Allison and John Dietz.

Lunn jumped up on the platform and inspected the men, looking for weapons, looking for him.

"Don't worry. They won't find him," Mrs. Shipley said softly. "They're much too smart to let themselves be taken prisoner."

How could Mrs. Shipley be so certain that Keely wished him no harm? Woman's intuition, or did Keely have sympathy written all over her face?

On the platform Lunn was shouting. "The bastards must have gone over the hill."

Keely's knees went weak. She nearly collapsed with relief.

Lunn shouted orders dispatching men. "I want every road, path, and buggy trail into Wallace guarded. We'll find them."

He turned toward the crowd and caught Keely's eye, smiling at her. She forced herself to smile back, but it didn't reach her heart.

Let him go, Lunn. Show me you have some humanity left in you. Maybe then I can learn to care for you the way you want.

But a demonic hatred shined on Lunn's face, a manic need to punish.

Keely turned away. She wasn't certain she ever wanted to see the detective again, or that she could even face him. Cold, so cold. But she didn't want to witness his death, certainly not the one the union planned.

Run, John Dietz. Wherever you are, run.

"You should be in theater, Patterson." Dietz lowered his voice and mimicked Patterson's threatening tone. "Now you take the one on the right, and I'll kill the one on the left." Dietz chuckled. His sides still hurt from laughing at the sight of the last two union dogs they'd encountered sliding down the steep gulch cracking brush and running for their lives, frightened away by the two of them with their guns drawn. The day had held little humor. Dietz took what he could. "You'd think they would have a little more courage—their side outnumbering us by about a thousand to two."

"You would think." Patterson made his way cautiously through the underbrush.

Darkness had fallen some time ago and the going had become more treacherous. Fatigue pulled at every muscle.

Patterson stopped and pointed below into the distance. "The wagon trail above Wallace. We're about a half-mile from Wallace on the depot side of town. If we can hop a train—"

"We'll be home free," Dietz finished. He surveyed the road, trying to get a fix on it. Four small figures carrying rifles came into focus. "Look, over there. Didn't think they'd be foolish enough to leave even a wagon track unguarded." Dietz slapped his hat against his leg. "I'm tired as the devil."

Patterson stood quietly a moment. "What do you want to do? Circumventing them will add miles to our trip—dangerous miles."

"It's dark. They won't be able to recognize us. I say we bluff them. I'm dead tired. The worst they can do is put me out of my misery."

"I'm with you. You take the two on the left and I'll take the two on the right."

Laughter bubbled up in him, splitting his sides. Though he tried to suppress it, Dietz couldn't help himself.

"What's so funny?"

Dietz shook his head. The stress made everything seem funny. "You kill the one on the right, I'll kill the one on the left. Shit, Patterson, can't you be more original?"

Keely sat on her bed in a pile of McCullough's things—the real McCullough. She was so weary, but sleep wouldn't come, not until she knew the truth. The private detective, Dietz, had lied to her about so much, had he told the truth about McCullough? *About anything?*

She kept remembering the detective's words, *McCullough was a first-class bastard.* He didn't even bother denying he'd killed McCullough.

She shuddered, trying to force the brutal images of killings from her mind. On top of everything, he had murdered McCullough, the man she had fallen in love with from his letters. Numbness prevented her from really understanding. In her mind the real McCullough and the detective combined—one man, not two.

But the detective had killed McCullough and assumed his identity. How could it be accidental? There hadn't been time for explanation, but John Dietz had claimed he hadn't meant for things to happen. Why then did he have McCullough's things in his possession?

Could John Dietz have fooled her so completely? Could he really be as evil as it seemed he was?

Patterson swaggered boldly next to Dietz. A few hundred feet more and they'd be in the relative safety of the train depot. The electric lights illuminating the train yard made Dietz nervous. He felt exposed, vulnerable to recognition and attack. They'd walked right past the four union boys without a problem. But Dietz never felt safe with his back exposed. The four union boys hadn't even spoken to each other as he and Patterson had walked past. Too casual.

Dietz glanced back over his shoulder. The two he was supposed to be covering ran over to talk to Patterson's two.

"We're in trouble," Dietz said.

In unison, he and Patterson jumped into the waist deep creek that ran by the station. Dietz cursed silently. *Damn, icy water again.* The creek ran about forty feet wide, but darkness covered most of it.

The union boys called out from behind him, shouting for the two to turn themselves in. *Like hell.* There wasn't time to make much distance. They waded to a dark spot across the creek and hauled up the bank into the timber to wait things out as the four men came running around the bluff into the light.

Keely twisted her garnet wedding ring around her finger, trembling, uncertain what she should do, uncertain whose ring she wore, not sure she wanted to wear either man's token. Letters covered the bed, some crumpled in anger, some tear-stained, others merely tossed aside.

Oh, McCullough, what a terrible bastard you were!

John Dietz had told the truth, the awful, horrible truth. McCullough had had a mistress, one whom he beat and left. One who pressed charges? Was that what sent McCullough her way, his desire to escape the law? Why had he written to her? Why had he proposed?

His letters, the journal he kept, both detailed a vigorous, violent life, and portrayed a man bent on destruction, a man without conscience or compassion. Whatever mysteries his letters evoked, they solved one puzzle—Michael's sudden falling out with him. Michael must have realized the truth about him.

McCullough's words, told in his own voice, repulsed her now. In a way John Dietz *had* saved her, or had he?

She stared at the ring again, beautiful, delicate, expensive. The marriage could hardly be legal. She was Keely Byrne. *Again.* What man would want her now? What man besides Lunn? Why couldn't she cry?

The light of the depot yard surrounded the union boys. They kept looking toward the cliff, their movements comical. Dietz could tell from their puzzled expressions, and the way they gestured, that they thought Patterson and he had disappeared into a crevice or something. But the miners knew they hadn't had time to get far.

Look under your noses, boys.

Fewer than a hundred feet separated them. Dietz held his breath, willing himself not to laugh. At last the boys left, running off in the direction of town.

"Probably going for reinforcements," Patterson said. "Let's forget the train depot and move out toward the hotel."

The ease with which they reached the Carter Hotel where the mine owners stayed surprised Dietz, but the reception they got did not. Two owners who had not fled town met with them at the back steps of the hotel. They begged them to leave, fearing for their own lives if they were caught with the detectives.

When they had gotten out of earshot, Dietz spoke, "Self-centered sons-of-bitches. It's not like our hides aren't in danger."

Patterson laughed. "Yeah, but we're paid for it. Come on, let's sneak up to French's private quarters and see if Ed Kinney is here."

"I hope he is. I'm hungry as the devil." Dietz followed Patterson into the hotel. "You know, you interrupted my breakfast."

"Yeah? My heart breaks."

The welcome Kinney gave them gave Dietz more pleasure than the owners', but the food Kinney offered stank.

"Sardines and crackers?" Dietz asked.

Kinney laughed. "Haven't had much inclination to go to the general store lately." He shoved a pair of dry long underwear at Dietz. "Put these on."

Dietz laughed again as Kinney handed a similar pair to Patterson. "Sure glad you listened to your mother and remembered to pack clean underwear."

"Who says it's clean?" The humor left Kinney's face. "You boys had better get moving. The union has guards posted everywhere. If anybody saw you come in, it won't be long before they come looking for you."

Minutes later they prowled through the streets of Wallace and headed for heavy timber. They seemed to trek on forever, but at last, about three miles outside of Wallace, up a side canyon to the southwest, they decided to try for a little sleep.

Sleep, Dietz thought. The way he felt now, he would be sleeping through the rest of his life—the rest of his life without Keely. What was she doing now? Was she safe? He said a little prayer—maybe she had rubbed off on him—as he stretched out on the hard ground and closed his eyes.

The sun stood full above Dietz and Patterson, beating down with fervent intensity. Flies buzzed around Dietz, no doubt hoping to land on his hot, damp skin. He swatted at them silently, irritated and tired, eager to get out of the sun. But the shade had its own demons—mosquitoes out for blood. Sticky residue left by aphids covered his arms and face and sleeves where bushes had slapped him as he walked by.

"Where's this German fellow you've been talking about, Patterson? I'm hungry. The crackers and sardines Kinney gave us didn't keep me the night."

"Have a few more huckleberries." Patterson wiped his sleeve across his face, cleaning away the sweat that dripped down.

Wild huckleberry bushes surrounded them. Most of the berries weren't yet ripe. Those that were, were tiny, not hearty fodder for a hungry man. "Sweet as they are, a man could pick all day and not make a meal out of those things."

They came to the edge of a clearing. Patterson stopped and pointed to a small, crude cabin.

"You sure he's not a union man?" Dietz asked.

"He's union, but opposed to the way the union's been operating this last year." Patterson adjusted his hat and reached for his trusty Colt's 45.

"Can we trust him?"

Patterson shrugged. "We'll find out. Cover me."

"Nothing like risking one's life for the promise of a meal."

"You complaining?"

"Me?" Dietz smiled. "Hell, no. Move out."

The German spotted Patterson and stepped out of his cabin, rifle drawn, almost before the first bush snapped beneath Patterson's foot.

"Who's there?" The German squinted into the sun.

Patterson stepped out from the forest edge.

Recognition flitted across the German's face. "Mr. Allison! What are you doing in these parts? You're a wanted man. Get yourself in here before someone spots you." He waved him over.

"News travels fast." Patterson motioned toward Dietz. "I've brought a friend, Dutchy."

"The other traitor?" Dutchy didn't seem surprised when Patterson nodded. "Well, bring him with you." Dutchy swore under his breath. "What a confounded business this is. If they catch you, you're dead, that much I know. And if they catch me helping you boys, I'm dead, too."

Best Dietz could tell, Dutchy looked worried. His gaze kept flitting toward the forest.

"Something the matter, Dutchy?" Patterson asked.

Dutchy let out a long breath. "I shouldn't be helping you boys. My partner's due back from town any minute. He's a stubborn Irish cuss. Not nearly as kind-hearted as me. He went to town to take part in the riots. He sees you boys, he'll kill you."

"Look, Dutchy, we're hungry. Give us something to eat and we'll be on our way." Patterson sounded tired.

Dutchy shook his head. "Not time for that. You fellows need rest. Come with me. I got a place where you'll be safe for a bit." He headed out around the cabin to a small stone shack just a few feet from the back door. He stopped and unlocked the door. "We keep our valuables in here, but he isn't likely to look in here for now." Dutchy held the keys out to Dietz.

Dietz hesitated.

Dutchy stepped back from the door and shook the keys at Dietz. "You can lock yourself in. I'll bring you some grub directly."

What the—? Lock himself prisoner in a dingy stone hut? Dietz didn't like it, not one bit, but presently his options were limited. He took the keys and stepped back and extended a gentlemanly arm to indicate Patterson should go first.

Dutchy headed back to the main cabin. Once inside the hut, Patterson and Dietz locked themselves in and settled down to rest. They sat in silence a few minutes—a heavy, oppressive silence that allowed too much time for thought.

"Heard his partner's a dynamiter." Patterson's eyes danced as he spoke. "What do you think, Dietz? Is he waiting for his hotheaded Irish friend to come back so they can blow us both to kingdom-come with giant powder?"

The correct response should have been, *I hope not.* But death held some appeal right then. "We're rats in a trap. But he *did* trust us with the key. Hardly the move of a man bent on murder."

Just then Dutchy called to them. "There's a tray of food outside the door. Hurry and take it in before Mickey gets back." Then he scuttled away.

Dietz pulled the food in. Moments later they each sat with a cup of coffee and a plate piled high with food.

"Last supper of a condemned man?" Patterson shifted his plate on his lap.

"Stop trying to raise my spirits." Dietz set his coffee
down. "I was condemned long ago, now I'm surely
damned as well."

"Got your own demons?" Patterson asked between
bites.

"What do you think they've done to her?" Why
couldn't he push his worries away?

"To whom? Miss Byrne?"

"Mrs. McCullough." Dietz laughed then, at himself,
at the situation. It rang hollowly off the walls. "I left
her there."

He ran his fingers through his hair, raking it so it
stood at odd angles. He didn't care about anything but
her. He rested his head in his hand. "I left her there. I
left her to the dogs."

"They won't hurt her—"

"The hell they won't!" He paused. "She wouldn't
come with me. Not that I couldn't understand her sentiments at that moment." He shook his head again, be-
rating himself. "I should have hauled her pretty little
ass out of there. Fought her every step of the way if
that's what it took." He looked around at the cold,
stone walls. "If that's what it took."

Patterson shook his head. "You'd have gotten both
of you killed. She made her choice."

"A choice she would never have been forced to make
without me." Dietz pushed his plate away. "Is what I've
chosen any better? Trapped, hunted like an animal,
wracked with worry about her. What if they hurt her?"

He pounded the dirt floor. "How can I live with myself? I chose my own safety over hers." He leaned back against the wall.

What did Patterson know of guilt? What did anybody? Dietz could blame whomever or whatever he wanted—circumstances, improper upbringing, a mother who abandoned him, but, still, it all came down to personal accountability. Maybe the detective agency had taught him that; where else he could have learned it, he couldn't imagine. All he knew was that he had made a choice to leave her. And he missed her, longed for her, worried about her. Life would never be the same without her. Who could have known it would be this hard? If only he could have escaped without her ever discovering his identity. Left her with dignity and pleasant memories, maybe then he wouldn't be feeling so low. Or maybe he only kidded himself.

"Does the ache ever go away?" Dietz spoke without thinking. He didn't want to appear weak and foolish before Patterson.

Patterson snorted and shook his head. "You're talking about missing her?" He sounded sympathetic. "Is that a rhetorical question?" He took a long, slow sip of coffee. He looked miles away with his thoughts.

"I have no right to, but I feel like a blasted widower myself. Like Blackbeard himself." Dietz fixed his gaze on the wall above Patterson's head. He couldn't look his fellow agent in the eye just now. "I killed her. Not physically, though God knows what will happen to her now. I killed something in her—something good and hopeful. Optimism, trust. Hell, I don't know what, just something I'd never experienced before. Something I had no right to." He stared vacantly, confronting the dark thoughts tormenting him.

"I don't mean to sound egotistical. It's not like Keely won't survive. It's not like I think she can't ever be happy again. It's that she won't be the same, and I'm responsible." He took an absentminded sip of coffee gone cold.

"Part of me, selfish bastard that I am, doesn't want her to forget me." He laughed at himself. "What a fool I am. It isn't likely she'll ever forget me, after what I've done to her. But that's not the way I want her remembering me."

"Never is," Patterson said.

"At the time, I thought I was doing the right thing, Patterson. The only thing I could do. I held her hostage." He gulped. Her expression, the feel of her in his arms, haunted his thoughts. "I tried to make them believe I had duped her along with the rest of them, that she had no part in all this. That she was innocent.

"Now, I can't be sure I did right. I was only trying to give her back her life, atone for messing things up." He rubbed his hand over the stubble on his face. "It was the hardest thing I ever did." Finally, he looked into Patterson's eyes. Maybe what people said was true. Maybe confession really was good for the soul. At that moment, he felt lighter, less burdened. "You lost your wife, but at least you have no guilt, no regrets to contend with."

Patterson snorted again. "Don't I? I watched my Mamie die slowly, wither away."

Dietz tried to interrupt, but Patterson cut him short with a gesture. "It wasn't the watching that I regret, nothing I could have done about that. It was the leaving her alone while I was off in the field. It's knowing that she waited faithfully for me while I consorted with all types of women in the name of the job.

"Sometimes I imagine what my thoughts would have been had things been reversed. It's knowing I left her alone with thoughts and fears no wife should have to have, and that she loved me still and waited." Patterson took a heavy breath.

The room felt close and hot around Dietz, weighted with Patterson's confessions and his own guilt.

"My job and my love of it deprived her of my protection and company when she needed it most. The only comfort I gave her was my paycheck." Patterson shook his head. "I left her alone to raise little Viola. Now that Mamie's gone the poor little thing's being raised by her aunt and uncle. Still, it's a better life than I could give her."

Patterson stretched. "Maybe you're lucky, Dietz. Being a detective is a life more suited to a single man. Didn't I warn you not to mess around with marriage?"

He sure had. Why hadn't Dietz listened?

Patterson paused. "No regrets, eh? Maybe you aren't as smart as I thought. Life is full of regrets. It's learning how to live with them that makes the man."

Lunn sat in Keely's kitchen. She felt his gaze on her as she performed her chores by rote. Some things never changed. Or maybe they did, you just had to look beneath the surface. But she didn't want to look, because when she did, she saw things she didn't want to, things like the open lust in Lunn's eyes. Like his ebullience over the violence and the victory.

When she pictured herself outside her body, looking in at the scene with the dispassionate eye of observer, she could almost believe that she had skipped back in time to just before the detective had arrived. But when she came back to herself she felt the hole John Dietz's absence had left, and the odd skew to her universe.

"You still wearing his ring?" Lunn twisted in his chair, following her movements.

She turned to stare at him. "It's valuable. I didn't know what else to do with it."

Wear it for the rest of my life? Keep it to torment myself?

Lunn frowned. "Give it to me for safekeeping."

"Thank you, but no. As soon as things calm down, I'll take it to the bank."

He shrugged. "Have it your way."

She could tell he was unhappy.

"What are you doing today?" Lunn's tone sounded too casual.

"The wounded are mostly taken care of and President Waters has called in a mortician to take care of the dead. But I thought I'd check in over at the temporary hospital anyway, just to see if there's anything more I can do. Then I guess I'll come home and do what I always do."

What I'll be doing for the rest of my life—mourning McCullough, as played by John Dietz.

Lunn shoved back his chair and stood. In two strides he was beside her. Before she could back up he took her into his arms and pulled her face up to look at him.

"Marry me, Keely Byrne. Marry me today in the midst of the victory, in the middle of the celebration." His words were less a question than a command. A manic light lit his eyes.

His intensity frightened her. "I—"

"You, what?"

He drew himself up to his full height and puffed his chest like a randy peacock, daring her to defy his wishes.

"I can't, Lunn. It wouldn't be fair to you... " She trailed off, hoping he would leave her alone.

"You can't love him after all he's done." His words exploded into the room. He squeezed her chin in his grip so tightly it hurt.

"The marriage," she said. "We don't know—"

"Brown will take care of it." He leaned to within inches of her face. "Listen, Keely, you need me. I love you and am willing to protect you. There are those that don't believe in your innocence."

She took a deep breath to keep from letting her fear show. He spoke the truth only too clearly.

"I'll protect you with my life. I promise."

"It's not that, Lunn." She needed to buy time. Tears stung her eyes, partly from the pain of his grip, partly put on for effect. She lowered her voice. "I didn't want to say. It's...so personal." She squeezed a tear out. "But of course we had...well, I might be carrying his baby."

Lunn released his grip on her chin and took her by the arms and shook her. "Do you know something for sure?" His fingers bore into her. If only she could run.

"No. But how could I come to you carrying another man's child?" She bit her lip. How to proceed?

"It wouldn't matter to me. It would be all the better for you. I'd pass it off as mine and no one would dare argue."

"I couldn't. I'd rather know for certain—"

"How long till you'll know?"

"A week and a half, maybe two." She couldn't hedge too long.

"Pregnant or not, you're mine. I've gone through too much to get you to lose you now to a baby. You understand?"

She nodded dumbly. Poor Lunn, what could he imagine he'd done? Did mere longing count?

"Good." His mouth came down on hers hard and ugly.

She fought shivers of revulsion. Even empty and numb she could not enjoy Lunn's kisses. His mouth was a cavern swallowing her whole, slobbering over her lips. When he released her, his eyes glimmered with excitement. She resisted the urge to wipe off his kiss with the back of her hand.

After being on the run and hiding out in the woods for two days doing what spying they could while waiting for the militia to get control of the territory, Patterson and Dietz presented themselves just before dusk to General Carlin at his headquarters at the Carter Hotel.

"Thank God, the cavalry has arrived." Dietz smiled as he spoke to the General, who laughed at his remarks.

The boy could still joke, but Patterson worried about him. Any man jilted in love was a loose cannon, and one carrying Dietz's burden qualified as a whole wall of cannons.

"Who might you two gentlemen be?" the General asked.

Patterson extended his hand for a shake. "Charlie Patterson and John Dietz, sir."

"Oh, hell," the General said. "I just sent two dozen troops out looking for you two."

Patterson smiled. He liked nothing more than being known for his stealthy moves. So they'd slipped in past the union *and* past the militia.

"A fellow friendly toward the owners warned me the union had sent men out after you," the General continued.

"Appreciate your concern, sir." Dietz sounded too polite, like his own personality had gone on vacation and now he operated on manners long ago drummed in.

"No time for jawing, General. We've seen President O'Brien and his henchmen hiding out in Mrs. Hollihan's cellar. You better get them before they move out."

The General smiled with genuine delight. "What I've heard about your agency appears to be true—you are the best damned detectives in the world." The General called for one of his aides and dispatched a company of men to bring in the rabble-rousers. Then he turned his attention back to Patterson and Dietz. "Can I get something for you fellows? You look tired."

"Oh, hell, we are, but that's nothing new." Patterson looked at Dietz. The boy looked more than tired. He looked empty and defeated. "A rest sounds good, but not before I offer my services. I was recording secretary for the Gem Union for nearly a year. I know most of the men involved in the action by sight, whereas your troops don't. Let me help finger the fugitives."

The General nodded. "I accept your offer."

"Just part of the job."

"Count me in, too." Dietz broke his silence. "I haven't been in the Valley as long as Patterson, but I know a few villains myself."

Patterson couldn't let the boy do it. He couldn't let the boy stay. If he did, the agency would lose one of its best detectives. Patterson knew all about loss. The boy had to mourn and not in plain view of Keely Byrne. Why add salt to the raw and bleeding wound? Besides, Patterson liked the girl. She needed her own chance to recover.

"No," Patterson said. "I can do all the fingering. Dietz needs a rest. I'm sending him back to the main office as soon as we can arrange for a ticket to Denver."

"The hell you will." Dietz spat the words out and gave Patterson a look meant to intimidate. The boy looked ready to swing at him. Fortunately, the kid knew better. Patterson watched him clench his fist next to his side.

"I'm the senior agent on this assignment. I make the decisions." He had to phrase this carefully. "You've done some fine detective work, risked your life for the job. I'll make sure McParland knows what a fine job you did. But there's no cause for the agency to pay two men to do the job of one. There's nothing but cleanup left here. I'll handle it."

Dietz swore under his breath. The boy looked haggard and beat.

"What are you afraid of, Dietz? That you'll be written out of the history books on this one?" Patterson smiled. Hell, he liked the kid.

CHAPTER TWENTY

October 1892

Dietz collected his mail and retired to his hotel room, his "home" in Denver. He'd just returned from his latest assignment—"testing" conductors on the western railway system through Colorado, Nebraska, Kansas, Iowa, and Missouri. Though the agency assigned half a dozen operatives to it, the job was a piddly one and not to his liking. While an interesting study in human nature, riding the rails left too much time for solitary thoughts and introspection, two things he tried hardest to avoid. Not to mention testing conductors was boring as hell.

Superintendent McParland either intended it as punishment or rest, Dietz couldn't figure out which. To say McParland had not been happy about his "marry-

ing" Keely Byrne would be to understate the case.
McParland had been a hornet.

As Dietz opened the door to his hotel room, he
scanned the letters in his hand. Ah, one from Patterson. He recognized the handwriting. Patterson had
been a regular correspondent these last tortured
months, sending news of the proceedings, carefully
omitting any mention of Keely, or any other upsetting
personages. Not that it did a damn bit of good—Keely
Byrne never drifted far from Dietz's thoughts.

Admit it—Dietz had been despondent. Still was.
He'd even been too depressed to sample the wares of
the whores who regularly traveled the rails, though
God knew he probably needed a good lay. But he needed Keely more. Damn it all anyway!

Dietz never knew what he felt about Patterson's letters. Patterson wrote in a humorous, entertaining style.
His letters sounded like the man. But the information
Patterson conveyed was not always pleasant, certainly
not funny.

Dietz kicked his boots off and plunked down onto
the bed before ripping the letter open with his fingers.

Dietz,

*Thought you might like to be apprised of the go-
ings-on up here. Our good friend Geo. Brown has recovered from the injuries he suffered when he lit the
fuse that blew up the Frisco Mill. I guess the silly fool
never went to school, or if he did he slept through class
the day they taught about concussions. Anyway, seems
though he can mete out union justice with the best of*

them, he couldn't scent out a boomerang in the making.

After he lit the long fuse they'd sent into the mill, he stayed in the flume with his ear to the penstock, listening for the joyous sound of an explosion. Course, you and I know that the shock of the explosion would come back up the penstock. I guess he found out. His companions pulled him from the flume he'd fallen back into after being blown out. Lucky fellow to suffer only a fractured wrist and a few other minor injuries, all, as I said, now on the mend. Too bad some of the others, the scabs killed in the mill, weren't so fortunate.

John Monihan has returned now that the military has taken over the Valley. He escaped the massacre at Cataldo Mission, where the scab hostages were taken, by swimming to a small island in the middle of the river and hiding out. Last count the missing scabs, most presumed dead, totaled fourteen. Bill Black is in prison for leading the bloody attack and mass robbing. I doubt some of the scabs will ever be found. One scab witness reports Black and others robbing bodies after the shootout, then slicing their stomachs open so they'd sink when dumped into the river.

I've made numerous trips to local hospitals trying to identify more perpetrators of the violence, and encouraging the victims. Seeing men with their heads split open, beaten to jelly and fighting for life makes me want to fight this kind of union terrorism to the end. It makes the threats I've received seem worth the risk.

Several occasions I've had to use my old Colt's 45 to get me out of scrapes. I've been trying to avoid taking any lives, but I tell you, at times it's tempting. When I went to the bullpen, the big temporary jail compound where they're holding the miners, the prisoners rushed me. The miners aren't forgiving types, I guess. Many of them are still angry with me, guess they always will be.

As you know, I've been in Murray giving testimony in the trials of some of the terrorists. That in itself has been an adventure. I've got me a nice bed in the local hotel, but I haven't slept there one night. The local deputy has been worried over rumors that 300 unionists plan to take over the town to stop me from testifying against the union leaders. He's warned me many times that he can't protect me. There are no soldiers in Murray. I don't feel particularly safe there myself. Which is why I don't sleep in my bed. Every night I act like I'm going to my room, then I sneak out the back and up the mountain and sleep under the stars. At least that way I'm fairly confident I'll see daylight.

Dietz chuckled. Clean up indeed. The assignment still called for courage, honor, and cunning. Dietz owed Patterson a big debt for sending him away. Dietz turned back to the letter.

That brings me to the main point of this correspondence. I regret to inform you that Lunn Gaffney has been cleared of all murder charges.

Dietz nearly dropped the letter. It began shaking in his hands so violently that for a moment he couldn't read it. They let Gaffney go? Much to Dietz's relief, Gaffney had been arrested just after the soldiers took possession of the Valley and charged with the murder of Ivory Bean. He took a deep breath, forced his hand to still, and took up the letter again.

Though we got numerous indictments against the union rioters, no one believed we'd have a chance of a fair trial or a conviction here in the mining district. To test their theory, the prosecutors tried the most conclusive case in Murray, with the stated result. We had many witnesses who testified that they saw Gaffney shoot Bean. If I would have thought your testimony would have made a difference, I would have summoned you. But I don't think any amount of proof would have swayed the jury, so biased were they.

Because of this debacle, the trials for the union leaders have been moved to Boise City. Lunn Gaffney walks free now, but...

Dietz swore beneath his breath using every curse and oath he knew. Would Keely marry Lunn now? He could hardly believe she would marry a known murderer, but if she believed he was innocent, that the trial had been fair...

Terrible doubts assailed Dietz as he remembered former reports he'd received from Patterson. Before Gaffney's arrest, he'd held off a mob that threatened to kill a local newspaper man for his part in writing inflammatory articles about the union and accompanying the General on his missions to seek out rioters. Dietz wondered when Gaffney had become so particular about other people's rights. Had it been to impress Keely? Had she been present at the scene? He swore again and returned to the letter.

*... with your help I'm hoping we'll nail him. We can't
retry him on murder charges for Ivory Bean, but you
and I both know he was one of the union's hired guns.
Thing is, I think you were closer to the information
than I was.*

*Look, I must be frank about this. Boise City is not in
the Valley. Memories and some people you wish, for
personal reasons, to avoid should not be present. But
the situation is far from safe. The union has put a price
on our heads with the murderous Irish crime gang the
Clan-na-Gael. Of course, this probably is in effect no
matter where we are, but they'll be looking for us particularly in Boise City.*

*I think we can arrange with McParland to reassign
you to this. Will you come?*

Charlie Patterson

Dietz dropped the letter and watched it float to rest
in his lap. Would he come? Hell, yes. Indignation at the
lawless terror wreaked by the union aside, he owed that
much to Keely. He'd be damned if he'd let her marry
Gaffney.

Gem, Idaho
October 1892

Lunn   pressed   Keely   tighter   against   the
boardinghouse wall, sandwiching her between it and
him. Why did he feel it necessary to trap her when she
didn't fight or block his advances? Maybe her acquies-
cence spoke for itself, told him of her absolute lack of
passion. But how could someone as dense as Lunn realize that?

His hands massaged the soft round of her breasts too roughly. Though both of them were fully clothed, he ground against her in a rough imitation of mating. Mating—that described it, like animals did, rutting, urgent, selfish. Not making love like people in love did. He tried to insinuate himself between her legs and encircle himself in the folds of her skirt.

Try, Lunn, but I will not give you that. She kept her knees locked, legs squeezed together. Through the fabric of her skirt his hardness assaulted her.

His mouth closed over hers.

Nothing. Try as hard as she could, she felt nothing. Shouldn't some instinct take over? Shouldn't his very maleness arouse something in her? Had John Dietz killed her so completely? Dangerous territory, thinking of him. She pushed her thoughts elsewhere, but the turn they took didn't please her, either, and didn't stray from the detective agent.

Could she disrobe in front of Lunn, strip as she had on her wedding night, hoping only to please him, ready to take Lunn into her body? Could she sleep curled next to Lunn, bear his children, handle far more intimacy than this time and again? Could she at least tolerate his attentions?

Disgust overwhelmed her—too much bumbled groping. Her breasts ached. Her experiment had failed, or maybe it hadn't, depending on how she looked at it. She had discovered most of what she had wanted to find out—it just wasn't the answer she'd hoped for. She pushed Lunn back from her. Her sudden action took him off guard. He fell back easily.

"The men will be coming home soon, expecting their supper." She ran a hand over her hair. Drat Lunn for mussing her up. "I don't want them viewing what they shouldn't." She stepped neatly around him into the body of the kitchen.

"I'm leaving for Boise City tonight. You still haven't given me your answer—are you marrying me?"

"I don't know, Lunn." She really didn't. Marrying him would solve many of her problems. But no doubt it would create as many as it fixed.

Her indecision didn't appear to set back his confidence. "Set the date, Keel. We'll be married as soon as I get back from Boise City."

She ignored him. What else could she do? But his confidence irked her. Was she indeed trapped?

"Why are you going?" Not that she cared for herself, except that it bought her time, just as his arrest had done before.

His smile gave little away. "The union needs me there. I go where I'm told."

The words chilled her. Word around the Valley had the Clan-na-Gael active again. She stopped herself short of warning him off of involvement with it. She wanted the choice to be his, then maybe she could make hers.

He stepped into her and pecked her cheek, giving her bottom a squeeze in unison. "When I get back." He winked and left.

She picked a dishrag up off the table. She shuddered as she wiped his spittle off her face, then slapped the rag back on the table and sat, mindlessly washing circles on the table.

If only she could be certain about Lunn. He'd been acquitted of the murder charges brought against him. All along he'd claimed the militia had invented the charges as revenge against the union's success, as a way to cripple the union. But Keely had heard too many disturbing rumors, too many accounts of the murder to be certain. And further, why was Lunn going to Boise City? The Clan-na-Gael? She shivered.

Maybe she could force herself to marry Lunn, tolerate his advances, and give him children. There seemed few options. Maybe she could re-establish her reputation in the Valley, and help to rebuild an upright, honorable union—one she could believe in. Lunn seemed to be the door to that path. But if he were involved in the Clan-na-Gael, she wanted none of him. She wasn't certain she did anyway.

She sighed. Boise City. It seemed so far away from everything, including her problems. Boise City? Her heart started pounding loudly in her chest.

She had money. She could go. What if she did and checked up on Lunn? What excuse would she give? She thought a moment. Support for the union, of course. Loyalty to the men who had fought for the cause couldn't hurt her reputation, either.

Boise City
October 1892
Dietz focused his attention on the mirror and adjusted his tie. All dandied up he looked sharp. He

smiled to himself. At least without the mustache he looked like himself. He eased away from the mirror and pulled on his suit coat. Ah, the fit of fine wool and clever stitchery. He stepped to the window and cautiously pulled the curtains back a crack. No use giving the Clan-na-Gael a clear shot at him.

Warm, brown mountains ringed the valley where Boise City sat, radiating their heat into the city. Though early, the day promised to be hot, no less so for the task at hand. Dietz let the curtain drop. Two days in town, and now, for the first time, he'd sit in on court. Not on Gaffney's trial, as he would have preferred, but on Waters'.

Damn that Gaffney. Rumor had him still in Boise City. He'd been spotted once or twice over the past week, but so far had eluded the officials.

Assault. Attempted hold up of a train. Thievery. Attempted murder. Dietz mentally ticked off Gaffney's crimes, sins that Dietz had spent a day elaborating to the U.S. Marshal. Based on Dietz's evidence, the Marshal had issued a warrant for Gaffney's arrest. Finding the bastard proved a problem.

A knock sounded, taking Dietz from his thoughts of Gaffney.

"Dietz, you in there? We got to get moving if we want prime seats in court." Patterson's ebullient laugh floated into the room.

"Coming."

Out in the hall, Patterson greeted him with a slap on the back. "You ready for today?"

"Ready. Court testimony is the worst part of this job."

"Is it now?" Patterson walked beside him toward the stairs. "Worse than being waist deep in cold sewage in Placer Creek?"

Dietz smiled. "Sitting still for so many hours in a row? Has to be. At least we were moving in the creek."

"So we were."

They rounded the corner and descended the stairs.

"Any word on Gaffney?" Dietz tried to sound casual. Mentioning Gaffney, his voice always betrayed his rage and hatred of the man.

"Marshal's got several troops out after him. Last I heard they had a lead on where he might be staying."

The courtroom was filling quickly. Keely sat toward the back, watching as people filed in, trying to decide where their sympathies lay by gauging their mannerisms. This made her third day in court. The process of obtaining justice, though intriguing, fascinated her less than the actual testimony. So much she hadn't known, so many things she'd missed while absorbed in her own life. The scope of the violence, the treacheries, how could she have missed so much of what had transpired early on? She turned her attention away from the gathering crowd and turned to stare sightlessly at the bench in front of her.

Michael had known. Was it merely his shielding that had protected her from seeing? It made her wonder about her own astuteness, and her goals. With the depth of the violence and hatred, could one woman, could one person make a difference? Was there any chance of the union being restored to what it should have been all along?

Her hatred for the mine owners had not lessened with time. Someone still needed to fight for the rights of the working man. She just wasn't sure that she was the right person. Hearing the testimony, passionate and stilted on both sides, made her realize, or was fear a more apt word, that she might never be forgiven. However innocent of the detective's identity, however much the victim herself, the bias that fear and ignorance brought ran deep and strong. Her association with John Dietz, and yes, her obvious love for him, made her unforgivable.

And Lunn Gaffney? She doubted now, more than before, that he would ever be the right choice for her. The stain on her reputation had set too firmly and could never be washed away, not even by such an advocate as Lunn, not even by wearing his wedding band. Days of discreet inquiry about him within the Irish community had yielded nothing of either his whereabouts, or his involvement in the Clan. Had he lied to her about going to Boise City? She had expected to find him in the courtroom. Had something or someone chased him or sent him away?

The courtroom doors opened again, bringing a cool, welcome gust of air from outside into the stagnant room as more people entered. She turned to inhale the freshness and observe the latest arrivals.

Her heart stopped as John Dietz, immaculately turned out and clean-shaven, but unmistakable still, walked through the door. She could neither breathe nor tear her gaze away from him.

Patterson rattled off another of his stories as he and Dietz broke through the courtroom doors. Dietz only half listened. His gaze swept the crowded courtroom, instinctively gauging the situation, looking for enemies or allies, spies and hired killers. Instead, he found Keely, able on her own to maim him in ways a man sent to kill him could not. Stunned shock crashed over him, rendering him defenseless and immobile. For an instant their eyes locked.

What did he do now, other than stare like a fool and listen to his own blood rush in his ears?

The green of her eyes that had haunted his memories mesmerized him still. Her looks always entangled him, but the beauty that had snared him ran as deep as her soul.

Think, Dietz. What did decorum demand—-nod, smile, look away guiltily? How did one, if one did acknowledge the widow of a character he'd once played, an ex-wife of sorts, a lover certainly? A woman he wanted to forget but couldn't, and still loved?

He nodded acknowledgment while his heart hammered at his ribs. He turned abruptly from her condemning gaze, colliding with Patterson who stared over his shoulder.

"Why didn't you tell me she was here?"

"I didn't know. Believe me, I didn't know."

CHAPTER TWENTY-ONE

Lunn Gaffney hid in the alley across from the courthouse. Finding the detective agent John Dietz in town was butter on the bread. Taking revenge against him could only be sweet. Lunn had come to Boise City to kill Charlie Patterson. The union had put an outrageous price on both detective agents' heads, but Dietz had not been spotted for months. Since the possibility of killing both men and escaping seemed remote, he shifted his target to Dietz. Personal satisfaction counted for something.

Why should the Clan collect the money? What did another man's blood on his hands matter at this point? More important matters pressed. With the bounty for Dietz he could make a tidy nest for Keely and himself. What a fitting irony—rid himself of a rival, mark himself as a hero, and by Dietz's death support his lady in style.

Keely. Lunn had been shadowing her since her arrival in town, wondering what had brought her to Boise City. She'd been making inquiries about him, trying to find him. Her actions pleased him, showing a turn of heart. Was she worried about him? He liked the notion. And the way she sat in court lending support to his union brethren could only help her reputation.

A sound at the back of the alley startled him. When he turned, he found nothing. He cursed under his breath. Could have been just a cat or a rat, anything. But for safety, as soon as he made this hit and collected his cash, he would run to Canada and wait for things to settle down. And he intended to take Keely with him.

Time to get back under cover. Time to plan his strategy for eliminating the detective. A public execution seemed fitting. A blind shot echoing from a building or an alley and finding a resting place in Dietz's chest would do the trick.

There was time before the court's first recess to devise a strategy. He would kill John Dietz today.

Dietz sat toward the front of the courtroom and felt Keely's gaze boring into him. How much longer could he resist the urge to turn around and face the charge she had leveled at him with a look?

Patterson leaned into him and whispered. "You look like a ramrod. Relax and enjoy the testimony. She can't kill you a look."

He was that obvious?

The witness droned on. Dietz had lost track of the testimony an hour ago, before it began, since he'd first seen her.

With a whack of his gavel, the judge adjourned the court for a recess. The sound brought Keely up out of her thoughts and set her heart thundering again. With John Dietz in the room there existed no place for her gaze to fall but on him. *I can't face him.*

For the last hours she'd been trying to analyze the look he'd given her. What had she seen in those violet eyes? But try as she might she remembered nothing but her own shock reflected back at her. And his curt nod—nothing but barest courtesy.

To look into those eyes again and see nothing but the impersonal look of a stranger would wound her. To see them filled with any tenderness at all, any compassion or look of fond memory, would condemn her forever to an inescapable prison of her own heart's creation. She lived there now, but barely.

The crowd began to rise and file out. She watched John Dietz as he leaned over and spoke with Mr. Allison, Mr. Patterson. He looked handsome in his dark gray wool suit and white shirt.

Admit it. He looks good in anything.

He rose and started to turn in her direction. She must exit, *quickly.*

She kept her eyes cast downward and her head bowed. Her chosen comportment offered her little view other than that of other women's skirts, men's pant legs and boots—so much safer, all of it, than faces. She filed slowly toward the aisle. Why hadn't she chosen an aisle seat, rather than politely moving to center pew? The people in front of her moved slowly, like sloths.

Hurry. Oh, hurry! Sitting so far back in the room, she ought to have been able to leave and been safely to her hotel room before he cleared the doorway. If not for these incredibly leisurely and polite people in front of her letting everyone pass first. Why didn't they cut their way into the stream of exiting traffic?

She didn't dare to glance up and check Mr. Dietz's progress, but if only because of her own desire to be gone, she felt him closing the gap. It wasn't that she assumed that he would pursue contact with her; well, maybe she did *hope*. It was more that he might accidentally end up near her, and what could that bring? Ruthless awkwardness that led to small talk and heartache?

The couple before her moved into the stream pouring into center aisle. Finally! Her heart pounded wildly as she stepped out of the courthouse moments later and strode into the sunshine. Freedom! She raced toward the courthouse steps as quickly as her narrow skirt permitted.

As she lifted the heavy wool folds of her skirt and prepared to descend, a hand on her elbow stopped her cold.

"Keely."

Her name on his lips sliced through her like a cold breeze. She closed her eyes and took a deep breath, not caring if he noticed.

"Mr. Dietz." Despite her best efforts, her voice wavered. "Is that who you are today, or are you playing another role?"

"I guess I deserve that." Did she mean to kill him so completely? She'd torn out of the courtroom, obviously intent on avoiding him. But damned if Dietz would let her go this time without offering some explanation.

"Just myself today." He forced a smile, trying to coax one from her. "You're wondering who that is, I suppose."

That did the trick. She actually looked him in the eye and a tiny smile played at the corners of her mouth.

"I might have cause to, you know."

He laughed, albeit a bit nervously. Up close, she smelled like he remembered, of flowers. Smell proved a potent memory stimulant. All he wanted was to take her in his arms, like old times.

She started down the stairs. "You seem to have escaped the Valley intact."

He kept pace with her. He wished he knew what she thought of him, if she still felt anything, but he could get no read. She seemed polite, nothing more.

"Barely. What do you think of the trial?" *What an idiot thing to say, Dietz.*

She returned her gaze to her feet as she carefully took the steps. "Interesting enough. You knew Mr. Waters well. Will you testify against him?"

Was she condemning him? Calling him traitor? He couldn't tell.

"No, I won't be called in this trial. They have enough hard evidence against him without me." He

stopped himself. Had he said too much? Damn this delicate pussyfooting. "Do you believe he's guilty?"

She continued her descent. "He's guilty sure
enough."

Her calm pronouncement took him aback. When she
stepped down off the last step she stopped and gazed at
him. "You look surprised." She smiled. "I may have
been blind where the union was concerned, but I have
never been narrow-minded regarding the truth."

"You no longer believe in the union?"

"I believe in what the union should have stood for.
The plight of the working miner is still abominable.
The owners oppress us. We need a union to stand up
for us. But what the union had become, no, I don't believe it served our purposes. Not at all."

She scrutinized him. How was he faring? Dietz
wished he knew.

"And you?" she asked. "Do you maintain the owners'
innocence in this affair?"

"I'm not sure I ever did." Did she believe him? He
grinned. "They're a selfish lot, greedy and not altogether honorable. That I escaped alive reflects little on
them." He briefly related the incident at the Carter Hotel. He thought she fought down a smile. "Still, regarding the union, anarchy cannot be supported. The laws
of the United States must be upheld and terrorism
fought at every corner of this country. That is all I've
ever stood for."

"Is it? Maybe we haven't been at such odds as we've
imagined."

Was it Dietz's imagination, or was there hope for them yet?

"We've got him in sight. There." The young lawman pointed toward the alley that ran perpendicular to the courthouse. Lunn Gaffney slunk into the shadows, a rifle with its sight trained on the crowd streaming out of the courthouse raised to his shoulder.

U.S. Marshal James Nelson eyed the fugitive cautiously. "You certain it's him?"

The lawman handed him the binoculars he'd been holding to his eyes.

Marshal Nelson grunted. "He fits Gaffney's description. Doesn't really matter who the fellow is. He looks like he means to cause trouble." He handed the binoculars back. "We can't have him taking potshots into that crowd of folks. What do you think? Can your men disarm and subdue him without any innocent being hurt?"

The younger man shrugged. "All we can do is try. In our favor, so far he doesn't appear to suspect that we're following him."

"Damn!" Lunn cursed and swore beneath his breath, using every expletive and slur he could remember. Down the sight of his rifle barrel he had a bead on Dietz. Next to Dietz, Keely strolled along, smiling at the cursed man. Jealousy, green, ugly and raw, tangled with his nerves. The gun poised at his shoulder trembled slightly in response.

His finger curled over the trigger. At this range, the trigger required a gentle touch. Too much force, the pressure that rage required, and he'd hit air over the bastard's head, maybe getting a ricochet off the courthouse. Damn Dietz anyway.

With the way the blasted gun trembled, Keely stood too close. Any miscalculation and Lunn would hit her instead. The couple's path would take them directly in front of him. *Hold on, boy, just a bit longer.*

He'd have to wait until they were close enough that the rage and the trembling would make negligible difference in where he hit the target. Heart or lung, Lunn didn't care where he hit Dietz's chest, so long as the shot was immediately fatal.

Keely's words set Dietz's heart scrambling at a breakneck pace. And she was smiling fully at him now. He had to take the chance that might shatter the moment. "May I buy you supper?" The moment the words escaped him, he knew he's said the wrong thing. Her expression told him.

"You ask too much." Her voice became soft and sad. She turned her focus to the distance, away from him. Contradictory as it seemed, her action gave him hope. She might try to hide her feelings from him, but she did a damned terrible job. What did she think to hide, her vulnerability?

He took her arm and pulled her around to face him. "Innocuous conversation is too much?"

"After all that's happened, how can any conversation between us ever be benign?" She sounded sad, almost wistful.

Damn, maybe she does still care.

"Buying you supper was supposed to be kind—a gentlemanly thing to do." He tried to sound light.

"Was it?" Her eyes misted over. "Then I thank you, but I decline. I'm sure you understand."

"Damn it, Keely! You must know I want to explain. Don't deny me this chance."

"Innocent conversation. You liar!" She broke free of his grasp, picked up her skirt, and hurried forward. He had to take long strides to catch and keep up with her. How did she manage to move so quickly taking those itty bitty steps?

"I don't want to hear your explanation," she said.

"You don't want to hear that—"

"That it was your job." Her words came out staccato, punctuated with hurt. "Why would you think that would make me feel any better?" The moisture glistening in her eyes slid down her cheeks.

She was crying now.

"Keely. That's not what I wanted to say."

Lunn smiled at the sight. Keely ran from Dietz, who, looking uncertain, had paused, letting her gain distance on him. *Run, Keely, run to me.*

In a moment, Lunn would have a clear, point blank shot at Dietz. Not the best shot. His position made detection more probable, but it would suffice. When would the opportunity come again? Time had run out. Gaffney set the rifle at his side and pulled a pistol from his holster. Better to use the right weapon.

A noise echoed from the back of the alley. This time Lunn didn't flinch. Cursed cats!

"Drop the gun, Gaffney! In the name of the law."

Lunn froze. At that moment Keely passed just feet in front of him. Instinctively, he reached for her.

Undecided how to proceed and explain to Keely, Dietz paused, letting her get several building lengths on him while he plotted his strategy. He'd just moved to catch her when her scream broke through the streets.

What the—?

Lunn Gaffney stepped from the shadows of an alley, an arm locking around Keely, pressing her against him with a pistol to her head. Suddenly the ordinary, a woman walking down the street, became surreal, like a painting out of perspective. Just a man holding a woman—in a deadly embrace.

Dietz froze, taking it all in, in an instant. Gaffney loosed a tirade of threats and insults directed down the alley as he pulled Keely into the middle of the street. It took Dietz a second to realize whom Gaffney yelled to and what was going on. The law had found Gaffney.

The crowd realized what was happening at the same instant Dietz did. Everything stood still—people, carts, carriages, horses, time. In the unfiltered sunlight, Keely's auburn hair made a red halo around her face. Gaffney's pistol gleamed dangerously in the middle of it all. Softness and steel collided.

People began stepping back, away from Gaffney until he stood in the middle of an empty street, surrounded at a distance of some twenty feet by a tide of people. Dietz saw only Keely.

Dietz drew his Colt and put a bead on Gaffney. Most emergencies filled Dietz with a welcome rush of energy that heightened his senses and perception. Now his gut tightened and burned and he had to fight down the shaking fear rapidly rising within him. Emotional detachment—he had none now.

"Drop the gun." Gaffney sounded edgy. He fidgeted, looking around quickly and nervously, most likely scanning for an escape path.

It might have been seconds. It might have been forever. Time in its weird way had skewed for Dietz. *Hold your head. Remember your training. Now is not the time to panic.*

A line of militia troops and lawmen formed around them. Without glancing around to check, he assumed they lined up for a chance at a clear shot at Gaffney. Whether Gaffney realized it or not, he was a doomed man. If only he didn't take Keely down with him. The bastard knew enough to keep Keely between him and Dietz. With supreme will of effort, Dietz's gun didn't waver, but there was no way he had any chance of a shot at Lunn.

Lunn whispered into Keely's hair—strange, fanatical declarations of love, distorted endearments, talk of escape and a life together afterward.

Keely tried hard to block it all out. She focused everything instead on John Dietz. At that moment, he looked like salvation. She wanted to live and live with that man—forever. Looking down the length that separated them, past his gun barrel at steely violet eyes, she saw concentration, cunning, and something she'd seen in them only once before—fear. Just like last July in Gem. Only then she'd been too angry and upset to judge it with any objectivity. Why hadn't she seen that he faced danger with something akin to excitement, except when it involved her? Mothers looked like that when their children were in danger, wives their husbands, and lovers their sweethearts. He loved her, just like he'd said. Why hadn't she believed it before? Maybe she'd needed the distance. Maybe she had to see it for herself, just once when he was himself, not in character.

If it came to it, dying while staring into those eyes was preferable to just about everything Lunn suggested as he hissed and warbled his strange, contorted feelings into her ear.

And die she might. Lunn frightened her. The gun he pressed against her temple trembled. *He'll kill me if he needs to. He'll kill me if he wants.* The thoughts echoed through her mind with shattering intensity.

She remembered John Dietz holding her hostage, gun at her ribs, and her complete certainty that he would not harm her. Thoughts of John Dietz pushing her from him flooded back, along with his words, *Take your life back.* And she knew what he meant—not her life, the blood pulsing through her, but the way she had come to live, her home, her friends, her causes. He'd risked his life coming back to save her. Every thought sparkled with clarity now as she saw their lives entwine. How ironic—maybe none of it would be.

Lunn would not be giving her life back.

"Drop the girl. You don't want to hurt Keely," Dietz called out. "Let her go and I'll drop the gun so that we can talk."

Gaffney's eerie laugh seemed to hang on the breeze. "You can't take my girl and my means of escape away that easily, traitor. Offer me something I want more than those two."

Damn Gaffney and his taunting.

Marshal Nelson had edged his way behind Dietz. "We've got men taking position in the buildings across the way."

Thankful for a backup, Dietz didn't much care how he'd gotten there. Not wanting to alert Gaffney, Dietz kept his gaze focused on him. Peripherally, he saw movements in several second-story windows across the street.

"Let me take over, Dietz," the marshal whispered.

Dietz shook his head. "Just keep me covered. He hates me enough to be distracted by me. Keep your men lined up to get a shot at him and coordinate with the militia commander in charge."

With his back to him, Dietz couldn't tell what the marshal felt about his orders. Probably didn't like them much, but Dietz trusted Keely's safety to no one but himself. No one else cared enough to sacrifice everything.

"What are you going to do?" the marshal asked.

An armed figure came clearly into sight in a second-floor window at Gaffney's back. Dietz made a mental calculation. Damn, the trajectory wasn't right. But with a little angling, he could maneuver Gaffney into position. Dietz threw his Colt's down and put his hands up.

Keely gasped.

"I'm unarmed, Gaffney. That's what you wanted, isn't it?" Dietz took a step toward him. *Modulate your voice. Soothe him. Keep him off guard against any other danger.*

"There's a price on my head." Dietz laughed sharply. "But I'll bet you know that already."

"Stop where you are." Gaffney's aim grew steadily shakier.

With two objectives in mind—get Gaffney into position so that the law had a clear shot at him, and get close enough to jump him in case all else failed—Dietz approached Gaffney. Dietz fixed his gaze on Gaffney, using peripheral vision to keep track of the crack shooters taking aim at Gaffney.

"I've heard it's a good price, enough to set a working man up in style for a while at least. I'm offering you a fair trade—me for the girl."

Shit, Gaffney scared him. The man's eyes looked like ice—crazy and glazed over.

"No, John, no." It was the first time he'd heard Keely use his Christian name, his real one, and it flustered him more than it ought to, more than he needed it to at this moment.

The lawmen in the windows across the street still weren't aligned properly. Dietz moved to the side, forcing Gaffney to sidestep and rotate to keep him in his sights.

Gaffney cackled. "It's not about money. It never has been. It's about getting what I want."

Gaffney had a wild, caged look. Two things Dietz hated because they made for unpredictable behavior. "And what would that be?"

Gaffney appeared almost sad, vulnerable. "Keely."

Dietz fingered the name for what drove Gaffney— obsession. He took another step toward them. He played a dangerous game now—get close enough to grab Gaffney, but stay out of the line of sight of a shot. Dietz also hoped to get Gaffney to take the gun away from Keely and draw on him.

Gaffney guessed Dietz's intent. "Don't try it."

Gaffney shifted Keely to his right arm, transferring the gun along with the woman, holding it at her ribs. With his left hand he pulled the pins from her hair until it fell loose. He wound the silky strands around his palm, tightly, until he pulled her head up against it. "Your life isn't worth shit, not even to you, Dietz." Gaffney snorted. "But hers is, to both of us."

Did Dietz look that desperate, or was Gaffney only remembering what had been back in Gem? In any case, Gaffney assumed correctly—Keely's life meant more to Dietz than his own. Dietz struggled to keep his expression unreadable.

"You smug bastard." Gaffney sounded angry. "You don't think I'll kill her, do you?" He laughed. "It doesn't matter what you think, only what I'll do. I killed to get her. I'll kill to keep her."

"Lunn, please."

Ah, Keely, Dietz thought. *Don't plead.* "Killed who?"

Gaffney laughed again. "You're hell bent on a confession."

It was as if Dietz's question suddenly made Gaffney aware of his surroundings again. He looked around, apparently taking in the troops surrounding him and the slim odds of escape. Desperation clouded his eyes.

"Confession, what's it supposed to be good for, your soul?" Gaffney sounded suddenly stricken. With guilt or pain, Dietz couldn't really say.

"I'll confess before we die then." Gaffney's voice went low and soft. "I killed Michael, my best friend."

Keely gasped.

"I'm sorry, Keely." Gaffney's voice broke. "I didn't mean to. I meant to play hero and save him. Then I figured he'd help me win you. Approve of the match. But things got out of hand. He died before I could save him. What I want is freedom from guilt, to go back and do it over so it turns out all right. Can you give me that?" His voice cracked and he looked miles away with his thoughts. An indescribable expression lit his eyes, something terrible and merciless that suddenly became relief. The tension drained out of his face and the tight set of his jaw relaxed. That look frightened Dietz beyond anything that had occurred. Gaffney looked like he'd just received the absolution he'd been looking for, last confession, last rights before he went.

Keely started to cry. She mumbled something.

Don't listen, Dietz, he warned himself. No emotions, not now. He forced himself to think logically. The only thought that surfaced—if they didn't get a shot off in the next instant he would have to jump Gaffney. He poised, ready to spring.

As suddenly as Dietz's intentions formed, Gaffney thrust Keely in front of him, holding her by the hair with one hand, the gun at her head with the other.

"Oh, shit," Dietz said.

"To heaven with both of us, angel," Gaffney said. Then he stared at Dietz with a look so chilling that Dietz wasn't likely to ever forget it. "Together in death. Cradled together, my body shielding hers."

"Gaffney." Dietz lunged for him.

The crack of a shot echoed off the buildings. Gaffney's head tilted sideways, blown back by the force of the blast before he dropped the gun and crumpled to the ground. Dietz thought that expression would be burned in his memory for life, like the image on a photographic plate.

"Keely!" Was it his own voice crying out, hoarse and horrified? He reached out for her as Keely stumbled forward into his arms.

"Oh, dear Lord. Oh, dear Lord." Keely mumbled over and over again through her tears as he pressed her into his chest.

Before him, Gaffney fell to the ground, half his head missing. It wasn't until that instant that Dietz became aware again of the crowd surrounding them. For a time, all his attention had focused on the narrow perimeter of Keely, Gaffney, and himself. Now, suddenly, he heard the lawmen and militia troops yelling, the gasps of the crowd. He saw the horrified looks on the faces of the spectators. Where had so many people come from? Last he looked just a small group had surrounded them.

The Marshal and his men ran to Gaffney. A newspaper reporter stepped out of the crowd and began asking questions.

Keely squirmed in Dietz's arms, trying to turn and look back, almost an automatic response. He pressed her more tightly against himself. *Spare her, Dietz, spare her.*

"It's all right, Keely. He's gone."

A fresh round of sobs shook her shoulders. He had to get her out of the crowd. Without thinking, he scooped her up into his arms and pushed his way through the crowd.

Seated at the table under the whirring of an overhead fan, calming, normal, in the small cafe, Keely wondered how John Dietz had gotten her there. She remembered the gentle gait of his footsteps as he carried her down the street and the way she swayed in his arms in time, sobbing, and nothing else. Absolutely nothing else. Not how far he'd walked, not what he'd said, not how much time had passed. *Nothing.*

As far as it went, she remembered nothing much of the last hour except Lunn, John Dietz, and herself, and mostly, John's gaze locked on hers, keeping her sane through it all. Everything else from the instant Lunn had grabbed her until now jumbled in her mind, desperately misplaced and out of sequence. She hadn't been aware of the forming crowd or the gathering of lawmen and military. The shot had come as a complete surprise to her. Who had fired it? Where had he come from? For the briefest instant, until she tumbled into John's arms, she'd thought Lunn had shot her or himself. Her focus had been so narrow everything else had blurred.

If she wanted to, if she forced herself to think about it, she might be able to create some order to things. But she didn't. She never wanted to think about it again.

John held a glass of water out to her. "Drink it. You'll feel better." His voice sounded soft and reassuring, reminiscent of a day long past when her father's voice could comfort her.

She spoke her half-formed thought without thinking. "Like a child after a nightmare?" She smiled at the thought.

"Something like that," he said.

She nodded. "A nightmare."

He pulled his chair up close to hers and leaned forward on his arms on the table. "Keely, I'm so sorry. So sorry for everything."

His words surprised her. How could he take blame for something that Lunn had done? "You weren't responsible."

"Like hell," he said.

The venom in his words caught her off guard.

"If it weren't for me, you'd never have been in that situation." He sat up straight, as if trying to brace himself against the blame, face it like a man.

"You saved my life."

He turned to look at her. Her conscience urged her to speak.

"You saved my life many, many more times than just today, and in more ways than I can ever repay," she said.

He looked puzzled and hopeful.

"If you hadn't killed McCullough, I would have married him..." Her voice trailed off and she shuddered. "He was everything you said and worse." She paused. "Or I might have married Lunn. He wasn't all bad, you know. He saved that editor and that took great courage and strength of character. I think accidentally killing Michael just sent him over the edge."

Silence sat between them a moment.

Finally, Keely smiled, weakly, but a smile still. "I have the worst taste in men it seems."

"Yeah," he said and nodded.

"Is there really a price on your head?"

When he smiled, his dimples showed. "That's what I hear. Quite a fine one judging from the union's hatred and the Clan's determination to kill me. You thinking of collecting?"

She found enough strength to sip her water. He was right. Cool, wet, refreshing, ordinary, it brought life back into focus.

"Hardly. I don't need the money. You left me plenty." She took another sip to help swallow the lump swelling in her throat. They seemed to be running out of things to say. What would happen if she let him leave, just walk out the door? What if they never met again? She had to say something, anything.

"Who am I now?" What a silly question.

He cocked his head to one side and stared at her questioningly. "Isn't that what you asked me a bit ago?"

She couldn't more than nod. He'd evaded the question neatly.

"I suppose," he took her chin in his hand and brought her face around to his, "you could be whoever you wanted to be. Just like me."

She nodded numbly.

"I love you, Keely." His voice broke with emotion. "Now may not be the time or the place, but I have to tell you before you slip away again. I love you. You could be my wife again. John Dietz's wife, whoever the hell that is."

She felt tears forming again and tried to blink them back, blasted things.

He looked at her guiltily. "I can't give up my job, Keely, or change who I am. Being a private detective's wife is a hard business."

She nodded. Suddenly a smile overwhelmed her. "Oh, I know, John Dietz. Believe me, I know. But I can't think of anything else I'd rather be."

He grasped the back of her head with his hand and pulled her into him. She kissed him with trembling lips and all the passion of her soul.

ABOUT THE AUTHOR

Gina Robinson lives in the Pacific Northwest with her husband and children. She loves humor, romance, suspense, and spies. Not necessarily in that order. She writes contemporary romance, humorous thrillers, historical romance and women's fiction.

Most days she writes while wearing slippers, flip-flops, or tennis shoes, depending on the season. But she loves a great, sexy heel and has a closet full for special occasions.

She belongs to Romance Writers of America and International Thriller Writers. To find out more about Gina, visit her website at www.ginarobinson.com.